Something Happened In Spain

By

Sydney J Roderick

MAPLE
PUBLISHERS

Something Happened in Spain

Author: Sydney J Roderick

Copyright © 2025 Sydney J Roderick

The right of Sydney J Roderick to be identified as author of this work has been asserted by the author in accordance with section 77 and 78 of the Copyright, Designs and Patents Act 1988.

First Published in 2025

ISBN 978-1-83538-923-2 (Paperback)
      978-1-83538-924-9 (E-Book)

Book Cover Design and Layout by:
      White Magic Studios
      www.whitemagicstudios.co.uk

Published by:
      Maple Publishers
      Fairbourne Drive, Atterbury,
      Milton Keynes,
      MK10 9RG, UK
      www.maplepublishers.com

This book is fiction. Changes and adaptions of events and occurrences are the authors own. Any similarities to any other persons currently dead or alive are purely coincidental and have no bearing on these characters within this story.

*"It's better to have loved and lost

than never

to have loved at all"*

-Alfred Lord Tennyson

CONTENTS

April 2002...6

1 - Nick...10

2 - Jed...15

3 - Seville...23

4 - Louis..26

5 - Liz and Lydia...34

6 - Russian lesson..45

7 - Marbella...58

8 - New Apartment..66

9 - Wall Street Institute...77

10 - Another Apartment..91

11 - New Friends...104

12 - Settling in..113

13 - Benalmadena..122

14 - Fiesta Season..127

15 - Nueva Andalucía...137

16 - Estepona...146

17 - Christmas Surprise..153

18 - New Year..162

19 - Three Kings...175

20 - Happy Birthday..184

21 - Maud's arrival..191

22 - House Hunting...201

23 - Jim Returns...215

24 - Sex and Drugs..224

25 - A Week Away...232

26 - Monday at School..242

27 - Pearls. 251

28 - Malaga 261

29 - Decisions 269

30 - Cruise 277

31 - Masquerade party..287

32 - Confusion...298

33 - Something Happened 307

34 - The drug deal..317

35 - Margarita 327

36 - Cajasur Bank..336

Newspaper report. 350

April
2002

He had a special weekend planned as he drove to collect her. It was time to spoil and indulge the love of his life. He knew deep down that she was unsure of their relationship, and he needed to put matters right. A weekend away was the perfect opportunity to discuss why he'd been away on business, more often of late.

He couldn't grasp the fact she'd announced she was taking a year sabbatical to Spain. He knew she'd always wanted to work abroad, but he'd preferred it if she had chosen another destination. There were so many other places that offered the TEFL Teaching programme.

He'd been trying to find the right moment to discuss the future with her. He patted the top pocket of his jacket as he smiled. He was ready to share everything and support her plan. He also believed once he explained everything, they could live in Spain together.

He sounded the horn of his MX5 outside her house as she came out immediately. She looked beautiful as she locked her front door. He jumped out and embraced her, popped her bag in the trunk and they drove towards Aldeburgh, which was on the Suffolk coast.

"How was Germany?" she asked eager to catch up with her man.

"Good, all the meetings went well," he replied concentrating on the road ahead.

"Any more trips planned?" she asked as these odd weeks away were bothering her more than usual.

"Only one, over lunch I'll tell you."

"Look forward to it," she said not sure suddenly.

Had he been seeing someone else? Surely, this weekend away was not to end the relationship, he could do that over the phone. He obviously had something important to tell her. She relaxed a bit. They had been dating for nearly two years, he'd remembered, and she inwardly smiled with contentment.

She recalled the first time she'd set eyes on him. He had worn a black suit and had resembled an undertaker, but his sparkling blue eyes had danced all over her. He had worn a pale pink shirt and a deep crimson tie. He was exceptionally good looking, and she'd been attracted to his whole demeanour. He had arrived at the recruitment offices where she worked for a meeting. He and his colleagues had required skilled engineers for their imminent project. They were to supply the London infrastructure with the underground development in readiness for the 2012 Olympics.

Her company had won the bid, and their meeting was to plan a strategy around Nick's personnel requirements. Their eyes had locked the instant he'd walked in the room, and she'd dropped her files an inch from the table edge sending unstapled papers to the floor to her dire embarrassment. He had come to her rescue and her boss, who she nicknamed Hawkeye, had glared at her for such incompetence.

From the very first time she'd set eyes on him and his very first touch and even as he'd embraced her now, her heart raced, and her insides churned. A feeling she'd never experienced with anyone before.

"You're miles away Gaby."

"Sorry, I was just thinking it's nearly two years, is this an anniversary weekend?"

"You could say that we haven't had much quality time lately, just thought it would be nice to spoil you. I've arranged lunch at the Brudenell."

"Oh, that's fantastic, how thoughtful."

"We're staying at the White Lion."

"Oo I am being spoiled," as she looked at him as he concentrated on the road. His cropped blonde hair was streaked with the sun and the check jacket he wore, reminded her of their first Christmas together. She smiled as he'd knelt by the Christmas tree of the Brudenell Hotel and had asked, *"Gabriella Daly will you be my girlfriend?"*

"What are you thinking about?"

"Our first Christmas when you asked me to be your girlfriend."

"Yeah, it's gone quick, we're here," as he drove into the car park. *"Come on, I'm famished, we've got all weekend to reminisce."*

He grabbed her hand, ruffled her long black hair, kissed her cheek and they laughed as they ran into the hotel as the rain started.

"This way Mr. Armand."

They followed the waiter who beamed at them as Gaby sat.

"This was our very first date," she said wishing she'd bought him something, he'd obviously had romance in mind.

He handed her the menu and got his glasses out and there was activity around the tables, as the waiter took their order.

The wine waiter arrived and opened a bottle of Moët & Chandon as Gaby looked on in surprise.

"Champagne honey?"

Suddenly he moved to her side and kneeling on the oak flooring, he looked at her and smiled,

"Gabriella Daly, I love you very much. Will you marry me?"

"Yes," she gasped and leapt from her chair and hugged him as he placed a diamond ring on her finger. The place erupted as the waiters were in on it and there was jubilant cheer throughout the bar and restaurant.

1

Nick

"What did you say?"

"I'm not a construction engineer Honey. I've been meaning to tell you for a while, but I've been putting it off. You need to know."

She placed her glass on the table, had she heard him right the first time. She'd too much to drink, this wasn't happening.

"I'm an undercover Detective working for British Intelligence assigned to the European division, hence my several trips to Germany."

"You're kidding me, Nick.

"No, sorry, I wanted to tell you before now. I should have confided in you ages ago."

"I don't believe you."

He got out his wallet and inside his driver license were other credentials as she read the I.D. and gulped some more wine. She was bewildered; this wasn't happening.

"Why are you telling me now, after proposing? Shouldn't you have told me before declaring your allegiance to me?"

"Shh, there's no need to shout. I'm sorry, it's a shock. Look let's check in to the Hotel and then we can talk about it."

She got up and stormed out to the car as the rain caught her face, as she waited for him. She was stunned and needed to think. It wasn't too bad; it could have been worse but there was more to it. She threw her scarf over her head as he came out and unlocked the car as they jumped in, not speaking until they parked up into the adjacent Hotel to check in.

"Tell me from the beginning," she asked as they sat by the fireplace in the lounge of the White Lion.

"I've been in the special forces division of the Police force for ten years. I've been assigned one of the major operations about to unfold in Spain. This means I'm going to be away for at least a year. If I'd known that I was going to be tasked with this, I'd have discussed this with you sooner. I didn't know until three months ago, that I was going to be a key part of the surveillance team."

"Three months ago? Hang on, this is why you'd prefer it if I undertook my sabbatical elsewhere. How could you NOT tell me Nick? I'm gutted you couldn't trust me from the beginning."

"Would you have dated me knowing I was an undercover Cop?"

"Of course, I would have understood your lapses of time away, quite frankly, you're a crap liar. You've never trusted me, have you?"

He looked away and said nothing.

She got up in disbelief at his reluctance to answer her question. She went outside, she needed to think. How could he betray her and not trust her, AT ALL?

"Gaby, its cold out here, come on. Let's get upstairs, we can talk more."

He grabbed her waist as he pulled her back inside as she wriggled from him. She was totally shattered and was trying hard to rationalise this predicament. She went upstairs as Nick followed with a bottle of wine knowing he'd screwed up.

She was crying softly on the bed as he run to her and tried to console her. She pushed him away, feeling crushed to the core as he felt her torment and anguish. He sat and sipped his wine and waited until she was ready. Eventually, she got up and went to wash her face. She came back and sat with him and said,

"You've only told me because you're going to Spain soon. You've never stopped me from planning my year in the sun; you've said nothing at all. Now, you propose, you think you can dictate to me, what I should be doing next? Oh no. You don't want me there as you are going to be somewhere undercover, is that it. You haven't told me because you might have felt that this relationship should be based on complete and utter trust! Two years Nick, it's simply not good enough."

"Calm down Gaby, its not that bad a deal. I'm sorry. Yes, I don't want you going to Spain, because it's a bit scary there, right now. I'm more than happy for you to do your own thing. I do trust you and I do love you."

"Have you had me checked out, followed and all that?"

He nodded.

Horrified at this disclosure she walked to the en-suite disappointed and before slamming the door, she said,

"Shame you've no faith in me at all; it obviously suits you to tell me now. Thing is, I'm not sure if I trust you anymore and can I trust you with my future?"

They left the hotel the next day and made their way back to her house. She was devastated at the few things he'd said.

"I want you to listen to me. I love you and want to be with you. I will make this assignment my last one, I promise you that. Go and take your year away and take that course. I promise to find you when it's over. We can live in Spain if that's what you want. I love you; you must remember that."

"How will you find me?"

"It's my job sweetheart, whatever happens, I'll find you. Promise to text me on this number once you get to Marbella, or Seville. If I don't contact you, you must understand it may compromise my cover. You do understand how sensitive and dangerous this work can be?"

"Don't patronise me, Nick. I fully understand your role; I'm seeing you in a different light. I admire this in you, but you've let me down. I need time to think things through."

She'd been checked out, she'd been watched and apparently, she had gone through vigilant screening all without her consent and knowledge. She was shell-shocked and he was visibly upset at her reaction.

The relationship in tatters, he placed a business card on the table as she ignored it. He went to kiss her as she moved her head away. He closed her front door as she quickly pulled the chain across and she groaned, crying inconsolably on the sofa. Her engagement ring scratching her face accidentally as she held and cried herself to sleep.

She loved him but he had violated her trust in more ways than one. She had given herself completely to this man and he'd been living a double life. He had totally broken her heart and at that moment she felt that she'd never be able to forgive him.

❖

2

Jed

"*For goodness' sake Gaby, we're all going out to "Quaglinos." The tables booked you can't stay cooped up at home for ever,*" Rosalyn urged her to go out with them.

She'd been off sick for three weeks and was now on antidepressants, she'd never seen her in this state ever before. However, she'd never been subjected to a big lie before, Rosalyn did sympathise, but her demanding job couldn't sustain her absence from a team dinner any longer.

"*I know you're on your years' sabbatical in August honey, but Hawkeye is contemplating your bonus entitlement which will affect your settlement, if you don't get your ass in gear. I'll collect you at eight; get your fucking act together for Christ's sake.*"

She was still in slow motion and had exhausted *Bridget Jones's* DVD to the point it now jumped in several places. She looked a wreck, Rosalyn was right. She looked in the mirror for the first time in weeks and was visibly shocked, she looked gaunt and old. That was it. She wasn't going to let the bastard get the better of her. She couldn't bring herself to say his name as she ran the bath and started plucking her eyebrows. Christ, it was going to take her all the three hours to reconstruct her image, what a mess. She threw on an Abba CD and she soaked in the bath and eventually started singing out loud, the odd tear cascading down her cheek as she brushed them away. She needed to get her act together, Rosalyn was right.

She'd lost over a stone in weight and although she'd not been overweight, the loss of several pounds accentuated her red glitzy dress, her curvaceous figure oozing sex appeal as she set her rollers in place before applying her make up.

Three hours later as she waited for Rosalyn to collect her, sipping a glass of red for a bit of courage, she knew she looked gorgeous. How could she have let him destroy her like this? The car horn sounded as she grabbed her coat and clutch and locked the door. Rosalyn's face confirmed she hadn't lost her looks but deep down she knew her sparkle and hot passionate flame, she had once possessed had been blown out for good.

***

"Do you come here often?"

Gaby turned around as she looked up at dark eyes as black as olives. He stared right through her as he handed her a glass of champagne. She laughed at the cliché line and accepted his drink.

"First time here actually."

"I thought I hadn't seen you here before. This is my club, and I know all of my guests," he said.

"Really," she wasn't interested.

"My name is Jed, pleased to be of your acquaintance. Would you like a dance?"

"No thanks, I'd rather not."

"Why are you alone, may I ask?"

"I'm not, my colleagues' are dancing. I didn't feel like it."

"Can I invite you for another drink? We can sit somewhere quiet."

Rosalyn and Hawkeye came back towards her as Hawkeye was nodding behind Jed's back as Rosalyn agreed with her. Feeling trapped in a corner she nodded.

Gaby sat with Jed the rest of the evening and eventually agreed to dance with him. It was late by this point and Rosalyn had gone home.

She had allowed this Italian to talk to her, and she was now letting him hold her on the dance floor. She was rigid and stiff as he held her close, the music was low and suddenly she realised they were alone.

Three months later; she was having an affair with him; his patience and perseverance had paid off. He had told her that he was married, and she was relieved. She didn't want a relationship with any man ever again. An affair was in order. She had never looked back. She had locked her emotions and feelings away and she had taken on a persona with no scruples and certainly she didn't care much about his feelings. After all he was married.

Jed had been surprised when she announced she was leaving for Spain. He liked being in control and he had never been able to dictate or control her. That was her attraction, her feisty free spirit. She was attracted to him; she had to admit he was gorgeous but his best feature apart from his cheeky grin and keyboard set of teeth; he was married and technically unavailable and no commitment discussions were required.

***

His probing tongue was down her throat as their tight embrace sent quivers down her spine as the last call was announced over the tannoy. They unlocked arms and as she went to walk away, he handed her a package which she placed in her handbag. She looked at him, surely, he knew it was over, as her name was called.

"Will passenger Gabriella Daly; please make your way to boarding gate 23 immediately".

"Or we'll go without you," as she looked at him, grabbed him for one last kiss as he muttered in her ear,

"A year isn't long; I'll come over and see you. Maybe, I'll be free to make an honest woman of you?"

"It's been great, but I don't want to marry you, Jed. Thanks for the fun time. I'll stay connected."

She hurried to the departures gate; her emotions aroused but in check. She had needed him, and he had come along at the time she was at her lowest. She had only wanted an affair, and it was time to be free of him.

The first rows of passengers, eager to commence their vacation were whispering about her as she walked down the aisle to the remaining empty seat. She muttered an apology to the man next to her who smiled and went back to his book.

The plane took off and Gabriella held her breath as they climbed up through the fluffy clouds towards Seville.

She ordered a large Gin and Tonic and opened the package he'd given her. Why had he given her a phone? Of course, he wanted to stay connected. She scrolled through the numbers and his contact details for several locations were already punched in. Maybe, she wasn't going to be able to shake him off as easily as she'd thought.

She'd only wanted an affair, he knew about Nick, and she'd slept with him, to get the hurt out of her system. Jed's sexual attributes and demands had brought her back to the real world, albeit this was an illicit affair. She also had an inclination that his businesses weren't all what they seemed, and she'd kept away from his day-to-day activities.

She looked across the aisle to the far window reflecting on their last night together, as she'd told him she was leaving.

They had had dinner at Harry's bar, and he'd lavished a bottle of Dom Perignon on her. Later they went to his club where he'd booked a cosy lounge for two. Champagne and oysters were ordered and served on their arrival, which had been passed midnight.

He had started fingering her under the table at Harry's bar, hence her long flowing skirt and as they settled in the lounge; he'd locked the room, and they had privacy at last.

She continued to stare through the window of the aeroplane as her eyes misted over as she felt Jed's entire body encapsulate her yet again.

His passionate kissing and her response had started with their lips locked together, his tongue probing inside hers, sending waves of tingling anticipation down her body. She'd felt the hot searing pain of longing go through her as she'd sunk back on to the squishy leather sofa. He had sat on her as they continued to kiss as she moved her hands over his tight body, reaching for his trouser belt; she'd wanted him there and then.

He moved her to lie down, the sofa sucking up her curvaceous curves but petite frame as she tried to reach him. She fondled him and could feel him growing with arousal as he continued to kiss every inch of her face, his stubble, grown especially, sending her wild.

As she lay there, he cupped her large breasts.......

"Another Gin and Tonic Miss?"

"Eh Yes thanks," as she frowned at being interrupted.

......stroked them with such tenderness and nipped them with such ferocity and eagerness it had sent her crazy. His urgency married by hers had sent them to heights that made this departure more wretched than she'd envisaged. She moved her legs apart as he knelt over her as his mouth moved towards her softness and his tongue......

"Can you lift your tray please?"

She glared at the hostess, as she placed her tray in the upright position.

He'd moved on to the sofa as she continued kissing her juices from his mouth. She shifted his legs gently and teased him with her deft tongue as she felt his hands reaching for her. Their tongues met as they kissed as he turned her upside down, her legs in the air and leaning over the sofa arm…….

"Please fasten your seat belts, we will shortly be landing at Seville airport," the message interrupted her thoughts as she looked at the man next to her and blushed.

She alighted the plane, finally retrieved all her suitcases and trundled through to the arrival's hall. She allowed her mind to concentrate on the task in hand. She scanned the sea of people, and she hoped he'd arrived. Louis, her friend was her landlord for the four weeks as she was staying in his apartment.

She moved her laden trolley to one side to retrieve her phone. She could remember what he looked like but couldn't see him in her radar. It had been three years since her last holiday, before she'd met Nick at any rate; now where was his number?

Louis tapped her shoulder as she turned around as the piercingly turquoise blue eyes smiled at her as she laughed with the phone in her hand; she'd forgotten how handsome he was. They hugged as friends as he nodded at the pile of luggage.

"This is more than a year, no?" his Spanish accent sending a ripple of excitement down her spine as she replied,

"No idea Louis, but thanks for meeting me," as they walked to his car with the trolley stacked high with purple suitcases. All thoughts of her lover evaporated out of her mind.

Louis had brought his Mother along and she couldn't speak English. As she couldn't speak Spanish either, she reluctantly immersed herself to her thoughts as Louis drove them to the apartment.

Louis rented his apartment to the language school every summer. The TEFL Teaching programme included accommodation and when she'd received her confirmation details, she'd been thrilled to see Louis was the apartments' landlord. They'd met on some painting holiday three years previously and had stayed connected. When she contacted him to say she was enrolling as a student, he'd offered to collect her from the airport.

She caught his eyes in the mirror, and she blushed as she wondered why his eyes and embrace earlier had surprised her. Her body had over reacted, and she was sure he could sense it.

She looked away and her thoughts went back to her estranged fiancé. She knew she loved him but his revelations that weekend had destroyed her and her decisions of late had become irrational. Consequently, she was a different person and her need to re-charge the batteries along with getting her lover out of her system was in order. If Nick found her, then she'd see if she could start again. In the meantime, she'd sold up and without anyone's knowledge, she had decided that she wasn't returning to the U.K.

3

Seville

The apartment was on the sixth floor as Louis casually mentioned as Mum assisted with lugging her suitcases to the edge of the staircase,

"There's no lift."

Gaby looked at him in horror and wondered if it may have been better to have stayed on the college campus.

"No problem, you go ahead, I'll bring them, and the exercise will be good for me."

Louis beckoned for his mother to go on up as he proceeded to help Gaby with four large suitcases and hand luggage as the six flights of stairs proved a challenge.

"This will keep me fit throughout my stay Louis," she chuckled and tried to see the funny side of her excess luggage.

The apartment once they were safely encased inside was larger than it appeared. It was old fashioned and typically Spanish with crochet doilies under everything that didn't move and crochet doilies over everything that wasn't to be soiled. The chair backs had a large version of the little round doilies, all pretty and all very dated.

Gaby's bedroom was light and airy in comparison, with a large en-suite bathroom. There was a small seating area comprising of a table for studying, a chaise lounge for relaxing and a double paned window. She overlooked the helicopter pad, a view which would prove fascinating. The apartment block was literally next door to the largest limb hospital in Seville as Louis gave her the guided tour as Mum prepared dinner.

"I'll leave you to unpack. Tomorrow, I'll walk you to the University in the morning; it's a short walk from here. It will take around thirty minutes, is that agreeable?" asked Louis as he stared right through her, making her shiver; she'd no idea why.

"It's all perfect, thanks Louis. I'll text my folks to say that I'm here. I'll join you in a while."

She sat on the enormous bed and found her phone charger along with Jed's phone. She wasn't sure if she wanted this phone as she didn't want contact with him, but right at that moment she set them both to charge. She located Nicks' business card and sent him the text as he'd asked. His revelations still hurt but she realised that she did want him to locate her, after all. She started to unpack her clothes as her phone pinged.

Surprised at a response from Nick, she sat on the bed and read his message as her eyes welled up.

"Get him out of your system, enjoy the experience but take care. Be safe and I WILL FIND YOU as I've never stopped loving youxxxxxx."

She realised that of course, he knew about her affair. He obviously knew her better than she knew herself. She wondered if he'd be pleased or surprised when he did eventually track her down, that she wasn't returning. She sighed, wiped her tears, and applied some lipstick.

She joined Louis and his Mum for dinner with her phrasebook, pen and paper in hand and knew she was going to relish her new adventure. He had given her permission to enjoy herself.

4

Louis

The walk to the Academy was a straight line as she swore under her breath as she'd packed all the wrong clothes. She'd needed to go shopping for lighter garments as soon as she had the opportunity. Louis was flirting with her as she tried to communicate in Spanish, but he insisted on talking in English, wanting the practise.

Gaby arrived to meet her new colleagues for the month and discovered three English girls amongst her class. Two of these girls were staying in the apartment. Louis was leaving for France to join his family for the summer months; he had a day to turn around the other two bedrooms in his apartment ready for these girls.

Nicks' only text for four months, had upset her far more than she'd realised as she sat with Liz and Lydia, her new colleagues, and tried hard to concentrate as Mike Charmers, the Director introduced the course.

He explained the do's and dont's of the Academy and then continued to describe Seville. He warned everyone regarding their personal belongings, especially everyone who had long strapped cross over handbags. Seville had the highest crime rate for any city in Spain.

Handbags would be cut away from the person walking on the pavement by a couple on a scooter. The kid riding pillion would cut the strap and take the bag before the victim would realise what had happened.

It was a sudden shock to hear this as Gaby clutched her handbag. She was carrying her money transfer along with her euros as she hadn't wanted to leave anything in the apartment. Suddenly the apartment seemed safer.

Liz and Lydia were both very bubbly in nature and over coffee the three girls got to know each other. They were going to move in the next evening as Lydia was staying with her parents in a hotel and Liz had joined them. Gaby declined their offer that evening as she wanted her own space for one more night.

She wanted to succeed this course and after the first day, it was evident that it was going to be intense. This was exactly what she needed; to focus on something else. Nick was undercover somewhere with no thoughts of her and the affair with Jed was over.

She smiled as she found the apartment block. The limb hospital towered over every other building, and it was easy to locate it. Not only was the building the tallest, but there was also a helipad on the top and the siren would sound every time the helicopter arrived with a limb. This helicopter seemed to land all the time, and the sirens became part of the month in Seville.

Opposite the apartment block was also a string of cafe`s and take- away shops, the closest one was a chicken rotisserie and pizza takeaway.

"*Gavee, over here,*" called Louis as he sat outside one of the cafe`s as she went towards him, laden with text books and files from the first day.

"*Café?*"

"*Gracias, Louis, Americano por favor.*"

Louis clicked his finger, and the waiter nodded and went to fetch his order.

"*You teach fast, Gavee.*"

"*You mean I learn fast, Louis,*" corrected Gaby. "*I've read my phrase book a lot that's all!*" as she sat next to him.

"*You have much books.*"

"*Many books. Yes. I didn't realise how much work this course was going to be.*"

It was years since she'd been in a class room. The coffees arrived as she ignored her own self-doubt.

"*Anyway, it's your last night Louis. Has Mum gone to her house? Shall we go out; maybe you can show me some of Seville? I've also met the two girls who are moving in tomorrow, they're great*", she said as his eyes went through her yet again.

"*Yes, I'm collecting Mum in the morning, we leave for France. Maybe, we go out later. Here in Seville, we go out after sun is down.*"

"*Fabulous.*"

"We have time to get to know each other. I help you with these books. There's so many, yes?" as he grinned at her.

She smiled at him; he was flirting again.

"Another coffee?" she asked breaking his gaze.

"Si."

The six flights of stairs were still a challenge as he carried the books for her. *This will keep me fit;* she'd thought as she tried to keep up with him, he was evidently used to having no lift. The apartment was ready for the two extra girls, he'd been busy. She was impressed as not many men would have turned the apartment round in a day, but there again, Louis had rented accommodation in various places, and he was probably used to it.

"Your mother has trained you good Louis," said Gaby as she opened the two en-suite bedrooms that Liz and Lydia would occupy.

"It's no problem, vino?" he said as he opened a bottle of red as Gaby nodded.

"I'll just put these books away."

She checked the mobile in the box, and she put her phone away. There were no messages from either man, she needed to forget them. She filed her new text books on the table and changed into a different top. It was so hot still and she'd brought four suitcases of the wrong clothes. It was already 38c and it was meant to get hotter as the month of August progressed.

She checked her money transfer and locked her passport and her funds away in one of the suitcases. A stringent discipline she continued throughout the four weeks stay at the apartment. She joined Louis on the terrace; the view of the helipad was the only interesting part of the imminent landscape, the buildings, and all tall, squashed in and close together.

Louis had Spanish guitar music playing in the living room and he got out olives as they both sat, chatting in both languages. The terrace, had several love seats built within the wall of the apartment, making clever use of space. The round table where Louis poured the wine was made with the traditional blue and orange mosaics. The numerous large yucca plants dotted round the terrace, along with trellis panels laden with potted colourful bougainvillea, rich reds and purple; meant privacy for the resident. The sun dancing in between the buildings creating shadows on the table adding intimacy to the evening.

"Do you remember the last time?" he asked.

"Yes, how could I forget? You were recovering from a broken heart, and your Mum had handed you the business all in one week! You were quite different then to how you are today, Louis. You've changed," smiled Gaby. He was a good friend.

"I am grown up now," he smiled.

"Do you remember how we met that week?" she asked not needing a reminder.

"Yes, you win a contract, yes? There was someone you also met. You hope he was the one."

"*Your English is much better Louis, yes. His name is Nick, and he's left me to work in Spain. I'm going to meet up with him, eventually.*"

"*Why, what happening?*"

"*He pretended to be in construction for nearly two years, looking back I always wondered why he was away so much. He was very guarded all the time.*"

"*What is guarded?*"

"*I mean, he was always careful, never totally relaxed in my company, I just felt there was something wrong. I kept him away from all my friends and family, for this reason. He proposed a few months ago.*"

"*You mean marry you?*"

"*Yes, I accepted if I could take my year away to relax. I've always wanted to travel for a bit, before settling down.*"

"*What happening?*"

"*I think I've made a mistake, because I felt let down as although he proposed, he hadn't been honest with me. I had a fling.*"

"*Fling.*"

"*Yes affair.*"

"*Oh, what happening?*"

"*When he proposed he also told me the truth. He is an undercover policeman and is working in the Costa del Sol somewhere. I was totally shocked and not expecting that at all. I felt betrayed.*"

"Betrayed?"

"I felt disappointed, he never trusted me."

"Oh, I see, but what about your affair?"

"Yes, I know, he told me last night that he knows about Jed, it was his job to know what everyone around him was doing."

"He's doing his job."

"Well, yes you could say that, but I still feel as if he should have confided in me."

"Confided?"

"Trusted me, to tell me from the beginning."

"Gavee, he couldn't. He probably didn't think his first date or two with you would go on for two years. Give him a chance, no?"

"Oh Louis, you're such a romantic, yes, I was hard on him. The mere fact I've had an affair is irrelevant. I accepted his proposal, but he left and last night told me to get Jed out of my system. He said, he would track me down when his assignment was over and then we could start again."

Before she realised, Louis was next to her holding her head to his chest as she started to cry. She held on to her friend as she let the tears flow. This was the first time she'd spoken about it to anyone, apart from her work colleagues.

It felt like torture, but she could sense the release happening to her body, the tension slowly drifted away as she cried for a further few minutes. Louis held her and stroked her long black hair as the sun drifted down to sleep, the shadows on the terrace starting to dance even more.

The acoustic guitar strummed in the background adding to the silence as she let out several deep breaths allowing Louis to fondle her long locks as she rested her head. It was a few minutes before she looked up into his piercingly blue eyes as she felt his lips brush hers. She responded with the need for comfort and felt his arms envelope around her as she moved her body towards him as they kissed. The holding of his embrace and his soft kisses all over her face and her lips made her feel wanted.

They moved to the love seat embracing, kissing, and fondling each other to the slow rhythm of the Spanish guitar. The orange crusted sun disappeared between the two buildings as the terrace was engulfed in darkness as Louis continued to kiss. She was vulnerable and emotionally charged and stopped his kisses and adjusted her top. She looked at him and in silence walked him to her bedroom.

She woke up early, the sun already blazing high above the buildings. She went in search for her friend and was dismayed to find a note on the living room table next to the acoustic guitar c d. "*Besos*" it read. She scrambled for her dictionary and realised that learning Spanish was going to be as important as waiting for Nick. She dismissed Nick from her thoughts as she found the word, "kisses."

She walked to the Academy that morning and felt free to get on with her life. She would move to Marbella as planned. She felt exhilarated; the tears had released a tension in her that she'd been harbouring for a while. It was time to put aside the men in her life and enjoy this new adventure.

5

Liz and Lydia

The first lesson of the day was the planning of the live lesson to real foreign students that afternoon. The surprise rippling through the class as the course tutor explained that this was intensive and to expect long hours.

The course leader Justin was introduced, and he needed to share the rules of the School along with being safe in Seville.

"I know you're all here to earn the certification of the Tefl Teaching, and I realise you'll all be out letting off steam on occasions in this lovely city of ours. I've been here five years and Seville is a beautiful romantic place. It really doesn't sleep but a word of warning."

Gaby felt a slight unease as Justin continued,

"The city doesn't stop, and it has the worst unemployment record of all cities within Spain. This means that shoplifting and pick pocketing is rife, especially in this area. The immigrants, mainly Moroccans have arrived here thinking the pavements are lined with gold. Mike has already told you, how they steal. Just be careful."

Lydia raised her eyebrow at her.

34

"Do not talk on the mobile in the street as you'll be targeted next time the kid in the street is on the scooter with his mate. They make money selling them on. These guys haven't been able to get work. It costs money to register for a national insurance number. Without this, you cannot work in Spain. Nearer the end of the course, I'll explain how to prepare you for work before you sit your exams. Thank you and be careful."

Gaby sat with Liz and Lydia. Justin proceeded to hand out the first lesson to be taught. The students made their way to the libraries where the research material was held. Planning lessons to beginners with the verb *"To be"* was already going over Gaby's head.

"We never learnt grammar this way," said Liz as she was struggling to find a topic for her class.

"I know," said Gaby. *"What's a gerund?"*

Lydia giggled in the far corner overhearing the two girls.

"My subject is "travel" I've no idea how to break this down."

Mike Charmers arrived and saved the day. He knew the older students would be struggling. The other graduates in their early twenties had studied grammar for the last few years and they didn't have issue.

"Ladies, follow these guidelines, Liz you're on the right track. Gaby, your past experiences, use this in what you're trying to teach.

*"What, "**To be**," I didn't know what this meant until this morning. Can I do role play as in a training session?*

"You've got it, show me before your lesson commences. Lydia let me talk you through this."

Gaby became immersed in her lesson and realised she wasn't daunted by the actual teaching. Her role in recruitment and the training she'd planned and instigated within the hospitality industry would hold her in good stead. She relaxed but knew deep down that the grammar and the teaching of it, would keep her occupied for the next four weeks.

With the first lesson under their belt the three girls walked back to the apartment. Neither female had the luggage she'd brought and suddenly she felt stupid. She should have backpacked like these two and once qualified as a *tefl* Teacher; she could have gone home and planned her next journey.

She shrugged those doubts and emotions, these girls didn't know why she'd made these life changing decisions, they didn't need to know either. She had no home; she'd sold everything as she felt her hidden purse in her bra.

"Oh, I forgot to say, we're on the sixth floor and there's no lift."

The girls laughed as they all clambered the stairs to the apartment. Gaby showed them their rooms, and they were pleased.

"I know we need to study but, I need more suitable clothes."

"Actually, I could do with a new bag and after what Julian and Mike have both said; we need to sort ourselves out. My dad would have a fit if I lost my phone," said Liz.

"Come on, I've got the "lonely planet" here and yesterday I came across this magazine, "The tourist," we can get to the shopping quarters, get what we need, have a coffee and absorb a bit of this city," suggested Gaby as thoughts of Louis lingered in her mind. She'd checked the other phone and nothing from Jed, she was beginning to feel relieved.

"It's only eight o clock; the city is only just livening up. Come on, we can study the rest of the time."

The *Quadalquiver* River meanders through the heart of the City. With the use of the local maps, it was evident by learning the bridges;' finding their way around was not going to be difficult. The transport system seemed easy, and they discovered a bus that brought them closer to their apartment than originally thought. Being near the limb hospital was an advantage.

There were four *"El Corte Ingles"* department stores and locating the one with women's fashion was more of a challenge than finding the boutiques and shopping areas. The cobbled streets were full of tourists and locals, and music was filling the area as shoppers strolled in the early evening sun.

"We'll get everything we need in here," said Gaby as they piled into the store and arranged to meet at the entrance when they were done. Liz and Lydia went together to the shoe department as Gaby started eyeing up cotton trousers with pockets. She saw Liz embracing Lydia and smiled, they were obviously very close friends.

A few hours later, it was time for a coffee as they ambled round the boutiques laden with bags. Being the middle of August, it was still around 38c and more importantly the *Rebajas/Sales* were in full swing. Near the magnificent cathedral were endless coffee shops and the three girls sat and took it all in. The two girls seemed closer than friends.

Two *Policia* passed on motorbikes and stopped adjacent to the café as Gaby admired them from her seat.

"I don't know about you, but these Police guys look like models," as the two men were basically observing everyone.

"Are they your type Gaby?" asked Liz lowering her sunglasses even though it was getting dusk.

"Most definitely."

"Oh, we should go clubbing, for Gaby to find her sexy Spaniard," suggested Lydia as they laughed out loud.

"You have to admit, they're pretty hot. Look at them, immaculate, maybe good looks and ray bans are part of the recruitment and uniform process" she giggled.

"Let's go clubbing, we've got all week and three weeks to get through to the exam," suggested Liz.

"Why not?" said Gaby, who couldn't think of anything worse but knew she needed to get her men out of her mind.

"Louis has given me a good one to go to, not just dance music but a combination of stuff."

"Who's Louis?"

"My Spanish friend, he actually owns the apartment," smiled Gaby thinking of last night.

"Tell us more," whispered Liz grinning at her.

"There's nothing to say really, he just gave me a few places for us to eat and drink and where the Irish bars are and a few clubs, that's all. I've known him for ages; he's in France for the summer, just a mate."

"Yeah right," said Lydia seeing right through Gaby as she laughed at them, they were obviously *"together."*

The three girls went to meet the bus as Lydia's strap broke from her shoe, and it fell off.

"Damn, I liked these too."

"Put a pair on that you've bought," said Gaby.

"No, I need a safety pin, let's go in there to the farmacia to get one," she said not wanting to open the beautifully wrapped packages she had.

"Por favor, haveh vou safety pin?" enquired Liz as Gaby started going through the phrase book knowing this was not a clever idea.

The lady wearing a white coat behind the counter, about to close was not amused as she nodded and said,

"Que?"

"There's absolutely nothing in this book to tell me what a safety pin is," said Gaby mortified as the lady started to look impatient.

"Quick draw one," said Liz as she grabbed the book, got out her pen and sketched a pin and showed it to the lady who smiled at them.

"Ah si, el imperdible," as she proceeded to open a drawer and handed over a packet of safety pins to Lydia.

"Of course, it is," laughed Gaby as she realised that without basic Spanish they would not be getting far in this city.

"We need to teach ourselves some Spanish," said Lydia as they embarked on the bus. As both girls nodded in agreement.

"We're going to stay in Seville after we qualify, where are you heading?" asked Liz as Gaby rearranged her shopping, checking her purse.

"I'm going to Marbella," said Gaby.

"Why Marbella?"

"I need the sea, and my boyfriend is working there somewhere. We'll get together when his assignment's over, he's an undercover policeman," said Gaby.

"Oh wow, what's he doing?"

"No idea, he's undercover," said Gaby. *"I presume you two are an item and you're both staying in Seville?"*

"You've worked us out already," smiled Liz.

"Wasn't that difficult," said Gaby. *"It doesn't make any difference to me. If I'm honest I don't fancy clubbing tonight, we've all got another lesson and homework, let's stay in and do that."*

"You're right, let's get a chicken from that rotisserie near us and work out a way to teach ourselves some Spanish and get our heads round this grammar."

"You go on up, I'll get the chicken," she said determined to practise some Spanish.

Two brothers managed the take away chicken outlet and they sold pizzas, bread, and drinks. They were open from six am until midnight and it was a busy shop. They acknowledged and recognised her from being with Louis the day before as she smiled at them, phrase book in hand,

"Un pollo por favor."

"Que?" said the brother with glasses.

"Uno pollo por favor," she clipped in a clear voice, was her pronunciation that bad?

The cute brother with glasses looked horrified, whilst the other bald brother stood behind him convulsing in hysterics. She beamed at him, and he went red and redder even to his ears as she smiled at him in anticipation of her poor pronunciation being understood.

"Que?" he whispered.

"Uno Pollo," she shouted and pointed to the chicken behind him which were rotissering nicely on the spit.

What was so bloody funny, as by this point bald brother was laughing so much, he was doubled up leaning against the counter? Three young girls were giggling behind her in the shop. She smiled, paid, and took her chicken parcel from the mortified brother and clambered up to the apartment. What the hell was all that about? She got in and told the two girls. They checked the dictionary and phrase book as Liz laughed uncontrollably as Gaby went red, she felt so foolish.

She'd ordered a dick!

"This Spanish language is going to be trickier than I thought," said Gaby as she went to her room to hide her purse, placed all her shopping on the bed, and composed herself, she felt a complete idiot.

Liz and Lydia were great and were chatting about the next day's lessons as she came back through to join them. The array of books and paper were strewn around the living room and Gaby was immediately at ease.

"It's so warm out on the terrace, let's eat out here," said Liz coming in from moving stuff around.

"Good idea."

"You've got to laugh, Gaby. I'd love to have seen his face."

"It was a picture, believe me," she giggled it was probably not the first time someone had ordered a dick and not a chicken and she laughed it was funny after three glasses of Rioja.

The Gypsy Kings on the cd spilled out on to the terrace as the girls stopped revising and raucous laughing and flirting began with dick being the subject.

"You don't like dick anyway?" whispered Gaby on her fourth glass of wine and thinking of Louis from the night before.

"Whatever makes you say that?" asked Liz intrigued by Gaby's statement.

"I thought you two were an item."

"Yes, but we still like a fuck," said Lydia as Gaby nearly choked on her wine spilling it everywhere.

"Have you tried batting for the other side, Gaby?"

"Not really, why do you ask?"

"Come here," said Liz as she gently grabbed her thick black curls and started kissing her on her lips.

She closed her eyes and responded as Liz embraced her, and Lydia looked on. They moved to the love seat, and they continued to kiss. Liz was expertly arousing her and started moving her hands all over her curvy body. Lydia appeared and took off her sandals and massaged her feet as Liz continued kissing. Gaby was sinking deep into a first kiss and didn't know where to place her hands. Lydia guided her hands to Liz's breasts as she started to fondle them through her silk top.

She felt the nipples harden as suddenly Lydia appeared from her feet. Gaby looked at them both and they laid her down gently and in one deft move she lay naked with the two girls around her.

She responded and suddenly she felt a mouth around her inner thighs and precious sweet spot as her body began to react. Her multiple orgasms that evening had engulfed her with great sharpness as she'd responded. She continued the lovemaking with both girls throughout the night.

In between the buildings, the early crust of the sun could be seen edging round the terrace as the three girls had lain entwined with each other. She'd watched Liz and Lydia making love and had been shocked at her feelings.

Not to feel awkward as they woke up, Lydia kissed Gaby once more, who had also stirred. Liz opened her eyes and smiled at both girls. Lydia moved her lips to Gaby's breasts and embraced her voluptuous curves. Liz moved to her inner thighs and between them brought her to a quick and satisfying release.

The sun began to rise, and they knew it was time to shower and leave for the Academy. They showered together in the large bathroom, and she knew these girls had saved her from all the nonsense of the past few months, two men and Louis.

6

Russian lesson

With events in the apartment unfolding, the three girls became close. Gaby continued to fret quietly as the grammar was harder than she'd envisaged. She'd no contact from Nick. Jed was becoming a distant memory. With the girls giving her much comfort, she was healing her broken heart. They'd only invited her once to the terrace over the past two weeks and for that she was grateful. She didn't want to start questioning her sexuality along with everything else.

It was nearing the end of three weeks, and the practical teaching was easy. She sighed as she went through the grammatical reasoning of continual sentences; this was truly becoming quite tough to translate into a lesson. Tonight, she had intermediate students, who asked a lot of questions, hence she'd buried her head in the text books all through lunch.

"You, ok?"

Lydia had appeared from nowhere as Liz had gone to look at an apartment and do some shopping; the boutiques were easily reached by a taxi during their lunch hour.

"I'm just finding some of this a nightmare. How are you absorbing it?"

"You know; it doesn't matter Gaby. You're already a great teacher, your practical classes are the best ones, even Mike our tutor has told us. Stop worrying, you need to relax."

"I know," said Gaby, *"But I don't want to re-sit the exam if I fail first time. I need to be in Marbella for Nick."*

"Fuck him Gaby. Go and live your life, if he wants you, he'll find you. I mean it. Men will always chase the one they want; he'll forgive you; that's the way it is."

She blushed, *"You're right. When does your class finish?"*

"I'll be home by seven," said Lydia.

"I'm early too, I'll get some supper, maybe we ought to chill tonight," suggested Gaby.

"Great stuff, I'll text Liz. We've got a Russian lesson before we split up to teach," said Lydia as the bell sounded to remind them, the lunch hour was over.

"Why the fuck do we need to learn Russian?" said Gaby out loud as Mike Charmers the Academy Director walked in. She flushed with embarrassment.

"Watch her technique, she doesn't speak English. This is to make you feel like the poor student," said Mike beckoning them not to be late as he left.

"Come on, you're stressed. You've done enough prep for your lesson, it looks good," said Lydia who never planned her lessons, but she seemed to get through each one, unscathed.

The Russian lesson was an eye opener as the young teacher managed to get all twenty-three students conversing in Russian. She gave them certain phrases and by repeating and drilling the phonetics they could pronounce the words and phrases accurately. The class including Gaby learnt how to improve on their own technique.

"***Mehr 3Obyt Gabriella!***" said Gaby as they left for their respective teaching class. *My name is Gaby and knowing the days of the week and month would certainly not come in useful,* she thought. What on earth had been the reason to learn about Russian firearms? Why couldn't they have learnt a bit of Italian or German, surely that would have been better?

She walked home to prepare supper for her friends. She suddenly felt better about the whole idea of teaching and looking for private work. She could walk six flights of stairs without gasping for breath; a lot had changed in a little time. It was all falling into place and her sun kissed body, showing all her light freckles especially her nose, had taken ten years off her face. The change of life was beginning to show, and she felt upbeat.

She prepared tapas and opened some wine, a week to go and they would be leaving this apartment. Liz and Lydia were going to stay together in Seville. The next task for them would be to find work. She'd calculated that in this Academy alone, there would be over a hundred *tefl* teachers, in the four months over summer. No wonder the tutors were giving them suggestions about Asia and the Far East.

She went for a shower and hadn't checked that phone for two days. Her own mobile was switched off mostly due to teaching; but she realised she quite liked not having any contact with the past. Maybe that was it. She needed to move on completely and start again.

An arm suddenly engulfed her waist as Lydia cupped her breasts from behind as she turned to embrace her. The shower continued to cover them as Gaby reached for the soap and started to massage Lydia's taunt body. They kissed and covered each other with lather.

The bathroom door opened, and Liz walked in already naked and eased into the cubicle. The wet room steamed up as the three girls lathered and caressed each other, enjoying the moment.

They shook soap out of their eyes as they moved to the wet room floor. She tied her hair up as the soap trickled down her face. They all knelt as Liz, holding on to Gaby's knees, continued to kiss her as Lydia trickled her tongue down her lover's back from behind, her other hand caressing one of her breasts.

Gaby moved her hands towards Liz's inner thigh; it was as natural as baby oil on silk sheets. They continued, their nipples responding to whoever's mouth were closest. All three receiving and giving at the same time, wrapped so closely around each other. Liz's vibrator appeared from the bag strewn on the floor as the shower continued to spray them as they lathered and played with each other. The steam from the shower enhanced their arousal as their juices flowed as they'd become greedy for each other.

They all moaned out loud together as they lay on the floor. Gaby looked up at the ceiling of the sixth-floor apartment and was relieved there was no one above them. They had been raucous; however, the shower had covered the sounds of passionate lovemaking.

"He CTPENRNTE BE MEHR" said Gaby out loud as they all laughed, as she needed to defuse the situation.

"Don't shoot me" she'd just said in Russian.

Lydia went to her lover and kissed her more. Gaby left them, their closeness apparent even though they'd shared her, used her even. She knew one thing; she would never forget this and hoped there would be at least one more time before she left them in Seville. Was she gay? She'd never thought about it until that moment.

She would have plenty of time to analyse this once she'd gone. Living the moment was required right now. No one had been hurt, no one knew; therefore, it was a waste of time worrying about it. It was too good a feeling to think anything but fabulous thoughts.

She got up and jumped back into the shower and quickly got herself out of the bathroom. The two girls needed to be on their own.

She poured a glass of wine and picked up the grammar homework. She would do this later. She went to cook some of the tapas she'd organised much earlier. It was nearly midnight and as she cooked, she felt exhilarated. Maybe she was gay, maybe she was a bit of both. She loved cock too much not to have any more, forever. She shrugged, perish the thought!

Lydia and Liz came in grinning, both wearing a skimpy sarong as did Gaby. The temperature was still in the high thirties. None of them could bear the apartment's air conditioning as it gave them sore throats. They ate some tapas and after a glass of wine the girls retired to Liz's room.

Gaby felt a new sense of purpose for some reason. She went to the terrace with the remaining bottle of wine and continued to study, making up for lost time. The exam was a week away and she couldn't fail.

***

It was exam week. Their first audited lesson was in the morning. The second audited lesson was in the afternoon. The two audits allowed for mishaps and nerves and for this alone Gaby felt good. She had no issue with the practical, but Liz was having problems.

"Why don't we combine your students with mine?" suggested Gaby looking at the list. *"You've got seven intermediates, and I've got five. I think we should do it together; will that help?"*

"That would be great, it gives us a further two hours to plan too, if we can move these to your slot," said Liz daunted by the practical assessment.

"Come on, let's suggest this to Mike."

"Yes, we can do this, but as you're sharing this lesson, I need something off the wall. Your theme is directions. I'll be monitoring this one, I'll see you later. Liz, you're next up in advanced."

"Yes, I'm ready, Gaby see you in an hour. Meet in the library to plan?"

"Yes."

Her theory was done; she was as ready as could be. Going through the material in the library and knowing this lesson could swing the exam result, she had a brainwave. With a copy of a street to hand she went to get pen and paper and planned furiously. Her objective for the directions was, right, left, over the hill and so on. She wrote down five key phrases and concentrated on them.

Liz appeared over an hour later and loved the idea. Together they made their plan complete. As the students were queuing outside the classroom, the two girls went inside to prepare. They re-arranged the furniture apart from two chairs for the auditors, one in each corner.

Liz got on to the blackboard and wrote the lesson objective as Gaby drew the street, with chalk on the tiled floor. They were ready. The students came in and looked-for chairs, there were none. The auditors sat and looking amused.

Liz, asked the students to queue to one side. Gaby explained they were going to walk the street. In pairs, they would be asking each other directions. Within minutes there were two teams walking up and down, left to right in the classroom, all reciting and drilling the objective phrases. Liz was having fun and with eye contact with Gaby, they managed to share the forty- five minutes. The lesson overran by five minutes as the students hadn't once looked at their watches, sometimes bored with the difficulties of grammar. At the end, everyone was laughing, and the students were all complimenting the tutors for a good lesson.

Wednesday arrived and the Academy was quiet as if someone had died. There were several examinations throughout the morning.

The last exam in the afternoon was three hours long with various tools used to check different forms of language teaching.

"I need a drink," said Gaby as the last exam of the day was over. They'd been quite daunting. Even today, there had been a question she hadn't understood but had given it her best shot.

"Let's go to the Irish Bar," suggested one of the graduates that Gaby had helped with his practical.

"Good idea," she said as they packed their bags leaving their books in the Academy.

"We're not needed back until late tomorrow afternoon. They've started marking already," said Lydia as she joined them all outside.

"Oh Christ, I definitely need a drink," said Gaby.

"You've already passed your practical, stop worrying," said Liz poking her in the ribs. Her reaction to her touch in public bothered her as they walked towards their favourite Irish bar.

The singing was mostly British even though a very efficient Spanish couple ran the bar. After several hours, the acoustic guitar was being strummed by the landlord as the shots and wine flowed. The bar was full of students and Policia, the Police Station being adjacent to the bar.

"We're going clubbing?" said Gaby determined to have a last fling with her colleagues. Sunday was looming, the day they were leaving the apartment.

"We're all going," said Liz very merry as Lydia was engrossed with one of their younger colleagues.

"Muy Guappa! Tu eres marido, no?!/hey beautiful, you're married, no?!"

"Si, si," giggled Gaby who realised there was no point trying to make conversation. In four weeks, she hadn't learnt any Spanish as she'd somewhat been distracted.

About thirty of them went to the club which opened its doors at midnight. The music was loud which meant she didn't have to converse with the good-looking men in their company.

They walked home from the club, very drunk but with three of the local Policia in tow. The guys were practising their English as Gaby held on to one, knowing she could easily fall if she wasn't careful.

Joaquin, whose eyes made her shiver as he spoke was intently practising his English with Gaby as they followed Liz and Lydia who were both arm in arm with two men. She managed the six flights considering she felt drunk on arrival to the apartment. On entry, she realised that everyone had disappeared, and Joaquin didn't waste any time either.

She took him to her bedroom and indulged him. She kissed his jet-black curls all over his body. She felt a sense of control as she felt more confident than ever.

They stirred as the siren sounded as the helicopter could be heard landing on the strip. Joaquin had fallen asleep wrapped around her body. They could hear movement outside the living room. She pulled a sarong round her and went to check. The two men were in shorts and the two girls were naked on the terrace watching the helicopter. Joaquin stood behind her, his hardness touching the base of her spine as she laughed at the girls waving at the helicopter in the nude.

Before she knew what was happening, Joaquin pulled her round and moved her to the love seat. The two men grabbed their girl, and the terrace suddenly became hot with bronzed bodies kissing each other as the sun slowly started to rise through the buildings, creating light and dark shadows.

Andréa was sat behind her as he slowly moved his hands over her body, fondling her and kissing the nape of her neck. She faced Joaquin's as his fingers moved within her, the searing hotness going through her body from his extra touch.

Liz and Lydia were enjoying Mario on the terrace floor and the whole morning passed in a whirl. There was no language barrier to making love or wanting comfort. Gaby, relaxed on the love seat as Joaquin was showing off his deft tongue as he encircled all of her throughout the morning. She massaged Andréa who had moved above her head. She didn't think, she wasn't questioning what she was doing. She was living for the moment; she'd never experienced anything quite like this and knew she'd never do it again.

***

They'd made love all day, in between the guys in turn running down to the rotisserie shop to get provisions. They'd all joined in after breakfast and after a short siesta had decided to continue from the shower room. By early evening they were all on the terrace, the three girls arousing the boys with their amorous kissing, setting the scene for the evening. The Spanish acoustic cd continued to play all afternoon giving the air of romanticism.

Andréa, grabbed her waist and lay down in front of the bougainvillea trellis as Gaby fondled him as he responded. Quickly Mario and Joaquin joined them in a row, with Mario's head opposite Andréa as Joaquin guided Lydia towards his erect member as Mario held Liz, squashed in the middle, moving immediately inside her. As if on cue and charged by the electricity between them, they moved together as one. Gaby and Lydia facing Liz in the middle massaged and nipped a breast each as they all began to react to their union.

Lydia reached to kiss her lover as the boys moved faster with this gesture as they became urgent. Mario grabbed Gaby's hair and pulled her towards him as his rapid response led her to wrap her arms round him as suddenly, they all groaned out loud together.

Mario's phone alarm went off and the men on cue finished what they were doing. They went to shower together. They left as they were on the night shift. It had been fun, and Gaby hadn't learnt any Spanish apart from words she couldn't repeat to any student.

"Shall we finish what they started?" whispered Liz as the apartment door shut.

"*Yes,*" said Gaby as she took the initiative and went inside Lydia's bedroom as the terrace was too hot to lie on the tiles.

Later in the evening, she started to pack her six suitcases, she wondered how on earth was she going to get all her luggage to Marbella? Lydia was cooking a chilli and Liz had gone to fetch a new bag for her as she'd far too much stuff. There were two bags of books, let alone new clothes and shoes. She checked her purse; it was safe, and all funds and the money transfer were intact and secure. Her spending allowance looked healthier than her initial budget. Everything was well. She placed it back in her bra for safe keeping, knowing her bra was not likely to come off in a hurry after these last few weeks.

She got Jed's phone from the box. There were three missed calls and three text messages. How bizarre. All they said, were *"Italy,"* she couldn't care less. Once she'd got to Marbella, she would change the chip. She didn't want contact with him anymore.

The three girls walked to the Academy for the last time the next morning. She'd had so much sex over the past few weeks, she continually felt sexy. The hot weather was adding to those feelings as she grinned at the two girls who'd released her sexual appetite. They hadn't discussed the company of the three men and Gaby didn't need to talk about it either. She'd also responded to both genres and was no longer sure what she wanted. All she knew that some people had no rules, and they were free.

Mike Charmers walked in, asking everyone to go to their course Tutor in turn, for their results. Leaving the Academy to celebrate was more a relief than celebration. She was packed and ready to go and went to the bus station to organise her journey to Marbella.

The sun had disappeared suddenly, and the rain had started as she made her way to the bus station squelching under her feet. Her new sandals were not geared for this sudden deluge of water. She needed a one-way ticket to Marbella and as she hailed a taxi to the apartment, she wondered how the hell she was going to cope with her entire luggage, of which she now had six cases and three bags.

All thoughts of Nick an indeed Jed were as far from her mind as England was a country. She was different; she was back to that Welsh girl, with vulnerabilities that she'd managed to hide all these years. She was entering a new world full of unknowns. Lydia pressed a package in her hand.

"We thought you may need these replaced and there's something to keep you occupied!"

She opened the bag, and it was a large box of condoms and a new vibrator as she laughed. She hugged them both, wished them luck and clambered into the front of the taxi as her luggage had consumed the boot and the back seat. The bus station wasn't too far and her bus to Marbella was leaving in forty minutes.

The rain had continued overnight, and she wore sandals, but the girls had quite rightly said, that by the time she arrived in Marbella, the sun should be shining.

7

Marbella

The journey to Marbella via Ronda had been an interesting one.

The thunder and lightning had been quite spectacular as they'd eventually left the bus terminal. The fork lightning had created colourful breaks in the dark sky, and it was followed by crashing thunder.

The driver had been totally confused at the amount of luggage she was claiming as hers. He'd said nothing apart from mutter something indescribable under his breath. She found a window seat and she could sit with her handbag hidden under her coat and doze off slightly. It had been an eventful four weeks, and she tried to digest how she'd behaved.

No one was the wiser. She would probably never hear from the two girls ever again as she relived some of their activities. She needed to bank her nest egg as she privately planned to find her home in the sun.

The rain continued to pour down like sheets of glass as they stopped in Ronda for an hour. There was no point spending the time to have a quick look around and she decided to buy a coffee and get back on the bus. The rain would ease by the time they arrived in Marbella.

She'd booked herself in to a hostel via the *"lonely planet"* book, which to date had become her bible. The hostel was in Old Town Marbella, easy walking distance to the whole area and her first task apart from opening a bank account was to find some work and an apartment.

She had a substantial sum on her transfer, and she didn't want to squander it. She was obviously easily led as past events had proved. That had been different. She'd allowed herself a pot of 10,000€ in a current account. Her money transfer of 287,000€ was to be placed in a high interest savings account. Even at the turn of the millennium, her bank had advised her to take her funds this way as she'd no idea which bank was to have her deposit.

She felt rested as the bus pulled into the terminal building of Marbella Town. The disappointment of arriving in the pouring rain didn't deter her. Her raincoat wasn't adequate for this deluge, but she wore it regardless. It was one less item to carry. She attached the straps to each case and bags and like ducks in a row pulled them out through the cobbled terminal to find a taxi.

Before she got in the queue, she located the address she needed and proceeded to move her cases and bags to the end. Immediately the raincoat was soaked through to her clothes, and her hair was saturated and sticking to her face.

Where was the bloody sun? She'd been ignored whilst the queue had dissipated several times. Totally resembling a drowned rat, it then dawned on her that the heap of wet luggage hampered a taxi to stop. She moved away from it and a few minutes later a taxi came around the corner and stopped for her. She immediately gave him her address, and he nodded.

She pointed at her luggage, and he waited for her to fill the taxi. He didn't get out to help her, the rain was relentless. She didn't blame him but this welcome to Marbella was a shock to the system. He proceeded to drive round for twenty minutes and stopped the taxi at the brow of a hill. He pointed towards it and in fast speaking Spanish scribbled a drawing, where she would find her hostel.

"Gracias!" she nodded as he quickly emptied his car and sped away as if his life depended on it.

"Charming," she thought as the rain pelted down like sheets of glass. *"The rain in Spain falls ...."* She couldn't get that phrase out of her head as she stood mortified, she'd been dumped. The suitcases and the bags piled on top sat in a pool of water as the rain flowed down the hill like a stream. Her kitten heeled sandals were ruined and she took them off. It was easier to walk in bare feet and move her luggage one at a time towards the top of the hill. The suitcases seemed heavier as they were canvas and wet. There was no one in sight and there wouldn't be in this weather. Who in their right mind would come out for a walk in the rain? It was also a Sunday, a family day, for a Catholic country.

Eventually, she got herself and her luggage to the top of the hill and she looked around the corner keeping her luggage in sight. Not that there was anyone around to steal them, she was horrified. There were probably a hundred stone-coloured steps sweeping up to the Old Town. She sat on the first step soaked through and tried not to laugh or cry.

She took two cases and about six steps at a time as she walked back and forth and moved her luggage up the hundred steps towards the town. An hour later, she had the hostel in her sight as she smiled and felt good suddenly.

She neatly stacked her luggage at the entrance of the hostel and walked in barefooted and soaked to the skin. Her long black hair dripped all over the tiled floor as she smiled feebly at the receptionist, and her mind went completely blank. She couldn't remember any self-taught phrases as the young girl smiled at her and tried to look sympathetic. She disappeared and quickly returned with a towel chattering in Spanish as Gaby nodded.

"Tener reserv/I have a reservation?" she said hoping she'd remembered right.

"Si, nombre?"

"Gabriella Daley."

"Si, Tienes bolsas?"

"Si, outside, uhm mucho bolsas," as she waved her arm to the front steps.

The young girl went out to look, shrieked, and turned back towards her and smiled.

"Un momento por favor."

She felt embarrassed as her hair created some water in the reception area even though the towel had helped. Before she grasped what was happening, three young lads appeared from the back room and took all her luggage. She was grateful as she paid for two weeks and handed over her passport, she was on the fourth floor. Again, no lifts!

It was only lunchtime. She threw her wet clothes in the tiny bath as she stripped and ran the shower and was grateful for the instant hot water. The rain was still pounding against the windows of her room, and she decided to have a siesta and then sort out her luggage.

She'd packed in a way that she only needed one case immediately. The rest could wait until she found an apartment. She felt quite alone suddenly, as this was now it. She'd been with friends for four weeks, she was now in Marbella, on her own. No work, nowhere to live and the realisation that she needed to speak Spanish; otherwise, she would not get far. All these things rolled around in her head as she went to sleep as the rain continued to hit the windows.

A few hours later, she woke up and realised it had stopped raining. Through the window, she could see bright blue sky and some fluffy clouds. She smiled and thought *"at last."* She wrung out the wet clothes in the bath and hung them round the room. She peered out the window and seeing blue sky, re- dressed in a skirt and a top with another pair of sandals. Her kitten heels were ruined.

Her hair, in a ponytail but still wet she made her way to reception to ask if they could direct her to the tourist office. Per her book, the tourist office was open on a Sunday.

"Donde, oficina de turismo?" she enquired and hoped to be understood.

"Si Sènorita," as the young girl handed her a map of Old Town. She pointed with her pen, the hostel and where the office was located.

"Gracias."

"Tienes paraguas?"

"No," Gaby replied not sure what she was talking about.

"Ok."

She walked outside; it was dry considering the amount of water that had been evident a few hours earlier. There was clear blue sky and a few clouds but a stark difference from the morning. By her map, she wasn't far from where the tourist office was located. A ten-minute walk-through cobbled streets and marble steps and Gaby arrived at Orange square.

There, she took in the scene in front of her. The orange trees were in full blossom. The odd pink or white flower could be seen floating off the trees and cascading over the tourists who were seated around several cafés. The lines of trees were as Gaby had visualised and the whole area had a pink tinge to it. People were milling around and there was a sense of calmness. She spotted the tourist office and went to ask advice on the area. Above all she needed a proper map of the streets and locations of language schools.

Her mobile rang which made her jump as she fumbled in her handbag to locate it. It was Liz and she sat and spoke to the two girls in turn. It was great to hear their voices, and they were calling to tell her that they were going to Japan. She suddenly felt quite envious as they had each other. But she had her own mission, and she wished them well. She didn't know at that time; she'd never hear from them again.

She'd been given useful information at the tourist office. The young man, who'd spoken perfect English, had been helpful. He'd even suggested talking to Antonio, one of the Head Waiters in Orange Square who knew of a few rented apartments. Armed with this information and which newspapers to buy for job vacancies, she went to the corner café to sit and enjoy a bit of the warmth which was coming through the trees.

She got out her phrase book and realised that they didn't speak like the book. She knew regardless that it was important to study and practise. She also needed an internet café and "top up" her phone. It was also essential to change to a Spanish number, all these things were on her list. She acknowledged the waiter as he handed an Americano coffee to her. She was here. How he was going to find her, she'd no idea. The girls had a point; she needed to get on with her life. She'd come here to re-charge her batteries. Her new plan to find somewhere to live in the sun and work part time.

Jed was history even though she kept his phone charged. If only Nick had been upfront with her, she would have understood the lapses of time away. He'd been crap at lying to her as all that time she'd thought he was seeing someone else.

Orange Square was thinning out of locals and tourists in general as she looked up and could see why. The sky was black again and she hurried to pay for her coffee. The café had closed, and everyone had disappeared as the first crack of thunder made her jump. The rain started immediately as the thunder rolled and rolled round the square, as she tried to find her way back to the hostel. The rain pelted down, and she was soaked in minutes. She buried the paperwork under her top, to try and salvage the information. She hid in a doorway as the relentless rain came, and the thunder continued to roll round the sky.

She tried to read the paper map that the tourist man had given her but within a second it disintegrated in the rain.

Her sense of direction was not her best asset as she tried to find the hostel. There was no one to ask as again everyone had seen the rain coming. She felt so naive and stupid. Eventually she arrived at the hostel, once again she was soaked as the young girl in reception smiled at her. She raised an umbrella behind the counter and gave her a knowing look.

*"Ah, **paraguas**, that's what she suggested earlier,"* thought Gaby as she nodded her head and smiled feebly. She clambered up the stairs barefooted; another ruined pair of sandals and ready to abandon the rest of the day.

8

New Apartment

Monday morning came and she was relieved to see a clear blue sky through her bedroom window. Her room looked like a Chinese laundry. The air was damp, and she'd written a new list of priorities.

The heat was as unexpected as Seville, and she unpacked her lighter clothes right away. She went to see Antonio at the café, but he wasn't working until middle of the week. She found a bookshop in Old Town and bought a tourist map and a basic Spanish dictionary.

She wrote down the name of the streets, where the hostel was located, and she walked to the beach.

The beaches of Marbella spanned over twenty miles, and the white sand was surprisingly hot to the feet as she sat outside a beach bar taking in the sun. The palm trees dotted around were hardly moving as she ordered a sparkling water. She poured over her dictionary and made notes of basic words to get her started.

It was already two o' clock and the waiter who spoke English explained that everything closed from two until four, some places until six. Most businesses would open again until eight or ten, dependant on their nature. This meant she had to sit in the sun, with her plans delayed until the afternoon. It was over 25c and after the extreme temperatures of Seville, which had been nearer 50c on occasions, this was comfortable.

She realised it was going to be impossible to achieve her list in a day or two. Not daunted, she half dozed, relaxed, and enjoyed her new-found freedom. How could these waiters work in this heat?

She needed to find an internet café. She hadn't been in touch with anyone for over a week. Part of her didn't want to bother, but she felt very vulnerable and quite a fish out of water for some reason. This didn't scare her, but she was aware how stupid she'd been, thinking she could arrive here, and Nick would find her quickly.

On reading the information and maps, she realised that the Costa del Sol was one of the biggest provinces of Spain. This province was the largest and the size of Wales. She sighed; he was obviously good at his job as he wasn't daunted by the task to find her. She knew that he had this number and once she bought a Spanish phone, she would send him another text.

Nothing appeared the same as she lay in the sun, thinking how much she'd changed. She felt that she hadn't thought this through thoroughly. These self-doubts were evident as she was on her own. She smothered her legs in sun cream; she could do it. She would have her life ship shape in no time. Above all, she had started to forgive him and looked forward to a fresh start with him.

At five o'clock, she ambled her way up towards the town, using her own directions that she'd written and feeling in control. The waiters had been helpful with locations for schools. Exhilarated by a feeling of new confidence she forgot one of the rules of Seville as the scooter came up by her side and before she knew it, the kid had swiped her beach bag and away they'd gone.

She felt sick, as she sat on the step of a shop, she'd been distracted for one moment. Her mobile was in the beach bag but nothing of value only sunscreen, the new vocab book and everyone's telephone numbers. Nicks' only contact number was gone. There was no email address for him, nada. The end. She felt quite nauseous as she sat thinking of him and at what had just happened.

She realised it could have been worse. Her money and documents were at the hostel along with her main cash. What she carried, cash wise was in her bra at all times. She walked slowly towards the old town and realised she was outside an internet café. She went inside and having lost her new vocabulary book, she managed to be redirected to a mobile phone store.

She knew these were her new challenges and she wasn't going to be disillusioned by this mistake. Mike from the Academy had made it clear that single people were targeted the most. Most people went about in pairs; they certainly did in Seville. She sighed as she also realised that there was no way she'd be able to contact Liz and Lydia. She hadn't thought she'd get her mobile stolen, she'd been so careful.

She stopped berating herself as she walked in to the shop to purchase a mobile. On leaving the shop with a new phone with the *"top up"* voucher, she felt remarkably better. One thing from the list done as she walked closer to the buildings of the pavement and not the road.

Over the main road and situated on the corner street tucked away, she discovered a language school. She would return the next day and ask them if they had any vacancies. She continued walking in a square as the town was built on a grid system and was pleased when she arrived at Old Town without a major panic.

Back at the hostel, she charged her new phone and discovered a message from Jed, which said *"not forgotten you."* A wave of annoyance enveloped her as she thought of him. He was no good for her, she knew this.

She might as well use Jed's phone as her English back up and left it in her room. She punched in family numbers that she could remember. She sorted her clothes; the wet ones were still damp. She rummaged through one of the wet cases and realised most of the clothes inside were also damp. A problem that would have to wait.

She went to have supper at the café where Antonio worked. She felt it would be prudent to eat at the same restaurant until she met him. The evening was balmy and warm for middle of September, and she had her first glass of red wine, *"I deserve it,"* she thought. She began to recognise the streets of Old Town, "**Casco Antiguo**" as she repeated it to remember.

She spent hours in the late evening studying and learning words as she'd popped to the book shop and purchased another vocabulary book. She was a little relieved it wasn't the same person serving her as yesterday as she couldn't explain what had happened. Talking in general was not going to happen very much unless she started to speak in Spanish.

Thursday arrived quickly and she went to buy the English paper called "**The Sur.**" On her usual spot on the beach, she sat and read the whole paper finding the job section. There was a vacancy for a teacher in the same school she'd come across the day before. This was exciting and she needed an internet café to print her C.V.

It was a nightmare trying to get a basic letter printed in the internet café as all their printers were offline and she couldn't print anything, let alone her C.V. She'd remembered that she'd seen another internet café and rummaged through her new bag to find the advert. She decided to find it. This opportunity only came across occasionally and she recalled what the tutors had said. *"There are over thirty qualified teachers' going for the same job and they all have more hours teaching experience than you. Don't miss any chance you have of applying for work anywhere you can."*

The café was the other side of town. The music was blaring as she entered, and the three girls were very chatty. One had a smattering of English as Gaby asked to print a few *documentos.*

"Si, si" the girl had replied, and she set to work.

Her C.V. was already done, and she added the hostel address to her details and her new mobile number. She wrote her letter and printed several copies. Two hours later after checking her mail and replying to the few friends who had contacted her; she walked towards the school to place her application through the letter box.

Arrabella smiled at her with a typical Spanish *"hola"* as she entered the reception, thoroughly pleased the school was open.

"Pardon, Yo no palabra español," Gaby explained, *"Tener C.V. para profesorra Inglés."*

"Si," said Arrabella as she opened her envelope and read the letter.

"Yo, I will give to Director tomorrow," Arrabella explained.

"Gracias, thank you."

She walked away and hoped she'd hear from them soon. She decided to take a different route to her hostel and find Antonio. The restaurant wasn't as busy as the weekend, and she observed two women sitting in the far corner talking loudly. She recognised a Welsh accent and decided to sit away from them.

"Una copa Rioja por favor. Antonio aqui?" she enquired.

"Si Señora."

Antonio, the Head Waiter appeared looking flustered but had an instant beaming smile as he approached Gaby as a long-lost friend.

"Muy Guappa, Señorita. How can I help you?"

"I apologise, I can't speak Spanish yet, but the young man at the tourist office recommended I come to talk to you. You might have a contact for me to find an apartment?" enquired Gaby conscious the two women had stopped talking and were listening.

"Si, Señorita. Come tomorrow at ten, we talk then, ok?"

"Si, gracias Antonio."

"Hi, we couldn't help overhearing, would you like to join us. We're on holiday here and overheard your Welsh accent."

"That would be great, ok," she said as she joined the two women.

"Hello, my dear, I'm Maud, this is my daughter Rebecca, pleased you could join us. What's a nice-looking Welsh girl like you doing on her own?" asked Maud sipping her Gin and Tonic smiling sweetly.

"I've just relocated from Seville, I'm a teacher looking for work," said Gaby reluctant to share any more information.

"We're on our last night of a ten-day holiday," said Maud.

"Mum is looking for somewhere to live," said Rebecca.

"Have you had any joy?" enquired Gaby thinking this information could be useful for her own plan.

"Not really, I haven't seen anything I like, they're all outside Marbella but I want to live here or Banús. Have you been to Puerto Banús yet?"

"No, I haven't; I've been catching some sun and looking for work."

"Any luck with a job?"

"Too early to say, have dropped in a C.V. to a school earlier. That's where I've been. I'm staying in Old Town."

"Our hotel is on the beach," said Maud.

"How far from here," asked Gaby.

"Five minutes' walk."

"Have you had a good time, you're both nicely tanned," said Gaby as their food arrived.

Maud was at least seventy and she was as brown as a berry. Her blonde hair was styled and immaculate. She adorned rings on every finger and had heavy jewellery round her neck. She was in white and looked expensive. She was very petite and attractive. Gaby suddenly felt very drab sitting next to her. Her daughter Rebecca was also dressed in white. She wore a flowing white dress with equally as much gold hanging from her ears as her neck. She wore one ring, a wedding ring. The two chatted loudly and made Gaby laugh, she'd missed female company. She'd missed conversation in general.

Maud ordered more Gin and Tonics and Gaby found herself immersed in the world of these two strangers. They were fun and thought she was amazing, coming to Spain all on her own. She thought she was amazing right at that moment and realised her man had a daunting prospect to find her. She cast those doubts aside and enjoyed the fun of the evening as Maud was insistent in paying the tab.

"On one condition, when I come back, you'll help me find somewhere to live?"

"Of course, I'll at least come with you, Maud," said Gaby knowing looking at property with Maud would help her. Her budget was four times Gaby's, but the contacts would help.

They parted as Maud took her number and would let her know, when she was next visiting. She went to her hostel and received a lovely surprise in her room. Her laundry had been taken down; the open wet cases had been emptied. Someone had laundered them all and they were folded on her bed with a message. She spent the next half an hour deciphering the housekeepers' note and smiled. It had been a good day.

She met Antonio at ten as arranged with her notebook and dictionary as his English was as poor as her Spanish.

"Come with me, yes?"

"Donde, where are we going?" she asked not wanting to get into a heap of a car with a stranger as he'd directed her to the back of the restaurant.

He showed her a box of flyers which advertised the restaurant, and she realised he wanted help in their distribution round the hotels. That would help her as she hadn't ventured out of Marbella town.

"Ok, Si," and she jumped in and placed the box on her lap.

Antonio was a terrible driver or an exceptionally good driver as he managed to avoid several collisions and clipping other car wing mirrors as they drove from one complex to another. Country clubs and six-star hotels all brimming with expensive cars outside the premises. The Pirelli monument at the edge of Marbella town was one landmark and she realised at that moment the taxi driver had fleeced her.

Dismissing that from her mind, Antonio also proceeded to tell her his problems as they got to the last hotel complex.

"Let's get back and we talk, ok," said Gaby hoping her empathy would result in some information about a flat.

Her phone rang as Antonio was parking his car, badly.

"De game/deh gahmeh/tell me," she said as this was what everyone said as they answered their phone. No one spoke formal Spanish.

"Gaveee Deahlee, éste es Wall Street Institute, Marbella. Can you come Monday at ten o'clock in the morning?"

"Si, Gracias. I will be there," said Gaby as she told Antonio. He was excited for her, and they sat in the restaurant which was closed until the evening.

For an hour, she listened to his woes, through broken English, of his failing marriage as she offered some advice. Eventually he took her to see a lady in the ironmongers around the corner from the restaurant. The lady owned three apartments, and one was empty.

"Profesorra Inglés Gavee, Maria. El necessito apartmento para seis meses," said Antonio as Gaby nodded.

"Si,"

"Go with her," said Antonio as Maria took her apron from her dress. Someone else appeared to man the shop as she followed Maria closely up the hill. She didn't have a clue what to say to her.

The apartment was on the top floor and the lifts were rather grubby with graffiti all over. *"It's only a lift,"* she thought.

The apartment was a two bedroom and small. The living room needed a coat of paint, and it was sparsely furnished. The main bedroom was clean and adequate, and she could see the potential through the sparse fixtures. The living room had a black leather sofa with wall-to-wall wardrobe mirrors down one side. Maria pulled one mirror open and there was an abundance of hanging space. The kitchen was tiny, but the hob was clean, and the cupboards were empty of crockery and glasses. There was a washing machine on the back terrace with room for hanging laundry. The second room had two single beds. Sufficient amenities until she found somewhere to buy, and it would suffice until Nick found her.

She agreed to pay two months in advance and then a month at a time. Maria nodded and between them she realised, Maria wanted cash. She returned to the shop later that afternoon and signed for her own place.

Maria would get her paint and everything she needed to start her new life, and she would have everything sent to the apartment. She gave Gaby a receipt for her rent with the dates included. With her new address, she couldn't wait to leave the hostel and get a couple of taxis to take her to her new home.

⊷⊷⊶◀▷⊶⊷⊷

9

Wall Street Institute

Old Town and its cobbled narrow streets and fancy boutiques suddenly looked amazing. Gaby, delighted her perseverance had paid off, spent the following day enjoying **Casco Antiguo.** The bougainvillea covered most premises in some form or another. Vibrant purples, blues, and pinks. An abundance of geraniums seemed to line the houses in terracotta tubs and Moroccan blue pots. There was a sense of romance on some streets with every house painted a distinct colour and flowers in abundance adorning each one.

Some streets had several unoccupied houses, with some in desperate need of repair and maintenance. No different Gaby thought to any town in the U.K. She'd lots to organise but decided to take in the scenery and her surroundings. She would leave the hostel the next day which was Saturday. The young receptionist who had warmed to her; would organise two taxis. She'd explained in poor Spanish; the taxi had charged her three times the amount from the bus terminal. The young girl had been horrified.

The sun was beaming down, and it was good to feel the warmth on her back. She had changed her footwear to flat sandals. She milled round the boutiques and bars, her mind working through how she'd make her little apartment cosy.

She'd allowed a daily amount since her arrival, and she was within her budget. She was pleased with this, even though she'd purchased clothes and shoes, she'd not overspent. The apartment was much cheaper than she'd estimated, which was a bonus. A little job next week or so and she would start to feel in control. Her next task would be to bank her money. She knew, before she invested all her savings and hard-earned cash on a property, it had to be the right one for the right reason.

A jazz quartet was playing in Orange Square adjacent to Antonio's cafe and she sat enjoying a long Gin and Tonic. It was early evening, and she felt she'd deserved it. After a few Gins with Maud and her daughter, she'd got the taste for the cocktail, and it was certainly hitting the spot. The only sad element of her evening as she ambled back for her last night at the hostel was losing her notebook and phone with all her contact numbers.

She dismissed it. She hadn't done too badly but felt alone in a strange town full of transient people. Two out of three people were tourists. There was another language school in the heart of the town, and she made a note of it. She would drop in a C.V., over the weekend once she'd moved her stuff.

The goodbyes in the morning were quite overwhelming as the young receptionist and her two brothers had organised everything. They came at ten in the morning and carried all her luggage to two waiting taxis. Both taxis had been given the address, and both taxis had agreed the same fare. Gaby couldn't believe it.

"Mucho Gracias, Marta. Hasta luego."

De nada Gavee, see us again, si?"

"Si, adios."

Gaby jumped into the first taxi as they both proceeded to leave the Old Town and three minutes on the main road of Marbella and half way up another hill, they stopped right outside. Both men placed the entire luggage in the lift, and she was amazed by the difference when a Spaniard got involved.

"Gracias," as she paid them.

The lift seemed to groan as she pressed the top floor, and she felt excited. Her very own place.

The lift was only ten yards to the flat door, and she turned the key to see that Maria had been over. There was paint, brushes and a pile of crockery, saucepans and she immediately felt at home. There was a pile of throws and curtains too. She dragged her luggage into the living room and shut the door. She sat on the leather sofa and felt so excited, she wished there were someone to share the experience with her. She opened all the windows as being on the top floor, she felt it was safe to let in some air.

It was Saturday lunchtime; it was time to forget her luggage and relax. She deserved to chill. She hadn't been on a bus or seen Puerto Banús. Maud had asked her, and she'd felt foolish that she hadn't been to one of the hot spots of the area. A trip to Banús was in order. She emptied her food and drink into the fridge, which was spotless and packed a lunch bag. She hid her passport and purse in her small suitcase; it was more habit than necessity. She found a plug in the double bedroom and charged Jed's phone and left it there.

With minimum articles in her bag, her money on her person, she locked her flat, placed keys in her pocket and went to locate the bus stop.

Puerto Banús was under twenty minutes from Marbella and one euro on the bus. The bus was full of tourists and relaxing Spaniards. She was beginning to tell the difference and wanted to look more Spanish. With her jet, black hair that was going to be easy. She'd already bought sexy flamboyant tops as the Spanish wore colour; this was evident on the bus.

She was impressed by the array of yachts, their size resembling liners all bobbing down the side of the quay, as she absorbed it all. The picturesque view to sea was obviously the magnet along with the clear turquoise blue water and smart open cafés and terraced bars. They were all situated around the harbour with the boats a stride away. The empty expensive boutiques were also dotted in between ice-cream parlours and estate agents.

There were estate agents every other outlet and looking at the properties on offer, she could see that her nest egg wasn't sufficient to buy a shed. She didn't want a huge villa, just a modest home. She decided she wouldn't worry about this. One thing at a time.

She walked the length of the area, and the sand was warm to her feet. She took her towel and sat with her book for a while; it was too warm not to take advantage of the sun. She carefully applied sun screen; she was not going to look like a leather handbag. She'd already seen a few sunburnt tourists and some evidently lived here. She could easily tell as their skin was aged and lined and that was a stark reminder the effects of the sun.

The harbour was lined with Aston Martins, Porches, and Ferraris as she walked round to the bus stop. There were a few sailing yachts bobbing out to sea and the sea was now turquoise green in parts. On the second line, she discovered a few hotels and clubs and late restaurants as they were closed. Banús was for night owls, a place Gaby was going to visit again. She was drawn to it, and she could understand why everyone else seemed to be. She couldn't wait to see it at night.

It was amazing how quick the roads and sand had dried up as there were still intermittent showers occurring. The buses to Marbella were every ten minutes. She was surprised to see the bus was full, standing room only. There was one seat unoccupied, and she sat wondering why people were standing when there was an available seat. She put the thought out of her head as the bus went around the first corner. There was a sudden gush of water, and she was soaked to the skin.

The two girls standing next to her stifled their laughter as she couldn't believe what had just happened.

She got up drenched and hooked a handle from the top bar and stood next to the two girls laughing. She couldn't help but smile as the next occupant, obviously, a tourist, sat in the same seat and again as the bus went around the next bend the water gushed in over the poor lady.

She couldn't help but laugh out loud at the incident, she was obviously having her fair share of local learning curves as she made her way up the hill. Later she discovered that the buses were called "bendy buses." Basically, two buses joined together by a rubber hose which retained rain water but the hose wasn't waterproof. It would disperse through the joints every time the bus went around corners. The locals knew this and a need to get involved with the Spanish was more important than ever.

She picked up a takeaway on her way home, her first night in her own pad. She got quite excited as she made her way up in the lift. A shower was in order and later she would sort out her clothes.

She opened her flat door and stood in shock at the living room where her suitcases sat. The whole apartment was crawling with cockroaches. Hundreds of them, fat juicy ones, baby ones, millions of them. She wretched, as she froze and closed the door behind her. They were crawling all over her luggage and bags. She held her takeaway to her and walked to the bedroom and wretched. They were on the bed, inside the wardrobe. All over her phone and she felt sick.

She gingerly went to the bathroom, and they were on the loo seat, she couldn't bear it. She flicked one family off the settee and sat for a minute to think. The windows were closed; she was sure she'd left them open. She panicked and wanted to check her passport and she sunk back into the sofa as the middle mirror panels of the wardrobe in front of her started to move. She nearly fainted as a Moroccan man came out and stood in front of her.

He was living in the wardrobe as the floor inside was covered in bedding. Oh, fucking hell, what was she to do now? She held her breath as a cockroach started to make a bee line for her food. She flicked it off and sunk back further into the settee as the man stood staring into space. He was drugged up to the eyeballs and he didn't see her and after a few minutes standing in the room, he went back inside and closed the mirror behind him.

She ran to the bedroom and closed the door behind her, it didn't lock. The crunch of cockroaches under her feet was nothing compared to the fear she felt right at that moment. There was a Moroccan man living in her flat!!!

"Think," she said to herself. She needed to get her stuff in one room and debug the room at the same time. She couldn't stay; it was appalling and where the fuck had this man come from. Her landlady knew all along, she was furious, angry, and disappointed all at once.

She flicked a dozen cockroaches from the bed and placed her food in the middle. She found a fly swatter in the closet of all places and tiptoed out to the living room and tried to stop herself from gagging. The top bag was covered in the little blighters; she gingerly found the handle and flicked them off as they flew and scattered throughout the living room. One by one, she flicked the insects from one suitcase, one bag at a time, moving them to the bed in her room.

She worked quickly conscious that the man inside the wardrobe may appear again and she wasn't ready for a confrontation with him. He'd obviously heard her coming in; she worked as quickly as she could.

She was dying to go to the bathroom but there were more cockroaches in the bathroom than anywhere. She sat on the bed with her luggage around her, flicking the odd one that tried to reach her or her belongings. What was she going to do now? It was nearly eleven o` clock at night and there was no way she could leave with all her stuff at this late hour.

She ate her pizza as the smell was certainly encouraging the cockroaches to attempt a coo on her bed. She ate, with one hand on the swatter flicking them off every other second. She would creep to the toilet and then leave in the morning. There was no way she could sleep with cockroaches around her. She felt sick as she crunched to the door and nearly gagged as she'd killed another one. She flicked it off her flip flop and froze.

As she turned the knob of her door, she could hear voices in the living room. She held her breath and flicked a cockroach from the light switch as she placed her ear to the gap. There were at least three voices in the living room and as she opened the door slightly, she saw the Moroccan man and three others sitting on the floor smoking joints and sniffing cocaine. They sat amongst the cockroaches and were as high as kites.

She felt fear of the unknown wash over her and she knew she had to get out of this apartment. They would all leave at some point. She sat back on the bed and reluctantly placed the heaviest suitcase by her door. She didn't want them attempting to come in to her room. Her passport and money were safe, and she peed into the salad container and left it in the corner of the room. She sat on the bed and flicked another cockroach away. Hot tears came quickly, the shock of her situation and feeling scared at what could happen to her. She brushed the salty tears away and sat in the middle of the bed and tried to read.

At 5am, she slowly moved to the door and flicked a dozen cockroaches from her suitcase and peered through the gap. There was no sign of anyone. She put on a jumper and secure sandals as she needed to move fast. She tip- toed out to the living room and it was quiet. She checked the bathroom and spare room and they'd gone.

She hadn't dreamt it, she'd seen them. There was no time to think, she had to get out.

She ran and called the lift and with one suitcase kept the lift door open and in three stages moved all her belongings to the lift entrance. She checked she had everything and locked the door behind her. She ran and threw the bags inside the lift, flicked the last cockroach away as she breathed a huge sigh of relief. What the hell was she going to do now?

She sat on her luggage on the pavement, of the main road of Marbella. It was 6.30 am on a Sunday morning and the town was sleeping from Saturday night. She had her straps and proceeded to hook the suitcases together and the five bags. She was crying with disbelief, shock and anger all rolled into one. She decided it was a long walk, but she would go back and see Marta at the hostel. She didn't know anyone else.

She passed one hostel sign and pressed the bell. There was no reply, but it was incredibly early, and she knew it was hopeless. After half a mile of moving her luggage slowly and deliberately, she saw another sign. She pressed the bell again and waited, but no one came. Maybe she would sit here until she saw a taxi pass.

"Señora, Señora."

She turned to see an elderly man walking towards her as she smiled at him feebly, as the man embraced her.

"Habitación por favor?" she whispered wiping a tear away with the back of her hand.

"Si, si, un momento."

The man disappeared as quickly as he'd appeared, and she wondered if she'd imagined him. Before she realised what was happening a woman and a younger man came running towards her and the three of them, the lady taking Gaby's hand walked her to their hostel.

Her entire luggage disappeared, and she was ushered into their kitchen. A coffee arrived in front of her as the old couple sat at the table and waited for her to compose herself. The younger man came to join them, and she suddenly realised she was amongst good people. She rummaged for her phrase book and found cockroaches and rambled in broken Spanish what had happened. *"There was mucho of them."*

"Start from the beginning," said the younger man in perfect English.

"Oh," Gaby said surprised. She explained. *"I'm an English teacher. My name is Gabriella; I went to rent this apartment and*

there was a Moroccan man living in the wardrobe and several men taking cocaine. The landlady must know, the place was full of cockroaches, and it's obviously being used to hide immigrants! I was scared and haven't slept all night and I'm now looking for somewhere to stay until I find a job and an apartment."

"I'm Sergio, Mum and Dad run this small hostel. I'll ask them to check their availability for you; you can stay here until you get sorted."

Sergio spoke rapidly in Spanish as his Mum checked their bookings. Dad on hearing what had happened reached for the brandy bottle and poured four glasses as Gaby gratefully sipped hers, feeling foolish. She'd been terribly upset and more shocked than anything else.

"Si, si," Dad was nodding as they were discussing if they could accommodate her. Mum had her hand on Gaby's arm and pouring more brandy in her glass as she continued to sip the liquor. She felt better as the cognac hit her throat as Mum kept pouring and patting her arm. The three-talked fast about her predicament. The two men disappeared and eventually returned. The son spoke as they all sat round the table again. It was only 7am in the morning and the bottle was half empty.

"We've placed you in room six, upstairs. Its en-suite and we've booked you in for ten days. We've placed your suitcases in the room already. You need to pay them tomorrow. I'm on the end of a phone if you need more assistance."

"Gracias Sergio," said Gaby taking his card and noting he was an *Abagado/* lawyer. She was grateful and Sergio took her to see her room. She blinked back the tears as she saw two

single beds, her luggage on top of one of them. There was a fridge and a kettle and a decent sized en-suite. There was even a bag of pegs on the line, which was running over her terrace, to hang the washing. A television on the wall, it was perfect.

She smiled and went downstairs with Sergio. The couple were drinking in the kitchen, and she joined them, laughing this time. She felt an overwhelming love for this humble family, she was grateful that they'd rescued her. With another glass of brandy consumed she left and promised to see them the next day after her job interview.

She spent all day, putting her domestic life in order. After all the chores, she sat at the tiny table on the terrace as her clothes flapped in the breeze and studied some Spanish. She prepared notes for her interview and decided a bath and an early night was in order. The traumas of the night before behind her.

The next morning on her way to her interview she located the landlady of the apartment and with her Spanish script written regarding the drug addicts in her apartment, she demanded a refund. The landlady feigned horror and apologised as Gaby flashed Sergio's card in her face. Seeing the Abagado details sent the woman to her safe behind the counter and she handed over her money in full. She apologised and gracefully Gaby accepted.

The ten o' clock interview became eleven o' clock as Gaby sat in reception and waited. The school was hectic with students in and out and Arrabella, the receptionist was kept in demand. She organised students' lessons, private tuition arrangements and some students came to her with grammar questions. She smiled at everyone all the time; she was an obvious choice for front of house.

The Director of Language eventually appeared and ushered Gaby through to his *oficina* where Gaby sat as he read her C.V. and letter. He peered over his steel rimmed glasses and smiled.

"You are first time in Marbella, no?"

"Yes, I've arrived from Seville to find work."

"How long are you staying?"

"Forever, I love Spain," Gabriella said with a passion.

"Last teacher only here four months, I need a teacher for one or two years?"

"Yes, that will suit me," her fingers crossed as her hands were clasped loosely on her lap.

The Director pondered and looked at her letter again.

"My boyfriend is a policeman and working in Marbella, we are looking for a house to buy," she added maybe he needed more security. It wasn't quite true, but he didn't need to know.

"Ah good. You can start on Octobre, I mean October. Ah, I need more Eeenglish lessons," he chuckled. *"First Monday of the month, Arrabella will give you the contracts later. Come back at eight o'clock and they will be ready. Are you ok to work 6pm until10pm? Those are the hours."*

"Yes, perfect," said Gaby trying to contain herself.

"Good, we shall see you this evening. Looking well for you to start, yes?"

"Yes, thank you," she smiled not wishing to correct the Director. She smiled at Arrabella, who was chin deep in an exercise book with a student. She waved a sign that she would see her later. She nodded; she knew already.

Gabriella Daly pleased at what she had accomplished walked on the beach side, back to her apartment. She purchased a large pot of flowers and a bottle of cognac for her new landlady. A new job starting in two weeks' time, she couldn't believe it.

10

Another Apartment

Señora Izzie was thrilled when Gabriella appeared early afternoon with a huge plant arrangement and a bottle of *Sobrano* brandy. She paid for her ten days stay and knew she would need to find somewhere else quickly.

"Ah Trabajo, si?"

She was excited. The husband appeared from somewhere and on being told her news went to fetch three glasses. She felt it rude to refuse and sat with the elderly couple and felt at home and so much at ease. She knew speaking fluently would have been the icing on the cake. Señor José had just let another room and the three of them conversed, with Gaby using her notebook, drawing items, and using her dictionary. After a few more glasses Gaby thought best to leave them to have their siesta. She needed one too, she had to be back at the school for eight and drinking brandy lunchtime was something she wasn't used to.

As she departed, the door opened, and a tall blonde man walked in.

"Hola, oh hi there," he said with a big smile.

"Hola" replied Gaby, as she thought he couldn't be family as he was too blonde compared to their dark-haired son.

"I've just arrived, I need to pay someone," he said.

She translated in pidgin Spanish and Izzie nodded. On cue, she left them and feeling buoyant, the brandy helping, retired to her room for a siesta.

At seven she got up and prepared for her walk to the school. On her way, down to the exit, she bumped into the blonde hunk on the stairs.

"Hi again, my name's Phil, I'm on holiday for a fortnight, fancy a drink later?"

"Why not," she smiled. *"I'll be at the Plaza de los Naranjos after 9pm, if you want to meet me there. I've got an appointment right now."*

"That would be great, eh where's that?"

"Orange Square, it will be on that map of yours," she smiled liking the knowledge she'd attained already.

"Great stuff will see you there," he said as Gaby walked to the school, feeling quite confident for the first time in a few days.

Wall Street Institute of Marbella had six classrooms and was open from 9am until 10pm. They were open Monday to Friday, and they paid €6,00 an hour. She signed a contract for twenty hours a week and she needed to bring her bank details and her NIF number on her first day.

The school closed for two weeks at Christmas only. She had to give six days' notice for any leave, and they would be unpaid for the first year. She would get paid for all the fiestas and the lengthy list was inside the paperwork that she signed.

She didn't mind that there was only twenty hours available. This gave her opportunity to find private work which was more lucrative. She agreed to start on the first Monday in October at 5.30pm. The teaching system was different to her *tefl* training, but Arrabella explained it was easy.

She folded the paperwork in her handbag and made her way to Orange Square to meet Phil. It was a good feeling to meet up with someone as she'd struggled being on her own. It was lonely more than feeling alone. It was also hard because of the language barrier. None of the elderly Spanish in Marbella spoke English. The younger generation conversed in both languages, especially the working age group. She reached Orange Square and Phil immediately descended on her, not giving her time to look around.

"Hi there," she said. *"You found it then?"*

"Yes," he grinned. *"Shall we stay here and have something to eat?"*

"Yes, ok. Antonio runs this café on the corner; we can go there if you want?"

They sat at Antonio's café, and he acknowledged her.

"Antonio helped me find an apartment, but it wasn't suitable," explained Gaby and then told him the story. He was mortified at this.

"You don't realise stuff like that goes on until you see it for yourself," he said.

"*It makes you a bit more vigilant, certainly,*" she agreed.

"*Why are you on your own? A girl as good looking as you should be married or with someone at least.*"

"*I'm meeting my long-term partner later in the year. He's here working but I'm unable to contact him. His job is sensitive.*"

"*Is he undercover?*"

"*I'm not at liberty to say Phil but you're on the right track. I can't talk about it. Whilst he's doing his thing, I'm looking to work a little and find somewhere more permanent to live.*"

"*Apart from the cockroach incident and the druggies, how's it been so far then?*"

"*Fantastic, I've loved every minute of it. I think adjusting to the heat is harder than the culture and the people. So, far at least.*"

"*When do you start your new job?*"

"*In two weeks,' time, first Monday in October.*"

"*Do you fancy exploring some of the coast with me? I've got a hire car and although I like my own company, I'd much prefer to have company.*"

"*That would be great. I haven't seen much yet. I've been to Puerto Banús, maybe we could go there tomorrow night as it's a place for night owls, I think.*"

"*Why not, we can do beach and then Banús in the evening.*"

The evening proceeded quickly, and Antonio eventually came to apologise to Gaby for what happened.

"It wasn't your fault, Antonio. She knew there were illegal's in there. Forget it," said Gaby. *"How's your wife?"*

*"We are better, thank you, **Besos,**"* he replied and went away smiling. He swiftly returned with two large cognacs.

"On the house," he smiled at Gaby who nodded.

"What's Besos?" asked Phillip.

"Kisses."

They strolled back to the hostel and Phil insisted on a nightcap. He'd bought a bottle of brandy as he'd been given a glass by the landlord whilst he'd paid his accommodation.

"I thought I'd better get a bottle in to be polite," he said as he poured two glasses, and they sat on his tiny balcony chatting.

"What about you then, Phil. Why are you on your own? Most men need company; I don't know any bloke that's gone away on his own."

"I'm actually a top gymnast and my discipline is the rings and the horse and I'm about to compete in a major competition and I need to rest in advance. I've also broken up with my long-term girlfriend of ten years and needed to get away."

"I'm sorry to hear that, what happened?"

"We've just outgrown each other; it was amicable in the end. We both agreed it was more habit than love."

"That's sad," said Gaby feeling for him.

"Better now than when we got married. That's what broke us up, talking about marriage."

"It wasn't to be then," said Gaby wishing she'd behaved better with Nick. *"My boyfriend proposed, and I accepted. That was before he told me he was an undercover cop."*

"What, you didn't know?"

"No, not until the day he proposed, I felt foolish and let down by him. He didn't trust me implicitly to tell me at the beginning. He's somewhere in the Costa Del Sol and he's promised to find me when he can."

"If he wants you, he'll find you regardless. A man will chase who he wants, Gaby. Believe me."

"It's funny, one of my flat mates in Seville said the same. I've had my original mobile stolen and he'd have to track me down."

"Then let him find you. It's his job after all. If he's in the Costa somewhere, when he's ready, he'll come to you. Especially if you think there's a chance of reconciliation."

"Yes, you're right. I'll come out with you tomorrow, then I'll have to concentrate on finding a new apartment. I've only got just over a week."

"Of course," said Phillip as he reached to kiss her goodnight.

She brushed her lips on his cheeks and whispered goodnight and left.

The orange sun seemed hotter the next day as she met him at ten. He was sporting a baseball cap to cover his fair hair. She jumped in his car, and they drove to *Guadalmina* beach which was a few miles past Puerto Banús. The beach was deserted in comparison to two weeks before. It was peaceful.

The deep blue sky had no fluffy white clouds, and the palm trees stood erect and still.

They got two sun beds, parked them near each other, close to the rocks with a few palm trees, acting as shade from the blazing sun. Gaby had brought her Spanish books, and Phil also had a book. They settled to their reading after covering themselves in sun cream. She was deep in her studies as her mobile rung.

"Gavee, éste José, Hostel, si?

"Si, una problema?"

"No, tiener apartmento por seis horas para les tardes, vale/ okay?"

"Si, gracias, seis hora para les trades, ok?"

"Si, Hasta luego"

"Your Spanish is good."

"Gosh, not at all, that's pidgin Spanish. I've realised they don't use half the words. I'm just copying what they're saying really. Anyway, he wants me to go and look at an apartment at 6pm. isn't that amazing. The Spanish have been really helpful."

"That great, we'll make sure we're back in time for you."

"Thanks, I appreciate that."

They had some tapas in the *chiringuito/beach bar* at around two o'clock and relaxed, both with books in hand. She was deep in thought as Phil interrupted her.

"Shall I put some cream on your back; you're a bit pink."

"Fabulous," she muttered as she rummaged in her bag that was under the sunbed and handed it to him. He massaged the cream into her back, and she felt herself getting flustered. She knew he was feeling the same and let him carry on. He moved slowly up the backs of her legs, his hands massaging around the edge of her swimsuit.

"Shall I, do you?" she said lowering her sunglasses and looking straight into his bright blue eyes.

"That would be great thanks," he said, as his smile said it all.

She moved the parasol over the two beds and looked around and the beach was empty. She plastered cream over his back and was surprised at how strong he felt. He was lean but muscular and as solid as a tree trunk. She moved her hands over his buttocks and to the back of his thighs,

"Shall I do the back of your legs, they're very pink?"

"Go for it," he said not moving his head from the bed.

She continued to massage cream into the whole of his back and legs noticing he'd no body hair. She was fascinated by this as all her men had been hairy. She gave him back his tube of cream as he pulled her towards him as he brushed her lips with his tongue.

He moved sideways on the bed, as she sat next to him as they found their tongues underneath the parasol and his baseball cap. He pulled her closer as she felt the bulge of passion through his shorts.

She moved her hand over his body to the edge of the bed, to steady herself as his tongue probed her mouth. He untied her halter neck and caressed her breasts through her swimsuit. He held her tight as she carried on kissing him as she felt him pressing hard against her thigh. A sudden noise from the beach bar a bit further down the beach stopped his caresses as she adjusted her top and went back to sit on her bed. She was hot and not from the sun.

When they got back to the hostel, they agreed to meet at ten, and they'd head for Banús. She went to locate the landlord and was greeted with enthusiasm from the couple as she embraced them. She genuinely liked them. Their son was there in the kitchen making coffee.

"Hello, how are you?"

"Well, thank you. My father has found you a studio flat. The landlord owns six studios and they're behind the hotel, over the road. I've checked Pedro, the owner through my offices for you and he's legitimate and registered as a landlord. My father asked me to sort this out for you this morning. I hope this is good for you."

"Thank you so much, can we see it now as I don't want to waste your time. You've done so much already."

"Yes, Yes, I'm coming with you and my father."

Relieved she had Sergio as an interpreter, the three of them proceeded to cross the dual carriageway and went to the reception area of Hotel Fuerte, where they'd already arranged to meet her new potential landlord.

A good-looking middle-aged man was waiting, and everyone shook hands. They followed Pedro to the block of studio flats; they were literally to the side of the hotel and three minutes' walk on to the beach.

The apartment was basically a large square room. The double bedroom was separate with an en-suite. The lounge had a leather sofa and a rocking chair next to the small kitchen which comprised of a washing machine a microwave, kettle, and basic furniture. It was ideal. There were two small windows on each side of the main door all with bars. On checking the lock, Gaby saw there were three dead bolts and a double lock. She pointed at the bars on the windows and looked at Sergio.

A rapid discussion in Spanish followed and Sergio explained. It was close to the beach and tourists; it was safer for the teachers this way.

"*Teachers?*" Gaby enquired.

"*Pedro only lets to teachers. He has six studios here and all five have teachers staying. He only takes in employed people. I've told him you start at the Wall Street on Monday. My reference will be enough. What do you think?*"

"*I think it's perfect, I can move in on Friday, or sooner I don't mind. I can pay two months in advance,*"

Sergio finalised everything with Pedro and he was happy. He handed Gaby two sets of keys and showed her how to lock the door from the inside and outside. The apartment was brand new. Although sparsely furnished, there was adequate room for Gaby to have her paperwork on the table and her clothes would easily disappear in the two deep wardrobes that were housed in the double bedroom. She checked every crevice not wishing to find another immigrant hiding in the wardrobe or under the bed. It was also perfectly laid out to house private lessons if she decided to teach from home.

She shook hands with Pedro as Sergio acted as her lawyer which she found amusing. In hind sight, she was grateful of their support. They'd helped each other, as she needed to leave. She arranged to meet Pedro on the Saturday to pay him; she could move in immediately. They made their way back to tell Izzie,

"Tell your parents that I'll move out Friday, in order they've the weekend to get the room ready," said Gaby. *"I don't want any refund; you've helped me enough already."*

Sergio smiled as he repeated Gaby's instructions, and they nodded. Izzie was delighted for her and got four glasses out of the cupboard and poured everyone a cognac.

She sat with the three people who had made her very welcome in Marbella. She stayed with them until gone 9pm and realised she was meeting Phil. She apologised for leaving the party and went back to her room to freshen up.

Phil was delighted with her news, and they went to Banús to celebrate and as arranged. The whole port was brimming with well-dressed people, the evening air balmy with a slight breeze. She felt good, her life was suddenly showing some order. All she wished for at that moment was to bump into Nick or for Nick to feel she was worth finding. He'd given her permission to have fun; she was sure this was his guilt in not telling her sooner.

They stood outside *Sinatra's* bar, which was two strides from the largest liner she'd seen close. The bars and the restaurants were full. There was music in the air and the front line was packed with tourists and locals all milling around. Her Gin and Tonic was certainly, quenching her thirst and she was pleased that she had someone to share her news. Phil was impressed by her achievements in such a brief time.

They laughed all evening and the Gin along with their amorous encounter earlier was making her feel frisky. She had to kerb her enthusiasm and her exuberance, but she was enjoying herself and all the important things had come to fruition. She had a job starting on Monday and she had a new flat, and she would move her belongings, the next day. Phil's offer of his car was greatly accepted as that would save her half a day. He didn't mind and he was happy to help.

"Let me show you the flat," she suggested as they piled into a taxi.

"Hotel Fuerte, Por favour."

"Ok," said Phil already with his arms round her shoulder.

The taxi dropped them at the hotel and Gaby walked him, literally next door. She opened the door as explained by Pedro and let Phil inside. He looked around and Gaby closed the curtains.

"It's great, what a location, right on the beach," he said as he went straight to kiss her.

Gaby feeling light headed but friskily responded. Phil was amorous and strong as he picked her up with ease and carried her to the bedroom. They stripped each other, both hungry for love and affection. They kissed for a long time as her heart beat faster with his urgency, as he kept saying, "*Besos, Besos.*"

He held her hands tight and pinned to the bed as he kissed and licked every crevice as she squirmed, her body convulsing in spasms of frenzied frustration as he controlled her. Her hands eventually free, roamed his hairless body which was incredibly strong and deceiving. He didn't waste any time as he immersed himself deep inside her as they moved and kissed without taking breath.

11

New Friends

The sun shone high in the sky as she relaxed before she commenced her new job that evening. She was excited and a bit daunted with it all. Phil had gone back to England. They'd visited several new beaches, and she had the layout of the town pretty much sorted. Phil had been passionate throughout his last week, and she'd never had so much attention. It was time to concentrate on new friends and hoped Nick would never find out but also find her soon.

Armed with her details, she made her way to the school. Arrabella was smiling as always and kissed her on each cheek. A Mediterranean custom that Gaby liked.

"Hola, Gavee, Cómo estás?

"Muy Bien, Arrabella."

"I must talk in Inglish as this is a Engleesh school," she laughed and waved for her to follow to the staff areas and classes.

"I'll show you the system and you have a class at seven, enough time for you to see how we teach."

"Great thank you."

"Your contract is here; did you bring your NIF and address?"

"Yes, it's all here," said Gaby as she remembered how painful it had been to secure her NIF number from the Police station. The station was situated on the top of the cockroach hill, where her first apartment was located. On queuing for two hours, she'd eventually managed to complete the forms and get two copies. She had returned to yet another mile-long queue of people who were evidently non-European. She'd baulked at the thought of queuing again for two hours but the man behind the counter had rescued her the second time. He felt sorry for her cooped up in the waiting room with over a hundred black faced immigrants seeking paperwork. The *"no smoking,"* ban in public places was totally ignored as the waiting room had been thick with smoke.

"Good," said Arrabella, *"Let me finish your paperwork. Have a look at our system, it's quite easy. I'll be back in a moment."*

The institute had a room full of computers where students came in on their own volition to study the grammar before class. It was the teachers' responsibility to *"sign off,"* each module if satisfied with the students' understanding. Phonetics was important to the school and no student could move to the next module until their pronunciation was perfect. There was no age limit to each class. It all depended who had studied that module sufficiently to book a seat in the classroom. The students ranged from sixteen upwards.

There were six classrooms with only twelve to a class. Currently there weren't many students in the evening classes.

This was the result of the last teacher, on several occasions not turning up and had subsequently been sacked.

She just thanked her lucky stars that her timing had contributed to this job. There was another teacher who also worked in the evenings, but she was covering a day shift until the following week. There were always two girls on reception and someone to ask if she wasn't sure about anything. With the seven o' clock class, she realised they were only forty-five minutes long with fifteen minutes in-between each lesson. This would give her ample time to prep the next module, as necessary.

She felt pleased with herself as she said goodnight to her last students at nearly ten. She felt good and knew she would enjoy the experience. On her way to see Arrabella to collect her paperwork she was even more delighted,

"Four students have told me; they think you're good. They've all booked the next module; this is excellent work, Gavee. I need a bank account detail by end of next week, ok."

"Thank you, Arrabella, see you tomorrow. I'll sort out a bank account this week," she said taking the envelope from her and skipped down the hill towards her hotel.

She felt exhilarated and wanted the night to continue and didn't fancy going back to an empty studio. She decided to have a coffee in Orange Square.

Antonio's cafe was buzzing, and she waved at him as he was flying around serving late night drinks. She sat in the corner, near the line of orange trees and a black lady turned up and beckoned to sit opposite her, the place was full.

"Si," she nodded as the lady sat.

"Are you here on holiday?" the lady asked.

"No, I live here. I'm Gaby," she said thinking that sounded peculiar.

"Me too, I'm Jasmine. I own the language school in Old Town."

"Never, I've just started work as an English teacher at Wall Street."

"No way," she said. *"I'm looking for a teacher."*

"No, really?" as the coffees arrived.

"Yes, I have a gap in the day, are you free?"

She couldn't believe this was happening. It was surreal.

"I work six 'til ten, that's all. My days are free now. I live ten minutes' walk from here. What's your set up?"

"My school runs from nine until four. There's also a Saturday school but that won't be up and running until I have ten students. They're all between six and eleven years old."

"Maybe I should come and have a look. I'm happy to take in extra work, part time. See how you teach and look at the modules you follow."

"Would you that would be a great help."

Several coffees later; the two ladies departed with Gaby agreeing to meet Jasmine the following morning at eleven.

She walked back to her apartment upbeat and confident; she would soon have enough work to maintain a new home after a purchase. That reminded her, she still hadn't banked her money. She must do that immediately; Arrabella had also reminded her. She would find a bank the next day.

Getting in to her studio, she felt relaxed. She'd purchased a few lamps and left them on to create a warm glow as she entered. She made a sandwich, decided on an early night, and laughed when she saw it was nearly two o'clock in the morning.

The next morning, she went to see Jasmine's school. There was a huge amount of chatter and general noise coming from the open windows. This school was hugely different from Wall Street. Jasmine seemed relieved when she walked in and was at reception organising a few children, once the kids had gone, said,

"Come, let me show you round."

The school was on three floors and there were two classes on each floor. The toddlers were on the ground floor, and they got older as they reached the top floor. There was only ten in a class, and she was a teacher short. The buzz was infectious, and they followed a standard American English curriculum. She wasn't sure how she felt about some of the spelling she could see on the blackboard as it conflicted with her English language.

"What do you think?"

"There's a great atmosphere; the kids are having fun."

"I'm glad you can see that. I try and instil fun in all the classes. The teachers I have are all up for laughing, learning and lots of general talking. It's all about speaking the language rather than writing it."

"I couldn't agree more; I've already worked out from my first night that pronunciation is important. Last night's students were good at the grammar, but they couldn't pronounce the language properly. I spent more time drilling and repeating the module than anything else."

"Gaby, that's what I need. Can you work some hours for me?"

"What about three mornings ten 'til two? Does that help at all?

"That would be great, shall we meet tonight at the bar and discuss. I need to liaise with the others which days are better."

"To be honest Tuesday, Wednesday or Thursday's, I'd prefer if you don't mind."

"Ok, let's meet up tonight, thanks again for coming in."

She walked back to the studio, collected her bag, and went to sit on the beach, it was already two o'clock and the banks had closed. She must sort out this money, how easy it was to let the day disappear. She got back to her pad at four thirty and at five thirty made her way to school. She was teaching three advanced classes and one intermediate business class. She hoped their modules were straightforward and looked forward to the company.

She wouldn't dwell on it, but she was lonely, and she'd never felt this alone before. She knew it was the language barrier but then shook off her doubts. She would soon make new friends, especially if she worked for Jasmine's school. Lynne, the teacher, was back on evenings the following week. She hoped she would strike a friendship with her. She met Jasmine after work and agreed to work for her on Wednesday and Thursday mornings. She offered her 7,00 € an hour. They also agreed to meet one night after her classes, for which she was grateful.

Her classes were an enormous success and by the end of the third night and before Friday, her classes were full. This was unprecedented and Arrabella was running around flushed and looking at her in awe. The Director had already noticed the difference in momentum in the evenings & had increased her hourly rate to 7,00 €.

Friday, she had three beginners' classes, and the last class of the week was a full hour with business advanced. She was quietly dreading this one as the intermediate class in the week had proved a challenge. Apart from their terrible pronunciation, they'd all grasped the reflexive verbs. She was so grateful the teacher's modules had the answers attached to the exercises. She prayed this last class were going to be exhilarating and not exhausting.

The advanced students were astute with their understanding of the English language, but they all needed pronunciation practise. She asked them their names, where they lived and where they came from. They'd forgotten the basics as they'd all been studying the grammar so much.

She was surprised to discover that several students had never been outside Marbella. Mercedes was from Seville and had come to Marbella to learn English and she worked at Hotel Pyr in Puerto Banús as a housekeeper. Eugenio was the accountant at the town hall working for the Mayor of Marbella and he lived in Estepona, which wasn't far away down the coast.

José was a Bank Manager for Cajasur based in Banús and Placido was his assistant and they both originated from Granada. Isabella was a lawyer, and she dealt with children's law and social services. She originated from Asturias and was married to the most influential *Abagado/ Lawyer* in Marbella. They'd all been in the same class for over a year and quickly Gaby could see they needed to "talk."

Unanimously, after class they took her to the tapa bar around the corner as they wanted to carry on talking. She was happy to continue as it meant company and she agreed if they taught her words and sentences whilst they all had a drink.

José said he would open the bank in the morning; for her to deposit her funds and organise an account for her. Gaby was chuffed, this was what she wanted. She left them all at midnight and felt that her first week had gone far better than she'd hoped.

The next morning Jose` deposited her money and opened a current account for her wages. She went to Hotel Pyr and met Mercedes for a coffee. She made her way home, got her bag and sat on the beach, feeling relaxed.

She walked to see Antonio in the evening, finding the weekend to be very long. She called Jasmine who was out on a date, she was getting used to being alone quite a lot. She didn't want to find anyone or look for anyone, she came across her vibrator, and she placed it away in the wardrobe. All she wanted was for Nick to locate her. It had been three months already since she'd arrived.

She recharged Jed's phone. She'd deleted his numbers; she didn't want to see or hear from him again. It was time to concentrate on new friends.

❖

12

Settling in

Her new students were all in their thirties. Her Friday evenings were full on and sometimes she met Eugenio or Isabella on the Saturday for a coffee. They kept her busy and even Placido and José from the bank would call her up and invite her for a coffee in Banús.

The icing on the cake was seeing Jasmine one night a week. Her two day a week job was working out well and she wanted Gaby to join her full time. She preferred her students and kept refusing Jasmine's offer. Lynne had resumed evening work, and they'd hit it off immediately. She was from Northampton and single. This was a huge bonus. She also lived in Old Town, which was handy.

They started going to Banús over the weekends and sometimes in the week after work. Lynne's large family were based in Estepona, Manilva and Marbella. Some of the family lived in Mijas and Malaga and she saw them on occasions. They'd all lived in the area for over twenty years. Lynne had arrived three years previously and kept saying that it had been the best thing she'd ever done.

Her nephew Paul, ran a cold drinks company from Cataluña, and he had the monopoly on the Costa del Sol for importing English drinks to the province. He'd been managing the business for over ten years with his father, Ryan; Lynn's brother. He'd convinced all the family to move out and everyone had work, it was a good life. Lynn was already an English teacher, and she'd found work immediately.

"There's no shortage of men around Gaby but finding a decent one with no agenda is another thing, just to warn you."

"It's ok; I'm waiting for my guy to turn up once his assignment's done."

"What's that then?"

"He's an undercover cop."

"Oh, say no more," Lynn chuckled as they watched a polo match in Sotogrande, eyeing the talent.

"There are so many time wasters here; I've given up finding someone like minded."

"Don't give up Lynn; someone will come along when you're least thinking about it. Surely Ryan must have contacts with his business?"

"You should meet some of them!"

"Maybe not then," giggled Gaby. *"Come on let's go back to Sinatra's and have a G & T before we go home."*

Lynn's mobile rang, *"Talk of the devil, Ryan and his gang are in Banús this afternoon and just asked if I'm about."*

"Perfect," said Gaby, *"Let's go, as I can't wait to meet them."*

Lynn drove a "*Skoda*" and Gaby knew that a car was on her list but until she needed one, she'd leave it. It was quite good not having to worry about driving on the right-hand side and she knew Marbella very well on foot. The public transport system was so efficient; it wasn't a priority.

"Tell you what, drive home and we'll get a bus to Banús and taxi home."

"Not a bad idea, time to seriously let our hair down and I want you to meet my family."

***

The Marshall family were on top form by the time Lynn and Gaby joined them in Sinatra's. The Bar had a pop-up extension to it and was as an island on the front line, adjacent to some of the finest luxury liners one only saw in high society magazines. The bar was crowded inside and busy outside.

"Hi, I'm Ryan, good to meet you. This is Mary my wife; Paul over there is my son and his wife, Maria. Let's have a drink."

Ryan, was tall, handsome, bronze, and fluent in Spanish as he ordered drinks. It seemed everyone knew him. He was an influential figure, and his company employed over thirty people locally, he was popular with the local Spaniards for this reason.

The local *Policia* walked past in pairs observing everyone and Gaby's thoughts went back to Seville. She couldn't help but smile as they did look good, even in Banús.

"Your type Gaby?" said Lynn.

"Oh yes, but been there, done that. I'll tell you another day. As you said earlier, there's so many perfect women here having

fun, and I don't blame them. It's going to be impossible to come across someone who wants a partner."

"It's ok for you, your man will find you when his job is done. You can have fun in the meantime."

"I have already, don't you worry," Gaby winked, and Lynn started laughing, she fancied some fun.

The evening was incredibly humid for end of October and the "*Gypsy Kings*" cd blasted from inside the bar and the Gin flowed until early in the morning.

"Girls, c'mon, we'll get a night cap and taxis from the piano bar," shouted Ryan who was as merry as everyone else.

The piano bar was full of celebrities and after another round of Gin & Tonics, they made their way home. It was a wonder they could both stand let alone say goodbye to Ryan and his family.

"Tell me more about the Policia," asked Lynn giggling as they merrily got in the taxi.

"Another time, drop me off here, I'll see you Monday night."

"Night night; good morning actually," Lynn laughed as Gaby slammed the taxi door, carrying her heels.

She walked to her studio and as she proceeded around the corner she nearly bumped into her landlord.

"O, pardon Gavee, Buenos."

"Buenos, Pedro," she said wondering what on earth was her landlord doing skulking around the back of Hotel Fuerte at three o'clock in the morning.

She dropped on the bed and fell asleep and was woken up by her English phone ringing in its box. *I thought I'd turned it off,* she thought knowing only Jed had the number.

"Hi Gaby, how are you? Just wanted to make sure you were,ok?"

"Jed, why I'm fine. Where are you?"

"Sicily, text me your address as I'm coming to see you. I must see you."

"Ok but let me know."

The phone was disconnected, and Gaby laid there knowing she didn't want to bother with him or re-kindle a past affair. She'd already decided she was committed to Nick even though she'd had a few flings. She was going to give Nick until the spring to find her and then ....

Who was pacing outside her front door, was it her landlord? She could see a shadow walking back and forth as the sun was rising over the sea. A funny feeling came over her as she threw on a sarong and tiptoed into her living room. She checked she'd double bolted her door, yes, she hadn't been that drunk!

Not wanting to be seen, she gently drew back one of the curtains from the small window and nearly fainted as Jed stood there grinning from ear to ear. *"Fuck,"* she thought as she quickly, fumbling with shock rather than excitement and nerves, opened the door and yanked him in as they embraced. They kissed and without talking or wishing to know how he'd found her, made love all day. All thoughts of what she should be doing evaporated as he massaged and sucked her breasts, his tongue teasing every sensitive spot of her curvy body.

She was greedy for him as they moved to the rocking chair, their union in sync as the night they'd parted. Exhilarated they lay on her bed and held each other. Eventually she asked,

"How?"

"Polo match, Sotogrande."

"We went to Sinatra's after that, then the piano bar."

"Yes, I followed you. I've also been watching that creep stalk this place."

"He's my landlord."

"He's after a bit of skirt, or he's up to something. Watch him, sweetie, I don't trust him."

"Why didn't you tell me?"

"You don't answer your phone. But then I saw you there and once I'd done what I needed to do, I decided to stalk you myself," he pinched her ample bosom as she bit his arm in response.

"I could have been with someone."

"Your man Nick hasn't turned up yet then? If I can find you, he can. You'll have to choose my lover."

"You're married and until I see a divorce paper then you know the answer. Anyway, as you're here, let's not waste time talking."

"Quite right," as he pulled her on top of him as she held him close kissing his face, not wishing to miss a hair.

The sun had gone down as they showered together from an intense afternoon.

"Come on, let's go and eat."

"Ok."

He walked her to *"Skin"* restaurant, and they were seated, the table had been booked. An uneasy feeling crept through her as she ate her mussels listening to his chatter.

"Have you made good friends so far, honey?"

"Yes, Lynn you saw with me today is one of the teachers. I'm out with my Friday evening class most of the time. They're good fun and I'm learning Spanish the same time."

"Who are they?"

"A bank manager and his number two. A Solicitor, housekeeper from a hotel in Banús and Eugenio works at the town hall."

"Which bank is that then?"

"Why do you want to know?"

"Interested that's all. I'm serious; I'm coming to marry you once I'm divorced."

"Yeah, yeah. Nicks already proposed and you know he's let me spend a year away before I marry him."

She'd never disclosed Nicks' real work as that would have been the ultimate betrayal. Something wasn't sitting right, and she couldn't work out what it was. She ignored it for the time being.

"When do you disappear as quickly as you've appeared?" *"First thing, that'll give you time to recover and get to work for six!"* as he grinned at her, the deep brown eyes melting her heart for a moment.

How did he know what time she started work? She dismissed it and gulped down some Rioja. Her instinct was always right, but she'd have to dissect this whole thing once he'd gone, and she needed to change the subject.

"What do you reckon my landlord is up to then?"

"He's on the prowl for something, have you seen any of your neighbours in the block?"

"There are three teachers and two lawyers, but have only acknowledged them in passing, why?"

"He's either dealing or one of the teachers are supplying, just give him a wide berth."

"How do you know, or shouldn't I ask?

"Don't ask, trust me on this ok."

"Ok, let's get back. A fabulous end to my week, thank you, a lovely surprise."

"Carry your phone with you then it won't be a surprise next time."

"I've already lost one," as she explained.

"Ok, keep it at home, text me your Spanish number as I won't spring myself on you, it's not fair. I do get it."

They returned to her studio, as she saw the landlord hovering in the shadows and that same fear swept over her, as when she'd seen the men in the cockroach apartment. As she opened her door, she wasn't sure if this feeling was the creepy landlord or her lover. Indeed, something wasn't right.

She enveloped herself around him as she let him drop her sundress to the tiled floor. He carried her to the bed as she clung to him, her eyes locked on his with his mouth as eager as earlier as she responded feeling aroused quickly.

As she enjoyed his touch and felt him envelope her, the penny dropped, she knew.

❖

13

Benalmadena

Through blurry eyes he tried to focus on the ceiling, as he placed a hand on his forehead, the thumping headache continued. His head hurt so much; he couldn't lift it from the pillow. He grabbed each side of the single bed and realised he couldn't remember where he was. He gulped for some air and tried to relive the night before.

He'd been undercover for over six months, and they were close to getting the Drug Baron and Cartel that supplied the Costa del Sol. He'd gone to buy drugs with Aleksey who worked with the Russian Mafia. His head continued to thump, and a bronze arm appeared from his waist. He peered downwards and there was a naked body wrapped round his torso, a mountain of black hair covering his chest.

"Armand tu eres despierto?" as the arm moved over his chest as she looked up at him.

"No," he whispered as he tried to remember and moved her up next to him. She snuggled up and he hoped his memory would return before she talked or tried to move him.

She fell asleep again and on the single bed further in the room, Aleksey was entwined with a blonde girl, both crashed from an obvious heavy night. The air in the room was stale from alcohol, drugs, and sex. There wasn't an open window and Nick racked his brains, pacing his memory to return as his life could depend on it. He remembered he'd organised a meeting in Sotogrande. His head pounded even more as he recalled seeing her, how much he'd reacted and had over compensated to keep his cover. Aleksey had pulled the two girls who had been on their hit list as perfect decoys and here he was.

They were close to discovering the identity of the Drug Baron and there were three mules working for him. They had names and surveillance on two and once they'd found the third, they would swoop and arrest them at the same time. The two hookers were perfect cover, and they were being used to infiltrate the drug scene. The two girls had led them to the two mules, one to go.

He tried to remember where they'd been using. He obviously hadn't switched his supply to the bag of painkillers that Aleksey and he prepared and used daily. The girls were addicts and it was easier to act as an addict than become one. He'd obviously had a line or two last night, as he couldn't focus on the gecko that was on the damn ceiling. He remembered being in Sinatra's and making mental notes for Aleksey.

Gaby had been with Ryan Marshall and his cronies, and he needed to know her connection. He knew she hadn't recognised him as after all he'd changed his appearance and at first glance in the mirror, he didn't recognise himself either.

With their two hookers on their arm, she hadn't looked at him at all. He had to admit, she looked beautiful and with Ryan as a connection, he'd be able to find her. She'd either lost her phone or didn't want to know as he'd tried to get in touch. Once this was over, he'd find her and hoped they could start again. The arm around his waist moved all over his body and he threw himself into his Spanish character as he allowed her to arouse him.

He could see in the corner of his eye that Aleksey was in mode as his blonde was on top, her tanned body moving slowly as she held his hands. Armand brushed his lips over his girl and turned her on to her back; he needed to clear his head, and that gecko was still not in focus.

Benalmadena port was full of affluent tourists predominantly German and English. The harbour housed yachts and boats of all sizes, and it was the largest port outside of Banús. As it was a stones' throw away from Malaga airport, it had become a tourist attraction along with an easy target for drug smuggling and crime in general. The Russian mafia were evident in some areas but only to the local businesses.

A few hours later Armand untangled himself from his hooker and went to shower, checking his brown contacts and his dreadlocks were in place. They needed to get to Gibraltar as he nodded at Aleksey who knew they needed to follow up on a lead from last night.

"Adios mañana, Rubio/See you later Blondie," Aleksey waved at the two girls as Armand drove away.

"Ryan Marshall, what do we know of him?" said Armand driving too fast as they headed for Gibraltar to observe a cargo shipment.

"My people are watching him, Armand,' he's got the monopoly on all the soft drink import. We'll move in, once we've got the surveillance done."

"Is it a front for drugs?"

"No, but the business could be lucrative for this and other exports."

"What's the surveillance showing so far?"

"They're all working in the business and two of the family are teachers, his sister and niece."

"We want it, it's perfect for our own Cartel, but we need to take this lot down first."

"No, my friend, the Russians will be ahead of your lot, the British are too slow, but we're on the same side. We both need the main Baron. He's good, but not that good. He'll slip up soon and hopefully right under our nose."

"Talking about noses, did you not give me the right pouch last night?"

"No, they were switched; one of those whores was on to us."

"Yours or mine."

"Yours I think; you couldn't keep your gaze from that other girl in the bar. You can't afford to fancy anyone right now Armand, this job is too far over our heads. The boys will eliminate us if they've any inclination; you're not who they think you are."

"You're right, when does this shipment arrive?" as Armando drove into the passport lane for Gibraltar.

The passport office waved them through, and Aleksey gave Armando directions where they needed to hide out. With kit bags and no I.D. on their person, they moved through the car park and over the back of the shopping malls and disappeared.

❖

14

Fiesta Season

It was November the 1ˢᵗ already and it was all Saints day; a national holiday paying homage to all of Spain's hundreds of Saints. It was also a day of mourning for all the Catholic families. It was an opportunity to have a family day, visit the graves of your loved ones and reflect. Gaby decided to take up Jasmine's offer of tapas and drinks as she made her way to *Casco Antiguo*.

Since Jed's' surprise visit she'd felt vulnerable and uneasy about her living arrangements. He'd either tried to scare her, or he'd tried to warn her. Her landlord had never bothered her; she only saw him on rent day in the reception of Hotel Fuerte. Sergio, who'd acted as her lawyer had probably helped in this matter, but she'd been more observant since. She'd seen him skulk around the block and she'd also seen him leave two of the studios on various occasions. Those two girls worked in schools in San Pedro, and they worked daytimes.

It was none of her business; she hadn't exactly behaved like a saint. Jed had known everything about her, and she had this uneasy feeling. She no longer felt safe. She rang Jasmines' private doorbell as she announced herself. She would ask her if there were any spare apartments in Old Town. A move would now be prudent.

A party was in full swing as Jasmine explained that two of her sisters had arrived unexpectedly from America and she'd rung round some of her colleagues.

"Muy Bien, Jasmine, Fiesta!" Gaby shouted over the din of the music as she closed her front door quickly as to respect the Spanish day of mourning.

There were at least thirty people mingling round the classrooms and her quarters. She went to the living room and towards the kitchen, where a couple of people were helping themselves to some drinks.

"Drink?"

"Si, yes, I'll have a G & T, but I'll make it."

"No, it's ok, I can make a mean G & T," said the bloke.

Gaby laughed and smiled at the couple.

"I'll have a glass of white please," said the lady in an American drawl.

"You must be Jasmines' family?" said Gaby introducing herself.

"I'm Yvonne, her sister and this bloke, I don't know..."

He grinned, *"I'm just the plumber, Jas called me earlier to fix a leak, and I've decided to stay, I'm Jim, how do you do?"*

"Hi, I'm fine thanks. I'm Gaby, I work for Jasmine two days a week."

"Do you live in Marbella?"

"Yes, walking distance from here, and you?" as Yvonne smiled at them and took her drink towards the noise in the living room.

"Estepona front line."

"How long have you been here?"

"Here in Spain, about a year."

"Can I ask you why you came here?"

"You ask too many questions; why do you want to know?"

"Sorry, Jim. It's just I've been here since August and everyone living here seem a bit transient."

"You mean you haven't come across anyone who isn't on a fling or who hasn't an agenda. Tell me. Everyone has a reason to run or hide and they're all here. Are you running or hiding, Gaby?" as he popped an olive in his mouth staring right through her, making her quiver.

She could easily have lied to this bloke; she'd had enough of lies in general.

"I'm on a year away from my fiancé."

"You're running then, is he that bad you need to have a fling for a year?" he chortled sipping his red wine and staring at her.

She giggled, it did sound bazaar, as she continued to laugh as she let him pour her another drink.

"I'm an accountant in the U.K. I'm on a year off too, wanted a break from the humdrum of city life. I'm going back next September. In the meantime, I took a course on general building

and plumbing and here I am your trusty local plumber who will come out on a fiesta day and drink your customer's wine."

"And gate crash her party."

"Why not? Have you been in Marbella long?"

"Since end of September, I spent a month in Seville on my teaching course. The time is flying past quickly."

"Are you home for Christmas?"

"This is my home Jim, I'm here and fancy a beach day. Are you on your own for Christmas?"

"Yes, I guess your fiancé will be over, but if he doesn't, then call me?" as he gave her his business card with two mobile numbers on it.

"Jim will fix it. Plumbing and General Handyman"

"Ok, Mr. Fix it, shall we join the others?" "Yes."

"Gavee, pleeeeeeeese come and work for me full time," said Jasmine full of alcohol and tapas as she swung her arms over Gaby's shoulders as she was leaving.

She laughed; she'd had an enjoyable day but wanted to go home.

"See you Tuesday, Jas. Thanks for a great day, you've a lovely family."

"See yah."

"Hey, do you fancy a coffee; I think I need one before I drive home?"

Jim stood outside the school; his jacket slung over his white t-shirt.

"I thought you'd left much earlier," said Gaby surprised to see him seemingly waiting for her.

"I did, but came back for my jacket; do you fancy a quick coffee somewhere?"

"Yes, ok. Let's pop into Orange square, Antonio will be open."

"Lead the way, Señorita."

She needed a coffee, she'd had too much Gin, but she was still alert.

Orange Square was packed with families all eating and the buzz was infectious.

Antonio waved at her as he manoeuvred a table of two for them.

"You've got influence, or is this your local?"

"It's my local, it's handy from the school and half way from Wall Street, where I work. It's a long story but Antonio helped me when I first arrived. I can't believe it's only been six weeks, so much has happened."

"Really, tell me more."

"No, it's not that exciting, tell me more about you. Are you running from a Mrs. Jim?"

"Not really. I just wanted a change from my business. I wanted to be outside in the sun and felt the only way to move on with my business was to leave it and decide."

"Decide what exactly?"

"I'm going to expand into Accountancy abroad and needed to make contacts whilst I'm here, but I wanted to be sure, that I either expand or sell up and change career paths."

"Gosh, huge decisions then, so you're running from responsibilities?"

"You could say that; I just don't want to spend the next thirty years at a desk without exploring other options. What about you, when do you go home to marry? What will you do, continue teaching and have babies?"

"I've got an Operations job with a recruitment company, and it's been left open for me, I can decide nearer the time or take the redundancy package, I'm yet undecided."

"And your man?"

"He's waiting for me, he promised," she said looking straight into his eyes for the first time. She knew, he could see that she wasn't sure.

"Thanks for the coffee but I need to go home."

"Shall I walk you?"

"No, I'm fine, it was good to meet you."

"What about a drink sometime, I know about the boyfriend, if you fancy company, call me."

"Yes, I'll do that. I'll call you if I need a plumber," she smiled kissed him on both cheeks and they went their separate ways.

She had no choice but lie. No one must know any more than she was prepared to divulge. As Jim had said and he was right, there was no one to trust. Everyone seemed to have an agenda, and she only wanted to enjoy her time here and give Nick an opportunity to find her. She was an English Teacher and currently she didn't have to do anything but teach English. She cast her thoughts aside as a black Mercedes pulled up alongside her and the window came down.

"Do you need a lift?"

"Jim, I literally live next to the hotel, but thanks."

"Can we meet for a drink in the hotel then?"

"Don't you want to go home?" she laughed.

"No, not really; come on, I'll park up and meet you there."

She nodded as she made her way to the Hotel. She didn't want to lie to him and wished he'd just go home. They had a few drinks, and she discovered that she liked him even though she wasn't prepared to get involved. He seemed a genuine bloke and she agreed to meet him the following week.

***

It was the middle of November and soon she would have to think about Christmas, but whilst the sun was shining it was hard to comprehend winter, turkeys, and Christmas carols. Jim knew she had a boyfriend, but this hadn't deterred him from taking her out once a week. She'd spent nearly a month keeping him from any close contact, but it was obviously going to happen. He was the first bloke she'd met, lovers aside, who didn't seem to have an agenda, kept his life private and seemed to genuinely like her.

He was determined to bed her, that was apparent, but she had a boyfriend, she kept saying to herself. She was such a floozy as the boyfriend excuse hadn't come up in her head with the girls. That had been different, or had it? What about the Policia, that was steamy, she'd never done anything of the kind before. She was a good girl and all she'd done was let her hair down. All she wanted was one man to love her forever, was that too much to ask? She sighed as she realised that this Jim was making her question Nick's trust of her again.

The school was buzzing as she arrived much earlier for a staff meeting. The rotas were to be set for the remainder of November and December. The school was closing for ten days. Lynn waved at Gaby as she joined her,

"Did you have a good weekend?"

"Yes, I've met a guy, actually he might suit you as I want to be faithful to Nick," said Gaby.

"Tell me later," said Lynn as the Director of Language was about to join them.

"He's our age group and lives in Estepona. He's over here for another year; I reckon he would stay if he met someone. Anyway, he's a nice guy."

"Have you slept with him?"

"'Course not, I haven't even kissed him. Whatever made you ask that?" she remarked.

"Don't want your cast offs! Are you really going to wait for Nick?"

"Yes, but I'm not really sure, if I'm totally honest."

"What's happened, you haven't been yourself since we met Ryan in Banus."

"Let's take our rotas once they've printed them and I'll tell you after class, ok"

"Christ Gaby, whatever, is it?"

They were positively delighted with their rotas, and a pay rise as both of their classes were booked solid. Gaby had been given extra hours and feeling very buoyant they left, crossed the main road, and made their way to their favourite tapa bar. Bar Tougana, was tucked away down a cobbled street. No tourist could find this bar easily as there was no main door. It was down the side street and hidden by a sumptuous purple bougainvillea tree, which covered the walls and the top half of the door. The door had been carved to match the stone work, a very clever way of keeping a place to word of mouth. This was a discovery through Eugenio, her student. As a Spanish couple ran it, this helped their Spanish conversation. They found a quiet table in the corner and Gaby ordered,

"Una botella Rioja por favor, Carlos."

"Si Gaveee, un momento."

"I'll tell you what's happened since I got here," said Gaby gulping down a large amount of red wine as she started.

Lynn's phone rang as Gaby stopped talking; Lynn was drinking heavily as Gaby waved Carlos for another bottle.

"Ryan and the gang are in Banus Friday."

"That's great shall we join them?"

"Yes, that's why he's called. He's bringing some new guys he's taken on for us to meet."

"Ooh I say that's sounds fabulous. I'm going to ask Jim to come for you to meet him."

"Have you a date with him this week?"

"Yes, tomorrow after work, I'll not kiss a hair on his head until you've met him," she laughed as her phone rang.

"Talk of the devil, Hi Jim. Yes, no problem, why don't we meet up in Sinatra's on Friday, my mates are all going?"

"He's gone to Cadiz with a work prospect and will meet us on Friday," said Gaby relieved. *"See, he will be untouched by me at any rate, you can see what you think on Friday,"* she smiled as Carlos brought over another bottle of red as Gaby disclosed everything, including Jed's surprise visit. Lynn's reaction was a picture as she drank back the wine.

Lynn admitted she'd had a lover for two years and Gaby ordered another bottle of red, completely shocked by her disclosure when Lynn confessed, who he was.

15

Nueva Andalucía

Friday's classes were now packed. This had resulted in another pay rise and this lesson was all about dating and the proverb, *"A bird in the hand is worth two in the bush."* She could give them new vocabulary around dating and the class had become quite raucous.

"Well done everyone. I'm going to Banús with Lynn for a drink; anyone want to join us?"

"Yes, I'll drive you, anyone want a lift?"

"We'll see you there," said José as Placido agreed.

"I'll meet you there," said Mercedes.

"I have a family dinner, Gavee. Maybe you come to have tea at my house before Christmas and meet my family?"

"That would be lovely Isabella, thank you."

Banús was in full swing by the time they all arrived. It was still warm, but the island bar was inside, and the windows were covered in.

"Have you seen Dad?" asked Paul.

"We've just got here," said Lynn as Eugenio, Placido and José went to organise seats and drinks.

"I've got tables in the corner, tell the guys."

Lynn went to speak to Eugenio and most of the drinkers were a part of Paul's business, and the rest were made up of Wall Street students.

Mercedes arrived as the bar filled up with the odd tourist party, drinking in one bar and then leaving for the next one.

"It's begun to rain," said Mercedes as she'd walked from Hotel Pyr.

"Do you live close by?"

"Yes, not far from the Hotel."

"At least you can walk from here," said Gaby as a Gin &Tonic arrived in her hand.

"It's busy here tonight."

"Yes, Lynn's family are here. They tend to meet up monthly for a catch up," explained Gaby. *"Her brother employs a lot of Spanish and has been here over twenty years."*

"Really," said Mercedes, *"We didn't know."*

"No, it's not something she'd share with you."

"Gavee as we're not in class, can we talk sometime about private lessons for my staff at the hotel."

"Yes, of course. After Christmas, I'll discuss it with you."

"Thank you, yes."

"Is your boyfriend here?" asked Placido.

"No, Placido, not tonight."

"Let's go and sit, the bouncer says there's a problem," said José ushering them all to the back corner.

"Paul, have you got hold of your dad?"

"No Lynn, his phone is on answer phone."

"He'll be here soon, I'm sure," as they continued to chat amongst each other.

"Jim's on his way Lynn," smiled Gaby as she wanted her to meet him; after telling her everything Lynn had said one thing,

"Oh My God, I haven't lived!"

At least she'd felt a bit better about her reaction; she didn't need anyone around her judging. She felt she was existing until Nick turned up. Lynn had also shocked her by confessing that she was sleeping with Placido. It was a secret as his family wouldn't want him seeing a British girl. She'd been dating him for two years.

The blaring music suddenly was turned down a notch and the windows were being covered with the black curtains only used when the bar was shut.

"What's going on?"

The bar door was being closed and the three bouncers outside were having brisk conversations with one or two customers who were trying to get in.

"That's Jim, he's here," as Gaby waved for him to join them.

Jim looked harassed as he joined them. He brushed his lips on Gaby's cheeks and was introduced to Lynn.

"Something's going on; they've got Banús on lock down."

"What?"

"I don't know, the bouncer just told me, no one's leaving, and no- one can get in."

"What's happening?" said Paul.

"Ryan's not going to get here now Paul. Banús is closed. That's what Jim just said."

"What do you know?"

"Nothing really, go and ask the bouncer, he might tell you more than what he's just told me. I got here in time."

Eugenio passed a beer towards Jim as he took it and gulped a mouthful from the bottle.

"Come on, let's sit, we aren't going from here, we might as well enjoy the company and music."

The bar Manager and staff had dimmed the lights. Suddenly they heard gun fire as everyone stopped talking and crouched under the tables.

Gaby felt Jim's arm around her and felt comforted. The music went back up and the bouncer announced again that no- one could leave until the Guardia gave them permission.

"Let's carry on drinking," said José who looked less confident than he sounded.

Everyone laughed as Gaby looked across at Lynn, who was engrossed in an intimate conversation with Placido; his arm around her, it was obvious they were a couple.

"When we eventually get out of here, do you want to come back to mine for a nightcap?"

"That would be lovely," said Jim as he kissed her gently in the corner.

Suddenly there were more sounds of gunfire and even the bar manager crouched behind the bar, as he turned the music down.

"This isn't funny anymore," whispered Maria, Paul's wife who was five months pregnant.

***

Aleksey spoke rapidly in Russian holding his Kalashnikov rifle to his chest as he gave the order. The military had moved on the instructions and within forty minutes all roads to Banús were blocked. They were to allow one vehicle in and that was the Rolls Royce owned by Ryan Marshall. He was scheduled to drive to Banús for seven that evening. Armando held the Nagant M1895 pistol, his comrade had given him the day before, knowing this wasn't part of his brief. But this was linked to his mission, and he had no choice but continue his cover. They were going to kidnap this businessman, and Armando hadn't been told any more details.

He stood with Miguel and Aleksey at the entrance to Banús and he hoped that she wasn't in Sinatra's. There was no way of letting her know and he wished he could prevent the kidnap of this Businessman.

The rapid gunfire earlier had been a warning to some bunch of tourists who'd ignored the embargo to enter front line Banús. These guys weren't kidding.

"Coche."

Armando and Aleksey with Miguel moved towards the car park entrance of Banús as the gold Rolls drove in. The chauffeur indicated to the underground car park as Aleksey held up his Kalashnikov and stood in the middle of the road.

The chauffeur was ordered out of the car, shaking, he whispered *"Take care Mr. Ryan,"* as he was pushed to the floor. His boss sitting in the back seat stunned, looked at Miguel and Armando, who stood at each back door. Both sported black balaclavas and wore combat gear. He knew they wanted him, and he sat still, dreading what was to happen next. He could see someone tying up his chauffeur, his best friend who'd helped him start his empire over thirty years previously. His friend who had always wanted to be a chauffeur and it had been their private joke and arrangement.

"Leave him," shouted Ryan from the back seat.

"Quiet," shouted Miguel as he jumped in the back and Armando jumped in the front. A black Mercedes arrived as Ryan watched his friend being lifted into the boot as the car disappeared. Aleksey jumped in to the other side of Ryan as he visibly shook seeing the Kalashnikov pointed at his chest.

"Where are you taking me, what do you want?" asked Ryan.

"My boss wants a little chat," whispered Aleksey in his rough Russian accent as Armando drove the kidnapped man to Nueva Andalucía.

***

Sinatra's was hot and stuffy, and the bar had run out of tapas. It was four in the morning, and everyone was tired with drink, and a few had gone under the tables to sleep off the alcohol. Gaby was merry and she was pleased that Placido and Lynn, were an item. She was in the mood to get to know Jim and he'd been flirting seriously with her all evening, especially since the lock down.

"Jim, go and find out if we can go home," she said realising this guy had no secrets and it was time.

"I'm going home, your boyfriend is a nice man, Gavee," said Mercedes.

"They might not let you."

"I only live around the corner."

"There's been gunshot, wait for Jim to come back."

Jim was a long time and kept checking his phone as Gaby observed him from the corner of the room. He knew everyone, but then he'd been here longer than her. She didn't think no more as Lynn caught her eye and winked at her. She was giving her thumbs up and after what she'd been through with men using her, maybe it was time to forget Nick and concentrate on Jim.

"Banús is on lock down as is Nueva Andalucía. The Black Berets are all over the place, there's been a standoff with the Russians. We can't leave until whatever is going on is sorted."

"Oh My God, Dad?"

"What about him" said Gaby as Paul and his wife looked visibly worried.

"He's had some threatening calls from a Russian man over the last few months."

"What about?" asked Jim suddenly interested in Ryan Marshall.

"He wouldn't elaborate and told me to stop worrying, this was Spain and there was always something going on, that's all I know. With Maria pregnant, he hasn't said much to me lately. We've moved to Mijas, and we only see him here once a month. He hasn't mentioned anything of late, though."

"I'm sure he's fine Paul," said Lynn equally worried about her brother and felt sick.

"Tapas everyone," said the bar tender who had miraculously organised some more food.

Gaby was ravenous and glad that Jim was with them. She had an uneasy feeling all round and didn't want to go home alone after this incident. She could see that Lynn was in a terrible state, trying to not think the worst and Placido was comforting her. Mercedes came back,

"The bouncer is taking me to the hotel. See you Monday everyone."

"Take care Mercedes."

"I'm going too," said José *"I live next to the hotel."*

"Adios José"

Eugenio was drinking black coffee and didn't look happy with the situation as everyone began to show signs of impatience to leave. At nine o'clock in the morning, the Guardia knocked on the bar door and entered. The bouncers and bar manager were in deep conversation and eventually the staff started to open the windows.

"At last," murmured Lynn.

"It's safe to leave everyone," announced the Manager as shell shocked as everyone else.

"We'll see you Monday Lynn. Let us know Ryan's' ok, won't you?"

"Yes, I'm going to Lynn's house," said Placido pleased that everyone had accepted their relationship.

"Good idea, Placido. Call us when you've got news, Lynn."

"Of course."

"My car is in the underground car park," said Jim as he grabbed Gaby's hand and made their way to his car.

They drove back to Gaby's apartment in silence and the effects of alcohol much earlier that morning had worn off. Jim double locked the door as she closed the curtains even though it was morning.

"Can we sleep, I'm worried about Lynn's brother and the whole thing has unnerved me a bit."

"Good idea, I'm not going to let anyone hurt you, come here."

They found each other's lips and embraced each other as Gaby found his touch and kiss a comfort as she held him tight. She responded and moved her hands over his body. He was surprisingly solid and much heavier to the touch, and she felt safe and secure suddenly, with a man she was beginning to trust. They moved to the bedroom, and he let her get in to bed and pulled her to him, his arms over her chest as they went to sleep.

⚬⚬⚬

16

Estepona

The mobile rung non -stop as they stirred but neither of them could be bothered to move.

"Someone wants a plumber," whispered Gaby as it wasn't hers.

"They can drown," replied Jim as he pulled her round and started to fondle her. They kissed as the phone continued to ring.

"You'd better get that; it's distracting."

"Yes, you're right, don't move."

She snuggled down into the duvet and knew this moment was going to be special, she peered over the cover and Jim was getting dressed.

"What's wrong?" she said slightly alarmed.

"There's a flood in the building next to mine and they can't get hold of the caretaker. Sorry, sweetheart. Tell you what, I'll come back for you once I'm done and I'll take you to Estepona, is that ok?"

"Of course, I'll lock the door behind you."

"I think you're gorgeous, maybe we can try again later," as he winked and kissed her fully on the mouth.

She showered and tidied her pad and made some notes for her classes the following week. She marked a test paper for Jasmines' kids and was pleased that they'd all got over eight out of ten in their spelling. She texted Lynn, again no reply. She thought of her anguish over keeping Placido a secret, as he was a student. He was the same age as Lynn and she thought it was great news. She'd call her again once she'd finished her prep.

Two hours later and no news from Lynn, there was a tap on her front door. She moved the curtain, it was Jim.

"I thought you were calling."

"My battery's dead, have left the phone at home, are you ready?" as he kissed her again on the lips.

"Yes, can we go past Lynn's house? She's not texted me; I need to know she's ok."

"Sure, but Placido was staying with her remember. They might be otherwise engaged."

"That's true, let's leave it then. Show me Estepona, Mr. Jim."

The sun was warm still, but a cardigan was needed after lunch as the temperatures dropped. They parked outside a multi-story apartment building and walked towards the beach.

"I live in that block, for my sins. I'll show you later."

Holding hands like lovers they ambled through the gardens to the Esplanade. The immediate beach was over three kilometres long and literally ten minutes' walk from Jim's apartment.

There were a few families enjoying the warmth of the sun as they made their way to the *chiringuito/beach bar* for some "***espeto de sardinas***."

Estepona district was renowned for fresh fish and there were several highly recommended restaurants in the area. Jim took her the long way in order she could take in the view.

"It's awesome, as romantic as Marbella."

"Ah, but Marbella is man - made, but Estepona already looked like this."

"No, I didn't know. I must start reading up about the history, it's fascinating."

"Yes, it is. Each province seems to have its own unique history."

They sat at a beach view table as the waiter came to take their order.

"Aqua con gas, what do you want Sweetheart?"

"Con gas igualmente" said Gaby as the waiter nodded and disappeared.

"Is your man coming for Christmas or are you going back to the U.K?"

"I'm not going to the U.K. I'm staying here. I'm not sure if Nick's coming, why do you ask?"

"Does he exist? Something tells me he doesn't?"

"What's brought this on?"

"Last night in Banús made me realise we could all have been innocently killed in the middle of crossfire. Just want to know as I don't want to distract you."

"I'm a bit distracted already. Trouble is, he does exist and the only phone number he had of mine has been stolen. I'm reliant on him to find me."

"Why can't you just go home and marry him, you're not making sense."

"O.K., he works abroad and is rarely home. He is somewhere in Europe as we speak, it's a complicated job, he's got. I've no idea where he is or how to find him."

"He'll find you, if he knows you're in the Costa del Sol, then it's not too hard to find your school. Where does this place me, better talk about it before I get involved."

"Are you involved?"

"Yes, I am. I need to know what could happen here."

"I've promised to marry Nick. In the meantime, I'd love an affair with you, but you need to know, when Nick arrives, I will leave you high and dry."

"Or you may not."

"Well, that could happen. Thing is, you're heading home yourself in September next year. Are you sure there's no Mrs. Jim waiting in Sheffield for you?"

Jim didn't reply but they laughed, and they clinked their glasses, agreeing to enjoy the moment.

The sardines were exceptional and after lunch, they walked the beach and made their way towards Jim's block.

"Let me show you my place and then I'll take you home. I want you to trust me. I don't believe you love Nick; I'm going to take a chance if you'll let me."

Jim let her in the entrance as Gaby's head was spinning from the mere fact this guy was being open and honest which she found exhilarating.

"I'll give us a chance, if you know that Nick is out there."

He grabbed her waist in the lift as it proceeded to move up six floors. They continued to kiss as the lift door opened, and he guided her to his front door.

Once inside, he bolted the door and walked her to his bedroom, kissing her face, lips and caressing her hair. She dropped her handbag on the chair as he continued to caress her. She felt him all over and was again surprised at how tight his body and how heavy he was. The white shirts he seemed to wear drowned his fit body. She undid his belt and gasped as he unhinged her bra and with the other hand was already inside her special sweet spot. He continued to kiss her not letting either hand move.

She was weak, her knees buckling with the intense force shooting through her whole insides. He instinctively dropped her skirt and dropped his jeans in one movement. He gently moved her on the bed and started kissing her toes and his fingers kept inside her, as she moaned uncontrollably. His lips kissed and his tongue circled her ankles, as he moved further towards his fingers. She grabbed his head as he slowly made his way up towards her mouth. He kissed her mouth with such force and passion; she could feel the electricity going through them. He moved on top of her as she cried out with surprise and their eyes locked right at that moment.

They woke up in the middle of the night as the phone rang.

"Who needs a plumber this time of the morning?" she whispered snuggled to him and not moving.

"No, it's yours, answer it later."

"What time is it?"

"Four o' clock in the morning."

"They can wait."

"Could be Lynn."

"At this hour, probably a wrong number, leave it. She's with Placido remember."

"Where were we?"

She giggled as he moved under the covers and squealed as his tongue found her. She'd never been indulged this much since Seville. How could she........?

He moved inside her as she thought of nothing but this man she'd met for a month and this man who made her feel safe. He was a straight-talking bloke and she relaxed as she rolled over wanting to give him all of her. She was smitten.

After a walk on the beach, Jim drove her to his favourite *chiringuito* on route to Marbella. It was run by a British couple called *"**Cruseos.**"* Jim had helped them renovate the bar before they'd opened that season. It was ten yards from the water's edge.

"I thought you were a plumber?"

"Yes, and handy man. I helped Brian erect the roof. Shelly, his wife is running the restaurant and Brian is the honcho man."

"It's lovely, I'm glad you've bought me here. Shall we sit on the sun beds for a while?"

"Brian, Shelly meet Gaby. She's an English teacher in Marbella. We met at the school in Old town. She's my new friend," he said coyly as Brian cheered, and Shelly hugged her and welcomed her to their bar.

"New friend, eh?"

"What would you rather I say?" asked Jim as they sat on the sun beds.

"No, that's fine. I'm recovering from last night and this morning."

"Did you not enjoy?"

"Oh, come off it. You know damn well it was wonderful, for me at any rate, what about you?"

"I'm smitten but you're betrothed to another so let's just shag a lot and have fun."

"Fabulous," she said with a sudden feeling of sadness but dismissed it.

17

Christmas Surprise

Harry the hatchet dragged the body towards Miguel as the men sweltered in the lunchtime sun. John the Dig as he was best known had done a decent job. The grave was deep, and the gorse bushes and trees would hide the finished spot. Miguel with Armando and Aleksey holding their weapons to their chest stood facing outwards, covering all angles of the campo, forty kilometres from the coast.

The two black Mercedes were covered in camouflage drapes as the dust whirled round. The body had been stripped of all I.D. Aleksey helped Harry roll the body over in to the grave. He nodded as John filled the hole, not stopping to acknowledge Harry as he picked up the second shovel. Miguel helped them to place random rocks around the area along with olive tree branches, bracken, and some gorse.

Placido, gagged and bound in the back of the Mercedes knew he was next, but why, he'd no idea. He'd been drugged; his headache making him feel sick to the stomach. He knew having witnessed this; he wasn't going to live. The blood congealed on his lips reminded him; he had hours.

Armando nodded and Aleksey spoke in rapid Russian as Harry and John jumped in their car and sped away, creating more dust clouds.

"He needs to give us the info" said Aleksey as Armando made a mental note where the grave was situated. They closed the boot as Placido closed his eyes with dread.

"We'll take him to Cartageña; I know who'll break him."
Miguel jumped in the Merc with his men, knowing it wouldn't take more than one broken finger to break this poor Spaniard. There was nothing he could do about it; he was in too deep with the others, but they were about to deliver the Baron.

***

Jim dropped her at home as she tried to call Lynn but still no response. Something was wrong as why would she be calling her at four in the morning?

He had given her several logical reasons, and they'd even driven past her house, and she didn't appear to be at home.

She went to shower and realised that Jed had called her twice and that was all she needed. She'd been honest with Jim and now she may have to confess that she also had a lover, who she couldn't shake off. What a mess, she was making. She needed to ignore Jed as he was a loose cannon.

Jim occupied her thoughts as she stopped wondering where Nick was in the world. She needed to live and enjoy this year. She sat on her beach which was isolated but still warm enough, for her to unwind.

She was worried about Lynn but knew she'd see her in school a bit later.

Her phone rang and it was José.

"Digame/what do you want, José."

"Gavee, Placido is not in work, can you find out if he's with Lynn?"

"Of course, what's happened?

"Don't know, he didn't make his Mother's birthday party yesterday, the family have been in, I have no idea what's wrong?

"Oh gosh, that's not a typical Son behaviour. I've tried to call Lynn all yesterday and this morning and she's not picking up either. I'll phone you from school later. I've no idea what's happened."

"Ok, call me later."

"Yes, José, don't worry," she said as she called Jim.

"Hi sweetheart, you ok?"

She relayed her conversation to Jim, who didn't interrupt, his silence unnerving as she packed her stuff to go home.

"I've no idea what to say. Wait until you get to school and call me in your break. I'll come and meet you after classes, ok."

She felt a huge relief that he could sense she was unhappy that her friend and now Placido seemed to be missing. He'd understood and she knew then she couldn't be alone, anymore.

She walked back to her pad and decided she needed a car. It would give her more freedom; she'd ask Jim later to help her find one.

She walked to school in anticipation and eagerness to see Lynn. She got there early, and Arrabella was smiling as usual, as she said,

"Sad Lynn is leaving, no?"

"What do you mean Arrabella?"

"Ah, you don't know, she with Director right now."

"Ok, tell her I'm in the staff room."

She didn't understand and made coffee as Lynn walked in and hugged her.

"Gaby, it's awful," as she broke down and Gaby steered her to the sofa.

"Whatever's happened? I've been worried sick. You called me at four in the morning, and I've been trying to get hold of you ever since. Where's Placido, he didn't go to his Mum's birthday, José is worried too. What's this, you've resigned?"

Lynn groaned as she held her stomach doubled up in agony as the tears fell down her cheeks. Through her tears, she explained,

"Three men were waiting for us when we got in on Sunday morning. They grabbed us and threw sacks over our heads. They attacked Placido and one of the men threw me in the broom cupboard. He must have heard me try to call you as he came back in, punched me in the stomach, and took away my phone. After a while I heard a car speed away, but they'd barricaded the door. It took me all day to move the furniture and open the door. I had to push with my ass, it took forever. Placido was gone and

I'd have come to yours, but this is what they left on the kitchen table."

She handed a note to Gaby as her stomach turned as she read the threat.

"It can't be right, no way," she exclaimed.

"Yes, I'm leaving Friday, if I want to live."

"Lynn, where's Placido, we need to call José, he's worried. I need to call Jim and tell him……"

"I don't know that just it."

"This letter is it genuine. I mean, can they really threaten Ryan's whole family?"

"Ryan was kidnapped when we were in Banús. The Guardia are with Paul now. I got the news earlier, the Guardia can't protect us all and the note says; that all the Marshall family must leave, otherwise they'll kill him and then us, in turn."

"But how can you be sure, they won't kill him anyway."

"We're not. The Guardia has got Mary, Paul, and Maria under protection. We've all got to book flights by Friday and send copies to this email address, then they'll release him to the airport. Mary has booked their flights already."

"Where will you go?"

"Manchester, I've rung a friend, she's as shocked as I am, but has a spare room."

"What about your house, your stuff, Lynn, for goodness' sake, you can't just leave it all."

"If I'm threatened with my life yes. Gaby, you'd be the same. You can go and live in it, send me some rent. That's a clever idea, why don't you do that?"

"No, Lynn. I just don't believe this is happening?"

"How do you know they haven't killed Ryan already?"

"The Guardia seem to think that he's alive, that's all we've got, their expertise in this sort of thing."

"What has Placido got to do with your family? Don't tell me it's because you're shagging him. That's a pathetic reason to take him? "I know, I'm as confused as you."

"Lynn, Gavee, lessons need to start," said Arrabella as she popped her head round the door.

"Of course, yes," said Gaby too stunned to say anything else.

"Let's talk afterwards, don't go home until Jim comes for us," said Gaby texting Jim as she walked to her first lesson.

The lessons went in a blur as Gaby was unnerved at what had been said. She was feeling even more uneasy and couldn't wait for Jim to collect them.

He was outside on foot waiting and José was waiting for them in their bar, hidden from the outside world.

"O.k., I've been to see Antonio who has made some calls. I hope you don't mind Lynn. There's also a missing person alert out on Placido, as his family are connected to the town hall of Granada. His disappearance along with this kidnapping and threat for the family's expulsion to the U.K, has ruffled a few local feathers."

"Is this real?"

"Yes. Apparently, the Guardia seem to think it's the Russian Mafia wanting to take control of Ryan's business to capitalise on his distribution network and his contacts in the U.K. If Paul doesn't leave, Ryan will be killed, the Guardia know of his location but can't intervene until all the family have booked flights and they're ready to leave for the airport."

"You're well informed for a plumber," said Gaby going paler by the second, something niggling her.

"I'm working for Antonio, Marbella's top lawyer; I got him to do the digging. I'm decorating his offices."

"Is he married to Isabella?"

"Yes, how did you know that?"

"She's my Friday night student, she's invited me to tea after Christmas," as they laughed for a second and then Lynn started to cry quiet tears as José put his arm round her.

"José, what does Placido know that would make him a target in the bank, I mean?"

"Not more or less than I know. Ryan Marshall has seven accounts, and they were closed by the Guardia this morning, that's all I know," said José looking worried.

"Until you know Placido's connection, I think you need to watch your back," said Jim pouring more wine round the table as Gaby wasn't sure how she felt, listening to this.

They talked into the early hours and Jim insisted they both stayed with him. Gaby went in with Lynn to get a few things and she did the same at Gaby's studio. They all fell silent as Jim drove them to Estepona.

Lynn fell asleep as her head hit the pillow as Gaby held on to Jim all night; she was as shaken as Lynn.

The next day as Lynn showered and Jim answered plumbing calls, Gaby knew she was no longer feeling safe. Jim looked at her as he came back from the kitchen and put his arm on her shoulder.

"Two people can live here much better than one Gaby. Why don't you move in over the weekend? We'll see Lynn off and then we'll move you in here. What do you think? We'll have our very own Christmas?"

Lynn stood there and nodded at Gaby,

"Do it Gaby, don't be on your own, not after this."

"Ok," as Lynn smiled relieved.

"I'll need a car for work."

"Yes, we'll look this week."

"Can you drop us at Lynn's, so I can help her pack stuff she wants to courier back, we might as well keep busy until there's news of Placido."

"Yes okay, I'll find out through Antonio. I'll pop over before you start class."

The Guardia car parked outside Lynn's house until the Friday was a stark reminder that this wasn't a joke. Jim nodded at the officers in the car.

"At least you have protection until Friday, Lynn."

"I don't feel safe; Gaby can you stay?"

"Yes of course," said Gaby as she pecked Jim on the cheek as he dropped them at Lynn's; her sparkle had diminished overnight as Gaby felt her own candle that had been rekindled since her arrival, slowly being burned out too.

⸎

18

New Year

The last Friday before the school broke up for the Christmas season should have been a fun one. That morning Jim and Gaby made their way to Malaga airport to say goodbye to the Marshall family. They'd been advised not to take Lynn; she had to be escorted by the Guardia whose responsibility was to ensure their safety. There was no guarantee that Ryan Marshall would appear for his flight.

There were terse tears and emotional farewell hugs from everyone, as Lynn tried to keep her composure; she whispered in Gaby's ear,

"Find Placido for me, here are my new contact numbers. And Gaby take care."

"I will Lynn, I'm sure between us, we'll find out where he is. The Granada town hall apparently has sent people to find him."

"How do you know this?"

"Jim's working at Antonio's, the Abagado has told him everything. Antonio seems to have the right contacts."

"What's he actually doing at Antonio's?"

"He's decorating the whole building, inside and out but also talking to him about setting up a liaison office with his firm in Sheffield."

"Do you believe that?"

"Yes actually, why do you ask?"

"After what you've told me, just make sure that's all. No one here seems real."

"You're rightfully upset as I would be, but I think Jim is the genuine article, thanks for the warning though."

"Come on girls, time to let Lynn go," said Jim coming over after saying goodbye to the others.

There was no sign of Ryan Marshall appearing from anywhere and the distraught family left departures as Gaby fought to keep her tears at bay.

"He may be already in the lounge; the Guardia may have got him and taken him straight through."

"We won't know until Lynn phones us; I do hope they've kept their word."

"The Guardia know what they're doing sweetheart. Come on, let's find a bar on the way home for lunch and then I'll drop you at school. Are we still going to bar Tougana tonight? Try and get in the mood?"

"Yes, it's all arranged. José is distraught but will come, his fiancée is coming down from Granada to join him and then he's going back until the New Year. We're all affected by what's happened."

Gaby's phone rang as she looked at it and nodded to Jim, it was Lynn,

"Lynn."

"I see, ok, talk tomorrow."

She looked at Jim and holding back tears,

"He's not on the flight."

"Oh my god, that's terrible," said Jim as he manoeuvred the car into Benalmadena port for a spot of late lunch.

"They may have put him on a different flight, let's wait until we hear from them tomorrow. I think we should move your stuff this weekend, what do you think?"

"Yes, it's a great idea, I'm beginning to feel nervous about being on my own."

"No problem, I have also seen a car that's for sale in Estepona, we can go and look at it tomorrow."

"That's great, but before I move in; I need to tell you something."

"What is it?" asked Jim really cool.

"I want you to know everything; I don't want this partnership based on untruths."

"I know about the elusive boyfriend; we've agreed to give it a go and see what happens. I shall worry about him when he appears. What's bothering you?"

Over lunch she told him everything about Nick; when he proposed, he announced he was a High-Ranking Undercover Detective. Up until that point Jim had been unfazed by the story. He continued to listen as she explained that on this revelation, she'd snapped. She'd been bereft and had gone off the rails and had embarked on an illicit affair with the boss of an Italian Mafia ring. He'd subsequently turned up, the week before and promised to come back once his divorce was finalised.

"Blimey, like buses you've got two blokes after you. Where do I fit in?"

"That's just it, you've been the only honest bloke I've known, for the last three years. I think you've got a good chance if I can say that right now. I don't want to mess you about, but I don't want this relationship built on lies, I'm sick of it."

Jim stared out to sea; did he tell her? She'd had enough on her plate; he didn't think she could take anymore. He could see how severely affected she'd been over the Ryan Marshall kidnapping and the disappearance of Placido. The last thing he wanted was for her to feel more vulnerable. He chose to play safe and decided to protect her from the Marbella underworld as much as possible. By asking her to move in, would make her safer. In the meantime, he would carry on as he was, and they would try and make this work. He was getting involved. Knowing there were two guys out there who had promised her a future was irrelevant, if they'd wanted her, they wouldn't have let her go.

"You're deep in thought, Jim. What are you thinking?

"I'm thinking that we'll give this time together a good shot. There's every possibility I might want to stay. I'm sure you're flexible on that. I know where I stand, that's ok. Promise me one

thing, if either of them turn up, you'll tell me before you meet them."

"I promise."

"Ok, let's go, do you need anything from the studio before school?

"Yes, I need to change," she said with a glint in her eye. The first spark she'd shown since the kidnapping incident.

School breaking up for the Christmas season was manic and the only dampener on the celebrations were Lynn's absence and Placido. The advanced class were a tight knit group and knew the whole story. After Gaby's last class, they all proceeded to Bar Tougana for a final drink before going their separate ways.

To date and a week since his disappearance, there'd been no sign of Placido. There'd been no ransom demand, no indication if he were dead or alive. It was unnerving and Gaby was glad it was Christmas as it gave her time away from it all.

"Isabella, my boyfriend is working for your husband."

"Antonio, si?"

"Yes, he told me that's he's decorating his offices."

"Ah yes, Antonio's meeting me at the bar, you'll meet him."

"Great, Jim should be there too."

The bar was in full swing, and Antonio was holding the fort, and his presence towered over everyone. Jim was with him and in a black suit. He looked so different, and she felt a rush of pleasure go through her; she hadn't seen him in a suit before, and he looked dashing as Jim embraced her.

"Hola, Gavee, I'm Antonio, my wife thinks you are a good teacher, Si? Come, drink."

"Thank you; I'll have a Gin & Tonic."

"Gavee, can you talk to Antonio after Christmas, we need the three children to have private lessons."

"Of course, Isabella, that would be great."

"You look lovely," said Jim as he kissed her on the cheek suddenly.

"I changed at school; you look as if you've been in an important meeting."

"Met the Mayor of Marbella with Antonio earlier, he is setting up a liaison office for ex- pats and I'm in discussion with them to operate the English division."

"Jim, that's fantastic news, I wondered why the suit."

The bar was heaving as most businesses had finished for the party season. The music was on full blast and the wine was flowing. Tapas and paella were being served to tables and the staff were dressed up as Matadors and Flamenco dancers. The atmosphere was electric as Jim's hand moved over Gaby's waist on more than one occasion.

The laughter was loud, and Gaby's Spanish was improving daily. Jim was fluent and she hadn't realised until then, how fluent he was.

She listened to him talk to Antonio and he was too fluent for her liking. That uneasy feeling crept to her belly again but then dissipated quickly as she ignored it. She was becoming paranoid.

The next day, they emptied her studio flat, and Pedro came to say goodbye to her and gave her his card.

"Tu problema, hablamos mi, parle/you have any problems, you call me, understand?"

"Si, gracias Pedro."

They went to see Señora Izzie who was delighted to see them. She got the Sobrano out and they all had a drink in her kitchen to say goodbye. Estepona wasn't far but she needed to break away from Marbella as Jed knew where she was. He agreed; she should leave but continue to work at the school.

It didn't take long for them to hang Gaby's clothes and move her books into Jim's apartment. They decided to use the second bedroom as her office; Jim's third bedroom was his, which was full of tools, plumbing bits and pieces and piles of paper.

A ford fiesta was for sale on the Estepona Marina and belonged to the wife of one of the estate Agents. Gaby, armed with key words in relation to cars went to meet another Antonio, with Jim acting as her chaperone. She needed his Spanish but never made comment on how fluent he was.

"Cuantos, Antonio?"

"Un mil quinientos, senora" (1,500€).

"Puedo tomar el coche para una prueba de manejo?" (Can I take the car for a test drive?)

"Si, no problema."

Antonio got in the back as she got in with Jim by her side.

"Which is the best way to go around the block?"

"Go down the esplanade and then right, right and you'll see us back here again."

Driving on the right side of the road was strange along with trying to change gears with the right hand. She inwardly cringed as she'd not driven for over six months. It was a shock to the system and after hitting her knuckles several times on the door, she managed to get them back to the port without incident.

"I definitely need to practise driving on the right," as they all got out of the car. *"Shall we go to the bar?"*

"Si," said Antonio who was smiling at her.

"Un mil trescientos, Antonio (1,300€)."

"Ok, tienes dinero?"

"Si, tiener dinero, mañana mañana, aqui" *(Yes, I have money for you tomorrow morning).*

"Gracias, Gavee."

Jim ordered coffee for everyone and three glasses of brandy to celebrate Gaby's car purchase. Antonio shook her hand on the deal and left.

"I'll come out with you for the first few trips, if you want," said Jim.

"Yes please, can we drive to the school, park up and practise the **carreterars**, *especially the slip roads."*

"Of course, we'll do that tomorrow as soon as you've got the paperwork."

"What about insurance."

"We'll go into the offices next door; you can get car insurance there."

"Good job, you live here, otherwise I'd never have got this done."

"Don't be daft, look what you achieved in Marbella. Come on, we can sort out a parking space outside the flats for you. We need to get organised for Christmas."

"I thought we were going to the beach bar for Christmas day."

"Yes, but we need stuff for the house, come on."

Much later and full of shopping, they unpacked food and goodies.

Christmas on the beach was a revelation, and it was hard to imagine the U.K being cold and under a foot of snow as they both sat on the golden sand with a hamper of food and Cava. Apart from not hearing from Lynn and Placido was still missing, life was good.

***

New Year was amazing as Jim took Gaby to Marbella's hot spot for a function dinner with Isabella and Antonio which was sumptuous and extravagant. The entertainment alone was the group, *The Gypsy Kings*. The New Year tradition for when the clock's struck midnight was explained by Isabella as the tin of grapes per person came around each table with a glass of Cava.

"You must swallow a grape with every strike, is it no eh."

"You mean chime."

"Yes, one grape per chime and then drink cava at the last strike."

"What if I miss one?"

"That's the month of bad luck you will have?"

"Oh, we better not miss one then," she said laughing as she got the grapes ready as the compere on the stage started to count ready for the last twelve chimes.

"Ocho, siete, seis, cinco, quatro, tres, dos, uno.... Feliz Año Nuevo."

"Feliz Año Nuevo!" (Happy New Year)

They walked to Antonio's office, and he called two taxis. It was five in the morning, and they'd all had a great evening.

"Let me show you Jim's new office, Gavee. Has he told you?"

"Office, what do you mean?" she said looking puzzled, but Jim wasn't within earshot as Isabella was showing him the paint colour she wanted for her son's bedroom. Antonio showed her Jim's new office as the buzzer went for the taxi's arrival.

"Si, un momento."

"Taxi here everyone. We see you both for Three Kings, no?"

"Yes, that would be lovely Antonio. Thank you for a great evening. Feliz Año Nuevo,"

Isabella laughed, *"Your Spanish is coming better, Gavee."*

"Thank you Isabella, see you soon," as they all embraced as the taxis waited to take them home.

She didn't want to ask but wanted to know about the new arrangement in Antonio's office, but she set it aside for the time being. She responded to his passionate embrace as soon as they got home. She hadn't made love since Lynn's departure, and she was grateful he hadn't pressed her. Right now, she needed him as she moved her tongue around…...

Her phone rang, making her jump.

"It's Lynn. Hi Lynn, any news?"

"Oh my God, no....."

Jim's phone rung and he jumped out of bed to answer it in the hallway; wanting one ear on Gaby's conversation as he answered the phone in Spanish,

"Digame?"

"Antonio, como estas?

She placed the phone in her handbag and went back to the bedroom; she was in shock. She sat on the bed shaking, couldn't quite believe it. She felt afraid and hugging the pillow cried for her friend Lynn.

Minutes later, Jim's arms engulfed her as he sat behind her, holding her and letting her cry. She sobbed feeling a mixture of emotions as she got to grips with what Lynn had just told her.

"What is it?" he said gently but Antonio had already told him.

"*Placido's effects have been found in the campo and Ryan's body was found in a rented car outside Manchester airport,*" she gulped for air. Jim held her tight knowing she would need to know what Antonio had just relayed to him, even though it wasn't good news.

"*Christ, what the fuck are they doing?*"

"*Why, what did Antonio say?*"

"*He's acting for Placido's family and José has asked for protection. He rang to say that he's received a phone call about Ryan from the Guardia. First thing in the New Year, they've asked Paul to return and officially close the business. It's out of their hands they're not stupid; by killing him in the U.K., it takes the problem from here.*

"*Poor Paul, Maria is about to give birth, they've no homes, jobs, it's a mess.*"

"*Antonio is trying to sort out with the Guardia that they can return at some point to sell their homes.*"

"*Can we see Paul?*"

"*No, you must stay clear. We're not to know he's on his way here. Antonio just told us as he knows how terrible it's been for you. Isabella liked Placido too, so it's great he's taking some time to help. If he's going to act for José, then he'll keep us informed. Don't worry.*"

"*Why have you an office there, by the way?*" as she turned around to face him.

"*He needs an English accountant who speaks Spanish. I'm working with him part time, in-between my plumbing jobs, when I get any,*" he grinned.

"*Is that what you want?*"

"*Yes, he's paying well, so we'll be ok. You're under no pressure to find half the rent as you muttered the other day,*" as he kissed her freckly nose. It was going to be all right.

19

Three Kings

*F*iesta de los Reyes, The Three Kings is held traditionally on January 5th and 6th as Jim and Gaby prepared to attend Isabella's party. They were to meet in Marbella during the Three Kings' procession, and she was feeling buoyant for the first time since the news of Placido.

Jim had showered her with practical gifts over Christmas and some indulgent ones as she decided to wear some of his underwear for the occasion. She hadn't thought about Nick for a while, and she was suddenly reminded of him as her English phone suddenly bleeped. She looked at the message from Jed. She texted him back to say she was on holiday all of January, hoping he wouldn't bother. She buried the phone in the box and shoved it in one of her bags.

"Are you ready?" asked Jim as he came in to fetch her as she sprayed perfume over her throat. He smiled liking what he saw, and he seemed romantic suddenly.

In the living room as they prepared to leave, he turned to her and presented her with a black velvet box and said,

"Feliz Fiesta de los Reyes."

"Ooh Jim, what's this?"

She opened the long box and a silver chain with an exquisite hand- made pendant was inside.

"Jim, it's lovely, I'll wear it now."

He placed it round her neck and the pendant sat above her cleavage and suited her outfit perfectly.

She looked in the mirror and kissed him,

"It's lovely thank you."

"My pleasure sweetheart, let's go the taxi's outside."

Fiesta de los Reyes was in full swing as the taxi drove them to the main square. Marbella roads were closed, and the tree lined dual carriageways of the main strip was crammed with families expectantly waiting for the three Kings to arrive. The annual parade started at dusk which meant any time after the sun went down.

Eventually the carriages emerged from the Pirelli Tower, and they proceeded down the strip in slow motion. The carriages of the Three Kings were gold and emerald and were pulled by four horsemen riding bare back, wearing rich coloured tunics. These carriages were followed by men on horses all equally dressed in sumptuous robes of colourful velvet and silks. The Kings wore crowns and waved at the crowds as the horses cantered towards the Town Hall.

Behind the horsemen came floats and trailers of local peasants all dressed in colourful costumes and the women were throwing sweets to the children in the crowd. There were several cartoon characters walking alongside the procession and the band marched amongst the carriages and floats, keeping the pace.

The overhead Christmas lights and the sprinkle of dim lights from the bars alongside the carriageway created a magical atmosphere as the crowds cheered the Kings as they passed. The carriages made their way to the town hall where a stage had been erected for the Kings to call each child to receive his or her present.

Gaby and Jim were seated in a prime spot on the main highway courtesy of Antonio and Isabella. Once the procession had passed, they tucked into pre- ordered paella.

"Our party starts at midnight," said Isabella.

"Where are your three children, Isabella?" asked Jim.

"They've friends in the house and their own party until we get home. They didn't want to come."

"Are they too old for Three Kings?"

"Paulo is only eight, but his two brothers are twelve and fifteen, he's an old eight-year-old because of his brothers."

"That makes sense," said Gaby.

"I want you to private teach them once we get back to lessons."

"Yes, we can arrange next week," pleased private work seemed to be coming to her.

The paella was devoured, and they all walked up to Antonio's office to order a taxi. Antonio seemed to have a taxi company purely for his own service as they never seemed to wait very long for one and it was the same company every time.

Jim raised an eyebrow as their maid answered the door as Isabella ushered them in through the tradesman's entrance.

"The main door is for the guests," she laughed and then realised what she'd said,

"Oh Gavee, Jim, please forgive me, you're also guests...."

"No, Isabella, I think we're friends, better," said Gaby as they embraced.

"Good," said Antonio as he summoned them through to the ballroom where the guests had started to arrive. They had a butler on the door and Gaby noticed they all had embossed invitations.

"I feel quite privileged," she whispered to Jim as he acknowledged her.

"Uhm, your right."

She loved it, the whole party reminded her of the Von Trapp ballroom and the ladies in their finery and jewels mirrored the same. She was pleased with her flowing dress and the jewellery Jim had given her. She felt a part of the party and accepted by this family.

Delighted to see Mercedes and José had arrived and Eugenio was a lovely surprise especially as he'd brought his wife, who'd been sick. It was like a student reunion and Gaby felt close to these people who respected her as their Teacher but liked her too as a friend.

The classical music in the background provided a feeling of romance as the tuxedo clad waiters came with trays of Cava and cocktails. Throughout the evening, although there was a buffet, more waiters moved round subtlety with trays of tapas, with no expense spared. There was an abundance of Cava and Gaby realised she needed to slow down as every time the waiter passed, she replaced her empty glass with a full one.

Jim grabbed her and they spent a while dancing to the music, and she was surprised how nimble he was as he guided her through the odd waltz and slow moves. She felt a rush of warmth towards him as he was trying hard to win her. She was beginning to trust him completely. But she had to keep something back, she wasn't going to be let down again. She also knew until she'd dealt with the past, she was unable to think of the future.

In the corner of her eye, she noticed a big burly man arriving with three bodyguards dressed in black as she turned Jim round for him to see.

"Marbella Mayor," he whispered in her ear.

The atmosphere shifted slightly as another set of celebrities walked in, again with bodyguards as Gaby noticed Eugenio's face looked pinched as a glamorous woman joined the party.

"Who are these people?" she whispered as they continued to dance.

"I've no idea but Eugenio looks as if he does, let's go and see."

They both grabbed a glass from the passing waiter as Eugenio and Mercedes were in deep conversation as José and his fiancé walked in, waved, and came straight over.

"Ah, Gavee, Feliz Año Nuevo."

"Igualmente José, Margarita. Margarita, mi novio, Jim. (And the same to you, Margarita. Margarita this is my boyfriend Jim)."

"He's the Mayor, I met him at Antonio's last week," said Jim.

"Yes, he's involved with the Placido affair, I feel," said Eugenio quietly.

"Really, Eugenio, what do you mean?" asked Jim this comment piquing his interest suddenly as José moved in closer.

"Yes, he's been to the bank. His honcho man asked lots of questions which weren't really his business."

"What sort of stuff?"

"Which were Placido's clients, and did he have any personal issues or concerns with any of them?"

"Do they think he was kidnapped by one of your clients then?"

"No idea," said José, *"I've put in for a transfer after I marry Margarita. I'm going to my home town of Granada."*

"We all understand, José. I thought they'd all been kidnapped by the Russian Mafia," said Gaby

"What else do you know Eugenio?" asked Jim.

"I don't know, but Marisol Gonzalez, who's standing next to Gil y Gil the Mayor, is up to something, that's all I can say, she's, his assistant. I just have the feeling, is that how you say?"

"Yes, Eugenio," said Gaby not wanting to correct him on a fiesta night!

"Antonio seems to be the Abagado for everyone, including the Mayor, José. Either he's stupid or clever," said Jim and only Gaby understood what he meant by this. He carried on, *"I'd make sure you tell him everything, in order he can safeguard your interests."*

"She's going to sing, how fantastic," said Mercedes as she interrupted the conversation as they all turned towards the glamorous woman who'd joined the Mayor's party.

A string quartet magically appeared behind her and started the intro as Isabel Pantoja's voice filled the room captivating everyone standing. Jim stood with his arms around her, and she felt as if she was in the *"Sound of Music."* The soprano finished her aria, and the place erupted with applause and the band continued with a last waltz as several couples took to the floor.

"It's nearly seven; shall we go to my hotel for special three Kings Breakfast, for Gavee to see our tradition?" suggested Mercedes. Everyone loved this idea, and Jim went to order two taxis as Gaby went to find Isabella to thank her for a lovely Three Kings experience.

***

Hotel Pyr, on the second line of Banús harbour was full of families having the traditional breakfast. Later in the day, the tradition was to have dinner at home like the Christmas Eve dinner. Mercedes had already called ahead and the head waiter Alberto, waved the party to follow him. He'd prepared a breakfast table with the Three Kings cake placed in the centre. Refreshments arrived and more Cava as Mercedes was anxious to explain to Gaby this tradition.

"This cake, Gavee is the Three Kings Cake, and we have it for breakfast the day after the Kings' arrive. It is made of sweetbreads and as you can see it is covered in fruit that's dry, yes?"

"Yes, dried fruits, very good, Mercedes."

Smiling and pleased with the compliment she continued to explain,

"Inside there is a prize for the person that gets that slice with dry fruits but there is also a bean. If you win the prize, you must wear this crown all day as our Queen or King. If you get the bean, then you will invite us all next year and buy the cake. It will be your forfeit, yes?"

"Yes, I understand who's going to cut the cake?" *"I will,"* said Jim enjoying these friends of Gaby's.

He cut the cake into seven and handed it round. *"Feliz Año Nuevo,"* he said and raised his glass as everyone chinked their glasses and tucked in to the cake.

"Oh no, I've got the bean," laughed Gaby as she showed them.

"I'm the King today," said José as he placed the paper crown on his head.

The morning continued and Alberto reminded them it would soon be time for the restaurant to lay up for lunch.

"Crikey, it's nearly twelve already. Thank you everyone for a lovely time, I think it's time we went home," said Jim as they all got up as Mercedes refused to take a contribution for breakfast.

"It's our teachers' first time Jim. I'm pleased you come, enjoy the day, Besos."

Mercedes had organised a Taxi for them, and they were home by midday.

"Do you fancy a stroll on the beach or..."

She pulled him to her and kissed him gently on the mouth and wrapped her arms around him. She knew how she felt right at that moment and wanted to show him, as she took him to their bedroom feeling as romantic as the occasion.

⬥

20

Happy Birthday

She massaged him as he laid there thinking. She rubbed his member and worked on him as he tried to respond but his mind was firmly on the undercover job. They were close. They'd got the name and date when the Drug Baron was dropping the next shipment. Through this hooker, they'd managed to source the third mule; it was a waiting game and he'd be glad when it was all over.

He looked a wreck and he'd more dreadlocks inserted in his long blond hair, which he'd dyed brown much earlier. He'd had time to replenish the brown contacts before Ginger called by. She was already high, and he'd left another line out, for when she was done. He was high on adrenalin and started responding to her, even though his feelings were dead and had been a long time ago.

Knock, knock.

He shifted his hips and pulled her arse over as she enveloped him. With one hand on her perfect silicone breasts, he fondled her curly mound as she moved with his rhythm to please him. She came quickly as he grunted, she didn't twig that he was faking, he was good at being somebody else.

Miguel's knock, his signal, made him finish the act as he ruffled her hair, kissed her for a few minutes, and left her on the bed. He went to shower, and she was already sat on the floor snorting the line as he left.

He went to the living room where Miguel and Aleksey had the table full of plans. The room was thick with cigar smoke as Miguel lit up another as Armando came in.

"You're not screwing her mate?"

"She got us the third mule and the Barons' schedule, just keeping up the cover."

"Yeah right. She's high all the time to know any different, right, where is it?"

"It's going down in three weeks, here are the details," said Aleksey. The three men all working for three different organisations and all undercover, looked equally worse for wear and had blended into the drug scene perfectly. Their appearances had changed dramatically, and they switched to speaking Spanish most of the time. They were close now and the precision of the next coup was crucial to arresting the Big Fish along with the three mules.

"We need to get the mules, near each other, there's one in Estepona, one in Marbella and one in Mijas. We need them to have a get together or something," said Armando.

"Oh, by the way, Armand, that broad you fancied in Sinatra's..."

"What about her?"

"She was at the swarray of Antonio Marquiez Three Kings Party."

"Is he...?" asked Aleksey.

"Yes," said Armando, *"Antonio Marquiez holds court for the Mayor."*

"How's the surveillance on him, Miguel. Is he clean?"

Miguel snorted out loud, *"No one's clean on this coast it's a fucking nightmare."*

"Who's the girl?" said Aleksey. *"I thought we'd agreed no personal romances apart from the hookers we use for the job."*

"Yeh, it's ok, Alek, it's just a good-looking girl and I looked at her twice, that's all."

"Ok, let's get down to this plan, guys. Pass me a fag."

He was worried about her; she was now in the circle of Antonio Marquiez. He would need to know why and try and warn her. He......

"Armand......What's up man?"

"I've got it, Miguel; I'll do Estepona surveillance tonight, I've been in Marbella too many times."

"Ok, Armand, you do that, I'll take Mijas and see you both here tomorrow. Miguel, you cover Marbella."

"I'll drop Ginger at her sisters and see you all at midday."

***

She couldn't have been happier with her current life as school started, and she had full classes. Placido had been officially declared missing by the Guardia. Jim was proving to be attentive and caring along with sometimes being possessive, but she suddenly didn't mind. The incident reminded her that she could no longer live alone. She felt vulnerable and without Jim, she knew deep down, she'd have gone home, wherever home was in the U.K.

She'd turned her English phone off and threw away the chip and used it as a back- up phone. Jed was history, she hadn't thought of him since telling Jim. She hadn't liked the way he'd turned up unannounced and knowing where she lived had also unnerved her. She'd discussed it all with Jim, being open and honest with him. Jim was equally pleased about this statement and that had brought them closer.

"One down, one to go!" he'd replied as Gaby knew that Nick was bothering him and deep down, he was bothering her too. She wished he'd find her. That said she'd changed. Since meeting Jim, she was beginning to trust again. He appeared to be completely honest, had given her a chance with a man. Nick had lived a lie and Jed was married. Even though that instant spark wasn't there with Jim; he had accepted her and had pursued her.

She made her way to Jasmines' school and today she had a class of ten-year olds. Jasmine and Gaby had become close friends even though she hadn't taken up her fulltime teaching offer. She didn't need full time. With Isabella and Antonio securing her for private lessons along with her two hours a week at his office, teaching Business English, she'd enough work.

She also worked at Hotel Pyr and had three of Mercedes staff as students along with three Guardia soldiers who she had acquired through Antonio.

Jim, with his plumbing, painting, and decorating seemed to have enough work and between them they were comfortable. He had his accountancy business in Antonio's offices, and this was giving him the right contacts. He would soon drop the plumbing and concentrate on the accountancy work with Antonio. Life was good at last.

Gaby's driving had improved immensely, and she'd had a few driving lessons. The Spanish were loyal but submissive people in general, but they were mad behind the wheel. This had helped her confidence, and she began to relax. For the first time in two years, she felt she was in control.

Easter was soon upon them and having read about the history of the province, she was eager to see the processions and the whole celebrations. She got home after teaching Jasmines' ten-year olds and had two hours before she needed to be at Wall Street. She was greeted by a very amorous Jim who was home, which was unexpected, and he kissed her passionately as she walked through the door, promising a surprise......

There were candles lit on the dining room table as she looked around wondering what was happening. IL DIVO sung her favourite tunes on the c.d., as he led her to the bedroom kissing her and unclipping her bra at the same time. He helped her on the bed, and he undid his belt, dropping his trousers as he fondled her.

She responded through surprise and as he slowly entered her, he held her close and whispered in her ear, *"Happy Birthday Gabriella Daly, will you marry me?"* as he produced a red velvet box from on top of the bed as he continued to move slowly inside her, as she gasped as spasms of uncontrolled pleasure shot through her.

They turned over as she sat moving with him and opened the box and the emerald ring shone, dazzling her with its size and brilliance. His unique proposal technique threw her momentarily off balance as she laughed and bent to kiss him. With slight hesitation, she replied,

"Yes Jim," as his hands moved over her breasts as she moaned even louder, their union complete. The intensity and the surprise sent a burning satisfied thrill through the core of their bodies, as they'd both felt the charge together.

"You have the night off, sweetheart. I've arranged it with Arrabella," he said as he placed the ring on her finger. He disappeared and came back with three large boxes and a bottle of chilled Cava in an ice bucket with two glasses. *"Happy birthday, I love you very much, here's to our future."*

She moved up a bit on the bed and took the glass and sipped the fizz as it dribbled down her chin. She laughed and pulled him to her, took another mouthful of fizz, and dribbled it all over his hairy tummy as she proceeded to

………

The phone rang interrupting the moment.

"It's always your phone…"

"Hum no it's yours."

"I'll get it for you."

"Yes, one minute, it's Maud."

"Who?"

"Maud."

"Hi Maud, oh yes, yes, I remember, after Easter, yes no problem, text me your dates and I'll sort it for you."

"Who's Maud?

"I met her ages ago; she wants me to help her find a villa to buy. She's coming after Easter, and I need to find her a hotel."

"Tomorrow, come here," as he pulled her back to bed as she flung the mobile on the chair, Maud could wait.

❖

21

Maud's arrival

"My favourite pet is my rabbit. His name es Pedro."

"Well done, Ivan, who's next? Mirabelle, tell us your pet's name," asked Gaby as Jasmines' class of ten- and eleven-year-olds were doing simply great.

It was the first week back after Easter and everyone was delighted with her news of engagement. She knew that instant attraction *"spark"* wasn't there for her initially, but she ignored it, as thoughts of Nick still haunted her. What she felt right now was a whole complete love she'd not experienced before. She hoped when he found her, if he were going to bother, he would understand.

Maud was due to arrive in the middle of the week and Gaby had arranged to help her for two mornings. Jim had located a hotel in Old Town and through Antonio's office; she'd located an estate agent. She did wonder how she'd manage without Jim and Antonio. She had Valentino, Antonio's right hand on speed dial.

She was working all week for Jasmine as one of her teachers was on holiday. She had Friday and Saturday free to entertain Maud. Gaby made the appointments. She was glad she was busy as Jim and Antonio had announced they were going away. The business meetings were in Granada and her raised eyebrows had not deterred Jim from staying away for the three nights.

"Granada is only a couple of hours away. What exactly are you doing with Antonio?"

"He's so many business contacts; he's taking me round to meet his clients. I'll try and gain them for the accountancy side as Antonio is their Lawyer. This could mean, I can drop the plumbing completely, not that I'm in demand with it as you know. If this works well, we can look for a villa and live in a bit more luxury. What do you say?

"Sounds feasible. Why do you need to stay away?"

"Don't worry, you'll be ok. You can go and stay with Isabella, she's told Antonio, if you're nervous. The thing is, they work split shifts, and it's going to be evening meetings as well as daytime ones."

"Of course, I forgot about that. No, I'll be ok. I need to catch up with my students and Jasmine has me working more hours. I'll be fine," she said, those doubts had all gone.

Jim's amorous farewell the night before was still firmly in Gaby's mind as she went around the six youngsters in her class, talking about their pet. She'd made them draw the pet and colour it in as the next days' lesson would be colours. Jim had been extremely attentive, and she'd started leaning on him more than she'd realised.

Jasmine walked in to her class as it was coming to an end with a big smile but wanted Ivan to wait. Ivan was eleven and German and he'd been attending the school for nearly a year, and his English was much more advanced than his peers. He was a clever child, and he sat as he said goodbye to his friends.

"Everything all right?" asked Gaby looking at Jasmine and then Ivan.

"Yes, I'm just wondering if you can do me a favour. Suzann has called; Ivan's Mum but she can't collect him. Can you drop him off on your way home?"

Ivan looked alarmed.

"Ivan, there's no problem," said Jasmine reassuring the little boy.

"I live in Estepona, you can direct me from the carreterra, can't you?

"Yes ok," said Ivan his eyes wide as Teacher was taking him home.

"I thought you'd be ok with it; I'll call her back to confirm. Thanks for that Gaby. See you both tomorrow."

Ivan was quite the chatterbox and between slipping the odd German word in his vocabulary, she was impressed by his knowledge of the English language. As she followed his directions towards the mountains and away from the port area, she asked him,

"How have you learnt so much English if you've only lived here a year?"

"My Mum has friends all over the world come to visit. They all speak English cos they all from unusual places. English is normal for them. I listen always."

"How did you get here?"

"We were smuggled out of Germany, it was scary."

She decided that she didn't want to know anymore as she turned the car up the second brow of another hill towards their villa. The villas dotted up the mountain road were impressive in size and Gaby thought of what Jim had said. Maybe she'd like a villa but more beach side and not up a mountain.

"We're here, this one," pointed Ivan.

She parked the car and was about to turn around as Ivan got out.

"Come in to meet Mum, please," Ivan asked.

"Ok."

She didn't want to get involved with parents, but it was probably best to acknowledge she'd got him home.

He ran ahead and opened the gate as Gaby closed it behind her noticing his pet rabbit Pedro, running free on the shaded back terrace. She followed him as he was shouting for his mum. She walked in to a massive hallway and adjoining living room come dining room, the view ahead through the floor to ceiling windows took her breath away.

"Yes, it gets everybody, that view. You must be Gavee. Thank you for carrying my son home," said an exceptionally large,

burlesque blonde lady with bright red lipstick, her German accent apparent.

"Yes, pleased to meet you. I'm Ivan's part time teacher. If I can help any time, don't hesitate to call the school."

"I've sprained my ankle," as she moved from the table and her ankle was in a cast.

"Oh, I'm sorry. I can drive Ivan home until Thursday if that'll help you."

"Could you really? That's good thank you. Would you like tea?"

"I'll have a quick cup; this view is amazing. How long have you lived here?"

"About a year, do you have leche uh milk?"

"No, plain tea thanks. I see you've been busy baking," as Gaby could see the kitchen table had pestle and mortar on it, weighing scales, mixing bowls, and rolling pins.

"Um, yes, Ivan is going to make cookies in a minute, he's a good baker. All my kids can cook," as she handed Gaby a mug of tea and hobbled back to the living room.

She admired the view and privately agreed with Jim, they needed a villa. Suzann interrupted her thoughts,

"How long have you been here, on the coast?"

"Only nine months, not that long."

"Do you like it?"

"Yes, love it. My fiancé and I are really happy here."

"That's good, it's not for everyone."

"*No, it's not,*" said Gaby not wishing to enter into any conversation. She sat with Suzann and finished her tea as her Skype started to ring.

"*I'll leave you; you're working. I'll drop Ivan off for you. Thanks for the tea.*"

"*Yes, no problems thank you. It was nice meeting you,*" as she shook Gaby's hand.

She drove away. It would be good to find a villa with Jim; she ought to tell him about her nest egg, they could use that. She started to get excited about Maud's arrival as she could look at the same time. She might have lots of news for him when he got back.

Her mobile rung as she got home, it was Eugenio.

"*Digame Eugenio, como estas?*"

"*Si Gavee, possibleh see you this afternoon?*"

"*Why yes, before school or later in our bar?*"

"*Yes, Bar Tougana, perfect, see you later.*"

"*Ok, Eugenio. No problem.*"

School was noisy and there seemed to be more students enrolling on the course. Arrabella was smiling as usual, and she announced there was a new teacher joining them for the evening shift.

She was pleased at this news but also sad as she'd hoped that Lynn would come back, but this was evidently not the case. There was no news about Placido, and she knew Lynn would move on and lose touch with her. She understood this only too well. She still thought about Placido, and she would ask Eugenio later if he'd heard anything more of where he was or what had happened to him.

She made her way to Bar Tougana to meet Eugenio and José was with him too.

"What a lovely surprise. Do you need a lesson before Friday?" she laughed and then realised Eugenio looked drawn and José looked awful.

"What is it? Is it Placido, have you heard anything?"

"This is awkward, Gavee."

"Whatever is it, just tell me."

"It's Jim."

"What about him?" asked Gaby a sudden pang of fear creeping into the pit of her stomach.

"He's best of friends with Antonio. How is he, we don't understand?" *"Why do you ask, I don't understand the question, Eugenio, José?"*

"He's a plumber, no?"

"No Eugenio, in England he's an accountant and accountants and lawyers sometimes have joint offices to provide customers with a complete business service."

"What's happening with Antonio?" asked José.

"Jim has an office with Antonio, to provide his clients with accounts for their business as well as lawyer services. Jim has a company in Sheffield; England and he's going to combine it with this company here. This will give his U.K. customers a Spanish

contact for when they want to buy a house for example. It's pretty straight forward."

"That's ok, we're a bit confused that's all."

"Why do you ask?"

"He came in with Antonio to discuss Placido's disappearance and he had a file with him. This dropped out and I couldn't help but get confused, look," said Jose` as he handed her a business card.

She looked at it and that feeling of dread returned as she composed herself and took a deep breath. She dismissed the feelings as she knew she was being paranoid.

"This is a Guardia contact; I wouldn't read any more into it. He's helped us get information about Placido. I don't think we should worry about Antonio or Jim. I think between them they'll find Placido. This is only a contact number for them, why are you worried about this?"

"I've called it, Gavee. It's the Black Beret division; in your country that's SAS."

"What does this mean, José?" she whispered as she took a large gulp of Gin & Tonic.

"They're not involved in the Placido case as they referred to it."

"It could be a personal contact of Antonio. I know Jim has been asked to get involved with Antonio's account customers. He needs an English accountant. I still wouldn't worry," she said trying to convince them both as well as herself. *"He's back Saturday, I'll ask him."*

"Ok, shall we meet Friday night after class and talk some more," said Eugenio not convinced with her explanation.

"Yes, give me the card for when I ask him, don't worry."

She left with the two men, and they seemed more relaxed than when she'd arrive. She had no reason to think anything different to what she'd told them earlier. As she manoeuvred her car in her slot at the apartment, she felt uneasy for a second. She walked hurriedly to the apartment lift berating herself for being paranoid. She rushed into the flat and locked herself in and then looked at the card again. She sat down and opened a bottle of red.

She poured over in her mind the conversation with Eugenio and José and did she trust Jim? Her men in the past had all let her down. Of course, she trusted him, he'd been honest from the beginning or was it she had been brutally honest from the start. She took a large gulp of wine and decided she would go through his spare room which housed all his stuff. It was full of tools and papers, if there was anything untoward, she'd find it. Her mobile rang and it was him.

"Hi sweetheart, you ok?"

"Just checking your home safe and how was school?"

Several minutes later as she said goodnight, she felt a wave of guilt overwhelm her. She had to be sure, he'd been so sincere on the phone, and she didn't doubt him. Her friends had trusted and had worried enough about her to confront her with a situation which made them uncomfortable. She had the utmost respect for Eugenio and José. She had started to trust Jim and therefore believed that she loved him, she had to do it.

She wore her plastic gloves, the ones she wore for cleaning the terrace of bugs and she went through the table of papers that was literally by the sofa bed. Taking a photo of the pile to make sure she left it as she found it, she proceeded to go through every single piece of paper and file.

She ransacked the whole room and there was absolutely nothing present other than his company details along with his plumbing, decorating, and painting equipment. She found his company's registration documents and phone numbers. She took a photo of it all and made a mental note to call in the morning, to be sure. Satisfied there was nothing in his belongings to make her cast a doubt, she went to bed relaxed.

She hadn't slept all night as she called the company and was greeted by the receptionist, the very girl Jim had talked about. She made a lame excuse of needing their services. It was genuine and she blinked back the tears with relief as she made her way to Jasmine's. She wasn't going to allow any man ever again to betray her.

Her phone bleeped as she walked to Casco Antigo. Maud had arrived and she would meet her in the morning. Tonight, she would reassure Eugenio that Jim was genuine, not that they didn't believe that. It was going to be an eventful few days as she got to her first lesson.

———◆———

22

House Hunting

The children knew lots of colours and with their pet drawings from the day before, had lots of fun going through new ones as they got a bit boisterous. Ivan, being in the last class was full of mischief as they walked to her car, to take him home.

"Mums had lots of men this week."

"What do you mean, you've had people staying?" asked Gaby knowing his English wasn't perfect and couldn't take stuff that her students said, literally.

"She a escort, Uh I can't remember what it is in English."

"Don't worry, I don't need to know. Will you have someone to collect you tomorrow as I'm not in school?"

"Yes, mum has asked her boyfriend to fetch me."

"That's great. I'll drop you off."

"No, Mum wants to thank you; she said you come in for tea."

"Ok, quick tea then, Ivan."

He ran ahead as Gaby smiled at what he'd said, peoples' English reminded her of her "*pollo*" incident. She'd learnt not to take anything any student said literally.

She closed the gate, and a shadow moved in her side vision as she looked up, she felt unnerved. She dismissed it and went inside as Ivan was calling for his mother. The pc was on, and Suzann was on the terrace with her sister and a couple of men. She went out to say hello as Suzann moved quickly towards her vision and guided her back inside.

"I want to thank you for your help with Ivan this week, would you like tea?"

"No, Suzann, I'm teaching earlier tonight and got some work to prepare before class but thanks. It's been no problem; glad your ankle's better."

"Thank you, good to meet you."

She went outside as Gaby turned to leave; the computer screen caught her eye. She quickly looked away from it and left. She drove down the hill fast. Two black Audis were parked under the olive trees, which hadn't been there when she'd arrived, but then it wasn't her business. She didn't feel comfortable as she put her foot down, the sooner she got home the better.

She was meeting Maud in Nueva Andalucía and hadn't been to the coffee shop or the commercial centre within it since the Ryan Marshall kidnapping. She parked outside Banús and walked to the "*Centro Commercial*" and hoped the estate agent she'd contacted would be there. His name was

David, and he had houses from 280,000€ and 1.800,000€ in Puerto Banús and Marbella areas.

Mercedes had given her a parking spot behind the hotel. In exchange, she tutored her daughter for two hours a week. Even Eugenio had given her a pass for the town hall car park in Marbella if she needed it. Gaby spent an hour a week with his wife, who was sick and helped her with her Basic English.

David waved at her as she entered the Centro's cafe` quarter where there were three cafes` with communal seating in the middle. Tapas were being cooked to order and Gaby smiled at David.

"Maud not here yet then?"

"Hi Gabriella, how are you? It was good of you to think of me."

"You were in Antonio's office as Maud called, David. It was silly going anywhere else. Do you have properties in her price bracket...ah look here she is..."?

Maud swept over to them dressed for a party and not villa spotting and David's raised eyebrow was enough to make Gaby laugh. She waltzed over beaming, hugged Gaby, and shook David's hand.

"Coffee Maud?"

"Yes, Gaby that would be great. David, how are you, so good of you to show me round. Can you tell me what you're showing me today?"

She left them to discuss the plan for the day as she went towards Café Arias to order the drinks.

"Gabriella Daley, no it can't be, is that you?"

Gaby turned as she seemed to recognise the accent behind her and gasped, *"Rosalyn Mathias, don't believe it, what the fuck are you doing here?"*

"Oh fuck, Gaby it is you, what a fabulous surprise." "I live in Estepona, where do you live?"

"Here, in Andalucía."

"Oh, my god, we must get together, can you send over three coffees, and I'll write down my mobile for you."

"Yes, of course, how long have you been here?"

"Nearly a year. Look, I can see you're busy, let's catch up later."

"Yes, I'll bring the coffees over right away"

Gaby couldn't believe it, she used to work with Rosalyn in London, and they'd shared Hawkeye, the same Operations Director.

She went to join Maud and David who were strewn over various details of properties on the table and Gaby froze as she sat down. Adjacent to them were Eugenio and José with Paul Marshall. He was heavily guarded with three men in suits and then she saw the Guardia car parked to the side street. Her heart nearly stopped as she could see they were in deep conversation and José had papers on the table. Eugenio nodded at her, and she acknowledged him. Jim had said to keep away and even though she wanted to go and hug Paul, find out if Maria had had the baby and ask him about Lynn, she couldn't.

Rosalyn arrived with the coffee chatting to David who paid for the drinks as Maud continued to plough through the information.

"Any properties you feel you want to see?" asked David as Maud had plenty of choice in front of her.

"Right David, can we look at these, how are they logistically for us to view today……?"

Rosalyn came over with a piece of paper.

"Gaby this is for you, my mobile. Do you still see Jed?"

"Whatever makes you say that?

"He was here yesterday with some men?"

"Are you sure?"

"Yes, he was here, he looked at me a few times, he sort of knew me but didn't want to say anything, I'm positive it was him."

"He's meant to be in Italy with his wife; I'm here and have met a nice bloke called Jim"

"What happened to you and Nick? We must catch up."

"He's going to catch up with me at some point, why do you ask?"

"I've seen him here too," she whispered as she cleared the table of coffee cups as Gaby froze to the spot.

"Are you ready, Gaby? David has three properties for us to look at and three properties tomorrow, how exciting."

"Yes," said Gaby as she looked at Eugenio's table as Paul smiled at her through his dark glasses. Her legs wobbled as she followed David and Maud to his car.

Trying to digest what she'd just gathered from Rosalyn; she sat in the back of the jeep as Maud and David chatted away about living on the coast and a little bit about the first property she was going to view.

They drove to the east of Banús and there was an urbanisation being built on front line and Maud was looking at a town house. She couldn't get her head round the information she'd just heard and tried to shake off a fear that was gathering in a knot of her stomach. She had no idea what to think and decided not to worry and call Rosalyn that evening after school.

The front-line town houses being built and for sale for between 500,000 € and 1,500,000€ were being sold *"off-plan."* Most people bought *off- plan* and then re-sold the property afterwards. The purchaser could make an easy 80-100,000€ more than they'd paid for it. The downside of course, the builder could run away with your money and deposit, and Gaby was all ears....

She listened to David explaining the system as they all walked into the offices of Abdul Abdullah, who was the primary agent for the urbanisation. Another link in the chain meant Maud would be paying two agent fees. She could see how much of a money-spinning operation house purchasing was through agents as she made mental notes.

Abdul Abdullah, by his sheer name was of Arab extraction but Gaby couldn't help but stare at him. She'd never seen an Arab with piercingly turquoise green eyes, which were obviously contacts. It certainly made you look at him. He was charming, extremely good looking and wearing a slick Armani suit with polished shoes even though it was over 30c in full sun.

She found him entertaining, knowledgeable, intelligent, spoke flawless English and had a good sense of humour. Maud who was dressed for a nightclub, her low-cut top and hip white jeans were fitting her flirtatious behaviour. They all clambered into Abduls' open top 4x4 to view the front-line house that Maud wanted. Gaby couldn't get Rosalyn's comments from her mind as she tried to look interested in Maud's potential new home.

Abdul concentrated on Maud, which meant Gaby and Dave could wander round and look. Gaby mentioned to Dave about her wish to locate a villa on the beach side but with a budget of 280,000 € allowing for his fees. Dave nodded and gave her his card for another time.

"What do you think?" asked Maud attached to Abdul.

"The brick work is pretty awful, look at that," said Gaby as the bricks had substantial gaps in the walls.

"That's not good for a house valued at over half a million. Sorry Maud, it's terrible."

"I'm sorry," said David *"I couldn't agree more. Have you anything completed on front line, to show Maud, Abdul?"*

"Yes, follow me," said Abdul understanding what Dave meant especially as Gaby was more observant.

The completed row of front-line villas further down the coastline but walking distance to Banús were for sale at a much higher price. This villa was ready for occupancy and had sumptuous furnishings which were included. They sat on the terrace overlooking the sea and harbour of Banús and Gaby could see the value. You'd pay for the scenery, no questions asked. The living accommodation was upstairs to take advantage of the views, and the sleeping quarters were downstairs which meant they stayed cool and private.

"It's lovely Maud," said Gaby as she wandered round impressed by the furniture and layout. It was out of her reach at 1,200,000€ but Maud wasn't fazed.

There were six bedrooms and four en-suites on the ground floor with separate toilet, family bathroom and Jacuzzi areas. There were three terraces off three bedrooms with secluded love seats as Gaby was reminded of Seville.

Upstairs there was a huge dining room with floor to ceiling windows, the view was incredible. The kitchen was granite and stainless steel with grey and pale pink tiled floors. The sitting room also looked out to sea along with three separate rooms, and Gaby was suitably impressed.

Maud nodded to Abdul, *"I'll take it,"* she said as Gaby shrieked with excitement for her and Abdul hugged, kissed her on both cheeks, and said,

"Back to my office to celebrate."

The Moët et Chandon was opened, and Abdul had the receptionist running around to get glasses and nibbles as Maud took a glass thrilled.

"Congratulations Maud, it's beautiful. I'm so pleased for you," said Gaby reaching for a glass and clinking hers.

"Yes," said David thinking of his commission.

She was in full swing for a party, but Dave looked at Gaby as she nodded,

"We've got to go Maud. Dave is going to drop me at my car, and I've lessons at six. I'll see you tomorrow at the café if you still want to view other villas."

"Oh, aren't you coming to celebrate with us?" asked Maud now on a large Gin & Tonic.

"Why don't I meet you in Banús around eleven tonight. Will Abdul be entertaining you all evening?" asked Gaby looking at Abdul who was moving his hands over Maud's hips.

"I'll entertain Maud. I'll make sure she's looked after."

"Hmm," said Gaby and looked at Dave who wanted to leave as they'd concluded the business deal.

"I'll meet you in Sinatra's at eleven," said Gaby and Maud smiled and mouthed a silent thank you.

"Will she be all right with him?"

"Yes, they'll have sex at the house she's about to buy, she'll sign the deal, and they'll meet you later."

"Oh, is that a criterion then?" laughed Gaby at David's frankness as he dropped her at the Hotels' parking entrance.

"No, but neither you nor I are stupid," smiled Dave. *"It's all right when I find your villa, it won't be a requirement,"* he teased.

"I don't think my fiancé would approve," she laughed as she thanked Dave for his time.

"Can you let me know if anything remotely like what I've seen today but a fraction of the price, comes up Dave."

"Yes, leave it with me, take care now."

She drove straight to Wall Street and decided she would call Jim before class, she was still feeling a bit unnerved by Rosalyn's comments. She texted Rosalyn her number also saying that she'd be in Banús later if she was around. She didn't fancy dealing with a drunken Maud on her own.

"Hi sweetheart, how are you?

"Are you getting lots of clients?"

"Yes, I'll be glad to get home, I've secured thirteen and five pending. It's amazing how many contacts he's got."

"Great stuff, I can retire then," she laughed stifling a gasp of breath.

"Ok, what's wrong?

"I'm fine, looking forward to tomorrow. What time will you be back?"

"I'll be home before you know it, stay in bed. What's wrong?"

"It can wait until the morning," she said quietly knowing she wanted to see his face when she tackled him.

Her lessons went smoothly, and her friends were the last lesson, and they all proceeded to Bar Tougana for an hour.

"How was Paul?" asked Gaby as she wanted to know their news.

"Have you asked Jim?" he asked.

"No, he's home first thing, I'll ask him then, don't worry. Has he had a baby, is Lynn, ok? Tell me."

"They've had a baby boy, all is ok. He's transferring all their assets this week, he was heavily guarded. Of course, we saw you," said José.

"Any news of Placido?"

"Nothing," said José equally worried.

"None of the family is allowed back in the country. Since the murder of Ryan Marshall, the Guardia cannot be held responsible for their safety. Their houses are for sale, and they must organise a team of removals to take their stuff back or sell. It's terrible," said Eugenio.

"Oh, my goodness," said Gaby feeling quite sick at the finality of it.

"I won't hear from Lynn ever again them; it's probably not a good thing."

"You're right; we've all got to move on. I just hope wherever they've got Placido or wherever he's buried, someone will find him. It's awful, his parents are in the bank every week asking me and of course I don't know what's happened."

"José, I'm sure the Guardia will find him soon enough."

"Do we know who was behind it?"

"Russian Mafia, we think," said José quietly as Gaby winced with shock.

Gaby's text went off as she retrieved her mobile as Eugenio paid the waiter. It was time for them to leave and go their separate ways.

"See you both next Friday unless something happens," said Gaby as she embraced her friends outside and made her way to the car. It was time to locate Maud who was apparently at a party in the house she yet hadn't quite bought apart from say yes.

It was dusk and Gaby noted several black limos and cars in general parked down the street at Maud's new house. She had a funny feeling but decided to check she was all right and then get home. She wanted to have a luxury bath and moisturise herself all over with the anticipation of Jim's early arrival.

The place was amok with Arabs and scantily clad young girls wandering around, some with a tray of drinks in their hand. Others just milling on sofas and the bedrooms downstairs seemed to have a queue forming by the top stairs.

She took a glass from one of the girls to blend in and went scouring for Maud. The music was turned on high and the smell of drugs was thick in the air forming a cloud as she walked upstairs towards the living room. There must have been a dozen people in various stages of attire as she spotted Maud's' white jeaned ass in the air, on the floor, behind the rich cream leather sofa. She was concentrating on her task as she was giving her Arab estate agent some *head.*

Another blonde girl was kissing him as he was fondling her breasts that were smothered over his chest. Maud was totally engrossed as she walked away towards the kitchen and got grabbed by a tall blonde with thick red lipstick. Before she could protest, she was pulled round and her hands were held together behind her back. The girl facing her smiled and went to kiss her as she moved her head. She wriggled free and turned to see Suzann laughing but then she quickly apologised as Gaby's face was red with thunder.

"Sorry Gavee, bad joke."

What are you doing here?"

"We're the double act," said Suzann, *"we're waiting to get to bedroom three but Maud's doing a pretty good job, we may be redundant."*

"Why, has he booked you?" asked Gaby relieved she knew Suzann and her sister, but they'd given her a fright.

"Five hundred Euros a session each honey, you should try it sometime. I don't know why you're a teacher."

They walked away from her as she saw Maud getting up from the floor, her makeup smeared from sex and alcohol. Her top was loose down her waist as she stood there, everything hanging out. Another hand grabbed her left tit as she spotted Gaby and looked embarrassed. Gaby could tell her some stories and smiled at her as she mouthed silently to her,

"Do you want to stay or shall I take you back to Marbella."

"Yes, I'll stay."

"Take care, text me later."

"Join us there's plenty on offer."

"No Maud, I'm going home."

She walked away and knew she looked a prude and a stuffed shirt, but she knew she was as promiscuous. There was a time and a place. She was not to judge anyone. She got home thinking about Suzann. Ivan was right, she was a hooker.

23

Jim Returns

"*It's so good to see you, you must tell me everything. What happened to Nick? I just can't believe you're here. I kept trying your mobile to tell you, we'd come out here too.*"

"*I got my mobile stolen. I'd no idea you'd left. I thought you'd been promoted to Scotland?*"

"*I had, but then I realised my life was planned in front of me and I needed to live a little. I just let my house and came out not long after you left, to have a bit of fun.*"

"*I thought you were seeing the accountant from head office.*"

"*Yes, he's with me, he's working at the estate agents in Centro Commercial, for the guy who owns the apartment block.*"

"*That's pretty handy. Are you happy?*"

"*Yes, we love it here, but tell me what's going on with you?*"

"*I think you need to tell me as I'm not seeing Nick or Jed; I need to know.*"

"*Nick looks terrible, I'm sure it was him; he was here last week with three others.*"

"Did he recognise you?"

"That's what made me look at him twice; in fact, I disappeared behind the cafe` wall to really check him out as he looked completely different. If he hadn't stared at me too long, I wouldn't have thought any more. He has dreadlocks, down to his neck, he's so brown, and you could pass him as an Arab."

"Who was he with?"

"Two equally rough looking blokes they were talking in Russian. They met up with a tall suited man and the Guardia."

"Jed?"

"Good god no, I didn't know them, but he was here a few days ago. He was his usual flamboyant self, and he was with about four others. They were all suited with Ray bans and shiny shoes. You know what I mean. He acknowledged me, but I don't think he twigged who I was. He was really engrossed in some business...." as she leant in and looked around. *"Gil y Gil, the Mayor turned up with a few minders and then they all disappeared."*

"Christ, it all happens here," said Gaby as she told her about the Ryan Marshall kidnapping and murder.

"Oh, my God, that's awful." Have they found Placido yet?"

"No, it's horrible, he's been officially declared missing."

"Tell me about your new man, all of it."

"Gosh, he's the only person I trust," said Gaby as she filled her in.

"Christ, so much going on, Jim sounds a great bloke, we must meet up one night," said Rosalyn.

"*That'll be great, he's back tomorrow. I'll text you once I get chance.*"

"*No worries, I work here four mornings and afternoons a week, you can always turn up here and we can arrange something. It's not too busy, but it's good for socialising.*"

"*I must get to school; do you know the bar in Marbella, the one with no door?*"

"*No.*"

"*We'll take you there. Only Spanish use it, good contacts for Ben.*"

"*Ok, good, see you soon.*"

She drove to Marbella thinking about Nick and Jed. Nick was obviously undercover, and she wasn't sure if she felt comforted that he was close by. For all she knew, he'd already seen her with Jim and would not bother when he came out of hiding. She hoped he would at least contact her, even to wish her well. She wasn't going to leave Jim, she trusted him.

Jed, being on the coast unnerved her more. This made her feel uneasy. Rosalyn would recognise him; she'd been one of the few women who'd met him. Why on earth was he here? She hoped he hadn't come to find her. She also knew that if he'd tracked her down to the studio flat, he could easily track her down to Estepona.

She parked and made her way to the school and Arrabella was her usual smiley self as she walked in to discover Eugenio and José in the foyer.

"Ah Gavee, we're about to leave you a message," said Eugenio looking drawn again.

"I'm early let's go to the staff room, what's wrong?"

"It's Placido," said José visibly upset.

"They've found him," said Eugenio quietly as Gaby gasped and reached her arms out to them.

"Tell me."

"They discovered a body in the Campo. They think it's him."

"Oh, my God that's awful."

"We're waiting to hear for definite," said José.

"Why him?"

"We think it's because he was seeing Lynn, and the Russian mafia wanted her brother's entire distribution network. Maybe they think that Lynn told him secrets or things about the business, we're not sure. The Guardia seem to think that's the link."

"Jim will be shocked, he's back in the morning," said Gaby.

"Is he in Granada with Antonio?"

"Yes, he's had a good few days, I'm expecting him first thing."

"This isn't him then?" said José as he opened his phone and showed her a photo.

Gaby paled as she looked at Jim, in a suit with Antonio in Centro Commercial with the Mayor Gil y Gil and others she couldn't make out.

"When was this taken?"

"Two days ago, Gaby. What's going on?"

"I've no idea; Jim said he was in Granada. I'll ask him in the morning before I decide if he's lied to me."

"We need to know, if we can trust him," said Eugenio.

"Why?"

"The Mayor is working on big projects involving prestige players, Arabs, diplomats Gavee. Why is Jim involved? This is between us, by the way."

"I'll find out. We'll meet in Bar Tougana on Monday night usual time."

"Yes, will see you later for our lesson, we just wanted to show you this without the others," said José.

"No problem, see you later. Are you going to tell them about Placido?"

"Yes, once they've confirmed it."

"Ok."

Her lessons went in a blur as she tried to work out if her fiancé were lying to her, she couldn't get to grips with it. He'd been honest from the start. She'd been honest from the beginning; he'd never said anything about his past. She'd checked the business in Sheffield, it was real. His paperwork about his business was legitimate, she'd checked Company's House. All sort of things went through her mind, and she had to stop. She would confront him in the morning and wait for his explanation. She was more worried about Jed and Nick and in that order.

José and Eugenio came to their last lesson and Mercedes were joined by Isabella and all the other advanced students.

"We're going to debate today everyone. Split into two groups. Jose`, your group can start after you've had ten minutes to discuss the subject, which is-

"Do you trust your partner, if he's lied to you?"

"José's team is to give the argument with reasons why you will trust again. Isabella your team must debate with reasons why you can't trust again."

José and Eugenio understood why she'd set this debate; Gaby found the reasons for and against all made sense and was amazed at how forgiving everyone was at the conclusion. They'd all got new vocabulary from the session, which she'd contributed, and it had proved to be a very cleansing debate. She felt prepared for either scenario for when Jim got back in the morning. It had been a good exercise as Isabella also believed that Antonio was in Granada.

She drove home and passed several black Mercs on the way and her heart flipped thinking of Jed and his entourage. She was paranoid. She got in and called Maud, who had not needed her services after finding her house. She'd also texted to say that Abdul had spent the entire few days at her hotel. Gaby smiled thinking how much she missed Jim as she was getting used to a rather healthy sex life herself. She wondered how an earth had she managed all those years without so much as once a fortnight.

"Good on you, Maud. Stay connected for when you move out."

Once at home, she had a long soak in the bath and pampered her body with oils and went to bed leaving the main door unhinged. She was excited to see him but also had slight trepidation about that photo. She just wanted to be with someone she could trust. She tossed and turned all night and eventually she heard the door being unlocked and turned over hugging the pillow and feigned sleep.

He was quite a while before coming into the bedroom and she wondered what on earth he was doing. She heard the shower running. Eventually, he came in and slowly lifted the sheet and crept in beside her. He moved his hand over the back of her legs and thighs and moved his finger under her lacy shorts as he spooned himself kissing her skin. She started to wriggle and turned over and smiled as he found her lips as he whispered,

"I've missed you so much."

He felt relaxed in the dusk of the room as she realised it was early hours of the morning and not breakfast time as he kissed her, and they made love until the sun came up without the need for talking.

He got up eventually and made breakfast and bought the tray to bed. She sat up on the pillows not wanting to spoil the moment. He poured a coffee and handed it to her as she made room for him to sit.

"How was your week?"

"Interesting, you first," she said.

"I didn't need to be away. His business dealings are getting complicated. I don't know why he's dragging me round with him. Anyway, I've been here two afternoons this week, sorry sweetheart but I didn't know. To keep it simple, I've made so

many new clients; I can work here full time as an accountant and keep my Sheffield office."

"Jim that's fantastic news," said Gaby blinking back tears of relief as she brushed them away, but not quickly enough.

"Whatever's wrong?"

"You were spotted in Centro Commercial Nuevo Andalucía, and I thought you'd lied."

"No, you know everything."

"Can you go to the kitchen drawer and get my blue purse."

"Yes, what is it?" as he went to fetch the blue purse which they used for buying the gas bottles.

She opened it as he climbed back into bed, and she produced the Guardia card.

"Oh, that's where it went. Dropped it with Antonio. It's his contact," he said giving it back to her.

"No, I don't want it, give it back to him," she said satisfied. *"Sorry, I didn't, uh wasn't sure, I had to ask."*

"Gaby, look. You must be able to ask and tell me everything all of the time," he said as he moved the tray from the bed and placed his arms round her. She felt reassured and apologised for doubting him.

"What else is wrong?"

"Jed has been seen and Nick," as he looked startled.

"Explain," he said quietly as Gaby told him about Rosalyn and their conversation.

"I'm never leaving you again," he said as he pulled the sheet over her head as they went under. Satisfied with his explanation she gave herself to him as he took her, his need as urgent as hers.

❧

24

Sex and Drugs

"*The plan starts tonight; you know what to do,*" said Aleksey in his Russian accent. It was even thicker since he'd started smoking roll ups using coarse tobacco, which gave him a permanent sore throat.

The three men went their separate ways and would meet up in Mijas where the first part of the plan was to be instigated. Miguel and Armando drove to collect their hookers from Sinatra's. They'd all met their bosses, and they had a few weeks to get manpower in place. The main heist would be in Estepona. It wouldn't be long before they'd all be able to disappear and become themselves. A mission which had taken over a year to complete.

It wasn't yet in the bag; this next stage was the bait for the main mule along with the Drug Baron. Dolly and Daisy were waiting for them and Armando could tell that Dolly was already a little high. He was pleased about that as tonight they were going to work. Armando had several pouches of pain killers colour coded in his chest pocket, to join them.

These girls were going to instigate a party in Estepona of sex and drugs as they had the contacts they were chasing. Miguel smiled as he read his mate's mind. They had a quick Gin & Tonic at Sinatra's as Armando looked around wondering if she was all right. He hadn't seen her lately but then he and Miguel had been in Gibraltar. His disguise wasn't that impressive as Rosalyn had recognised him, even though she'd done a double take. He prayed that Gaby had bumped into her and be reassured, that he was close by.

His dreadlocks made him look fearsome and he was brown as a berry, making sure he kept up the suntan. His contacts were deep brown; he looked wild like a native Arab and not a blonde blue-eyed Londoner. The Spanish accent perfected, he grabbed Dolly's arse as they left the bar. They were going to rock tonight and earn their lines of coke.

Mijas heights, an urbanisation at the mountain top of Mijas looked down on the village. The white washed houses and villas looked quaint and romantic as they walked up the thirty or so steps to the secluded villa. The wad of notes in Miguel's pocket was the entry fee. It was a get together for selective business men, along with courtesans and well-paid escorts. The cars were parked away from the villa as instructed and the village bars below subsequently looked impressively busy.

The enormous bouncer dressed in black and wearing ray bans smoking a joint was checking credentials as two other men walked in front of Armando's party. He counted the wad and nodded, looked at the two hookers and beckoned for the four to go through. Miguel spotted the key mule almost immediately and relaxed as this was going to go as planned.

The flamenco music in the background was loud and having talked out a strategy with Armando prior to the night. Miguel grabbed Daisy by the waist and took her to the floor. She was a sexy dancer, and this was a perfect way to get the party going.

Ana Belen's voice sung from the corner hi-fi of the adjacent room in the main lounge. A beefy man wearing a black tux was taking round silver trays of cava and Armando grabbed a glass drank it back and grabbed Dolly and joined Miguel and Daisy.

The music seemed to get louder as the room started to fill up with men in dark suits, men in white suits and scantily clad women. A tall blonde with red lipstick was caressing a woman in the corner as Armando stared at her, giving her the come on as she nodded but continued to fondle the girl.

Armando poked Miguel in the ribs, his sign he'd made a connection as he started snogging Dolly hard as the music kept on getting louder. Dolly knew her cue and they danced towards the two girls in the corner. Armando had his hands inside her skirt, fingering her pussy as she moved and cavorted seemingly wilder towards the two women.

Dolly turned to the blonde, fingered her wavy hair, and kissed her seductively as Armando let go. He moved her friend away to the sofa in the adjoining room. She seemed high and Armando nodded at a waiter to keep an eye on her. He spoke rapidly in Spanish and the waiter accepted something from him, nodded and went away.

Dolly had the big blonde tucked up behind the heavy drapes of the French windows. She started kissing her gently and fondling her ample breasts as the blonde responded eagerly. She hadn't had anyone this sexy and gorgeous for a while and she was eager to please. Armando, joined them, opened the blonde's top, and started teasing and massaging her left breast as Dolly moved her legs apart as the flamenco music got louder.

The room was packed solid, and Miguel and Daisy were in front of Armando and Dolly, protecting them for the moment, giving them ample opportunity to tease and give this mule a piece of cock and skirt.

"Do you have anything?" she whispered.

"Mine's the best honey, but you need to earn it. I only sell to the Horse, I don't deal with mules," as he let her unzip his trousers but moved, teasing her. She'd have to earn it.

"Show me what you've got, and we'll talk."

Dolly, immersed under her dress was making her squirm, she liked it. Miguel stopped her and she pulled away."

"What the fuck?"

"There's more of that to come, go and sink this and tell me if that's good enough. I've got tons on the way in a few weeks. She'll come with me, we do the deal, and we party once the goods done," as he fondled her breasts and nipped them through her bra hard. She wanted more as he dropped his hand, zipped himself up and stuffed a pouch in her thong. *"Tell me later."*

Miguel disappeared into the upstairs bedroom and was lining up coke, knowing they'd soon have company. Within minutes, the girl who was with the blond German opened the door and stood watching Daisy snort her line from the glass table.

"Knock you out honey," whispered Miguel wanting her report to the mule that it was a good kick.

She sat quickly at the glass table and taking the note, rolled it and snorted a line in seconds. She sat back and waited for the room to subside; it had been spinning before she came for some fodder. Where was Suzann?

"Lost your mate, honey?" asked Daisy who was feeling exactly right for a bit of ginger pussy as Miguel went to get alcohol, leaving the door open. He nodded at Armando who was still dancing with Dolly.

Three men in suits were in discussion with the blonde as the undercover tuxedo clad waiter came with laced alcohol that Armando had instigated. He was sure to leave once this drug hit the spot. He knew to watch Miguel. He'd already lifted the blondes' mobile and had got the numbers and details of her contacts. He stuffed it back in her friend's purse and continued to take the tray round. The three Arabs entertaining the blonde were sipping the drink as was she. Gil y Gil and three bodyguards appeared and there were deep discussions around the blonde.

Miguel picked up three glasses and a clean one for him as he went back to find Dolly and the German's escort. They were snorting another line each as he handed them a glass and left the spare on the table knowing the blonde would follow.

"Fancy some?"

"Just done a line in the other room, I'm good for a bit, come here."

Dolly got up and went to embrace the man she was reliant on, the man who'd looked after her for the last year. Her life was good, she didn't need to worry about her rent, as he'd covered it. She knew tonight she had to act as instructed by him, the evening before.

"Can I have some," said the girl.

"Come here, baby, let me sort you out," she said in her husky voice as Miguel moved to one side as the girl came to join her on the bed. Miguel needed to capture evidence and needed that blonde.

Dolly kissed the girl, who appeared drunk. She wore long, copper red ringlets down her back. She was green eyed, and her freckles joined up on the bridge of her nose. She was apparently kept by the blonde with red lipstick and was her house slave. She was sexually abused by her and anyone who fancied a spare at a party. She was illegal and she'd been smuggled into Spain with the blonde and her family. The better life consisted of housework and being the entertainment at a party. Maar didn't care, she was saving her earnt money and one day, she would run. Miguel had checked her out and needed to use her right now as Dolly started performing.

She unzipped her dress and let it drop to the floor as she moved her to the bed and laid her down, as the blonde sashayed in, her red lips intact and sporting a full glass of spiked cava.

"Ah, Maar you're in for a treat, hey big boy, fancy a quick one or one with the girls?"

"I'm watching, they'll get me hi," said Miguel his accent thick, *"Why don't you join them, and then you can fuck me."*

"Show me what you want honey."

"Will that do," said Miguel as he stuffed three hundred down her bra as she smiled and moved it to inside her stocking and went to the bed.

"That's more like it, its show time girls."

Miguel's video was on, as he watched playing with himself as they'd expect it.

The blonde started kissing Dolly with great gusto and fondling Maar's perk breasts the same time. Dolly knew she had a few minutes to make an impression and she unhooked Suzann's bra and in one deft move, only the wads of notes inside her stocking was left untouched. She fondled Suzann's breasts and suddenly Maar was behind, massaging her breasts as Dolly's tongue was inside the blonde's mouth probing and teasing her and suddenly the spiked cava kicked in.

Dolly's fingers moved inside the blonde as Maar moved her to lie down. She opened her legs as Dolly went towards her thick pussy, her tongue roaming her inner thighs. Maar, seeing her cue, lifted her arse and sat on her face. The blonde eager for cock after this pussy, licked with expertise as she held Maar's body over her as Dolly suddenly hit her spot. All three groaned together as Miguel came at the same time.

As if on cue an Arab walked in as Miguel zipped up and went to him, taking him the spare glass as the Arab sipped,

"Stuff's good, we need some."

"Let's go outside," said Miguel as Dolly's cue was to continue to keep the two girls occupied as he flipped his phone shut and placed it in his pocket.

Armando saw him and followed as Daisy was dancing with a Moroccan man in a white suit. He moved his head towards the bedroom as she nodded, acknowledging the blonde was with Dolly and continued to dance.

"How much?"

"Minimum twenty kilos."

"We need one, that's fine, what about fifty."

"Yes, there's plenty of it. We need to drop the same time as other drops."

"Who else is dealing, I've the monopoly on the Costa."

"'Fraid not, there's another drop we make, over sixty a month, you've got competition."

"I need to know who."

"Fraid can't do that, but the shipment will arrive the same day. You could bump in to each other, I suppose."

"No, we don't do business like this," said the Arab.

"Price has gone up."

"Only if I get the lot, no second party."

"He's been here longer than you," said Miguel looking at Armand as they both realised there was another Drug Cartel as big as the one, they were about to trap.

"Tell you what; this is what we'll do...."

25

A Week Away

Jim was slightly ruffled at the news of Placido's body being located. He was also unnerved to hear that Gaby's' friend had seen both her ex.'s. He would have to find them and put them straight. She was also upset about the news, and he needed to get this boxed off, otherwise they'd never be able to move on.

He was shocked when she'd told him about her nest egg and that she'd asked this Dave to look for a villa. He believed her, when she'd told him about the party at Maud's new house as it was happening everywhere.

He had no idea until this morning about her savings, and he drove to Marbella to see Antonio. He wasn't sure how he felt, especially after Gaby's revelation about her two men and Placido.

Should he tell her, but then he would lose her. He didn't know if it was best for her not to know as he hadn't done anything illegal. He answered a few cryptic texts as he got to his office, had a meeting with Antonio, and decided. He would take her away. He probably needed a break from all her goings on if he was honest. He texted her to ask if she could take a holiday. It was time to share something he hadn't told her from the beginning.

Gaby, in the middle of her lessons at Jasmines' school was pleased to receive a text to organise a holiday. How romantic, she thought.

She needed to talk to Isabella, regarding teaching her three children, after that she could fit in with his dates.

"Can you take Ivan home today?" asked Jasmine.

"Yes, no worries."

"Thanks, are you sure you don't want this full-time job, as I'll need to advertise in a few weeks?"

"Yes, I'm sure, Jas but thanks. I'd rather be your fill-in teacher or temp as and when you need extra."

Ivan was again in full humour and very chatty as they made their way to her car.

"Mum is having a party."

"Is she, that's good," said Gaby as they jumped in her car.

"Are you coming?"

"When is it?"

"Don't remember, but I want you to come."

"Ok, I'll ask Mum when we get home," said Gaby not wanting to attend a hooker's party. She didn't really want to talk to Suzann either as she intimidated her a bit, especially after that incident at Maud's villa. She knew Ivan liked her and she was more concerned about him.

"Who's coming?"

"All her important friends from away," said Ivan as they pulled off the carreterra and climbed the hill.

"She looks as if she's got a houseful of friends here already," said Gaby as she pulled up outside the villa, just about enough room for Ivan to jump out.

"Please come in, Mum wants to see you."

"Ok, I'll turn around."

She turned the car round and managed to park on the grass verge and off the hill, in-between three black cars.

"What's with the black cars?" she thought as she went inside.

Suzann's sister was sunbathing on the lounger and there was a couple swimming and messing about in the pool. Suzann walked in as Gaby called out a hello.

"Gavee come, do you want tea?"

"No, I'm fine, Ivan said to pop in that's all. Are you well?"

"Yes, please some tea, have made it how you like, look."

Suzann went to the kitchen and the table was again covered in baking equipment as before. She came back with a jug of iced tea with lemon and two glass mugs.

"Si, veery Inglish, yes?"

"Ok, yes thank you," she laughed and sat on the sofa looking at the magnificent view of the coast.

"The view is amazing."

"Yes, that's why I choose it, yes?

"Yes. Ivan is doing well in school; his English is better than all the students in his class."

"That's good, he wants to be a lawyer, and I think he better speak Inglish better than us, for that reason I send him privately."

"He's ambitious for an eleven-year-old," said Gaby.

Suzann's mobile rung as she got up, apologised, and went to the terrace to answer it. Gaby finished her tea and got up. Her eyes went to the pc again, and there was a driving licence on the screen. She couldn't help it; she picked up the paper licence on the side and it was a copy. She felt a moment of dread and quickly moved away from it. She noticed a pile of passports to the side as she put her glass down and looked away towards the view as Suzann came in.

"I must go Suzann, all the best."

"Come to our party, in two weeks, bring your friends."

"Let Ivan know when it is, I've promised my fiancé to go away for a week, I think it's the same time but thank you."

She drove down the hill knowing that not only was Suzann a hooker, but she was forging driving licenses and passports, no wonder the villa had a constant stream of visitors. What Ivan did on the holidays now made sense? In class, he'd said that he'd been collecting information about people, during the summer. Of course, he was pick- pocketing the tourists, whilst they had their guard down on the beach. She felt sick.

***

Isabella's maid ushered her into the guest living room which reminded her of the traditional Welsh parlours. Everything pristine, in its place but here with floor to ceiling windows showing off the view of the Sierra Blanca mountains. The rich carpet of Moroccan blue and rustic reds hanging on the wall along with paintings showing Antonio's wealth as a major player in Marbella. There was a huge painting of King Juan Carlos 3rd in his uniform and another one of a matador in the bullring of Seville, the home of the bullfighting. She sat and smiled as Paulo the youngest came in and said hello.

"Hello Paulo, how are you?"

"Fine thanks, my Mum is coming with tea."

"Thank you," she laughed the Spanish were all trying to perfect the traditional English drink.

"Sorry Gavee. How are you, Paulo get my organiser from my office?" as Isabella walked in with a tray of tea and bon-bons. *"How's everything? When is it good to teach my children?"*

"Do you want me to teach them all the same evening? It would make sense."

"Can you teach them all on a Wednesday evening, half way through the week? Is that good?"

"Yes, I don't work in Wall Street on Wednesday nights. We can teach in their study room, that's where they're more comfortable."

"Gavee, that sounds good. When can you start?"

"After next week Isabella, once I've seen their school work and report."

"Yes, that's fine, is the tea good?"

"Perfect. Did Antonio enjoy his trip with Jim?"

"Yes, they've done lot of good business, I think. Antonio doesn't tell me much about his office business. We have enough to talk about with the children. He does tell me if there is a big meeting or client."

"He is highly regarded in Marbella. Who is his biggest client?"

"Yes, he's worked hard for the prestige, no? It's Jesus Gil Y Gil, the Mayor. He's bringing lots of work now as he's preparing and building a huge project which will be good for Marbella."

"That's good," said Gaby.

"I'll let you go; I shall see you Friday at school and then we confirm when I can start?"

"Thank you Gavee, I'll pay you weekly, better for me."

"That's perfect, it will be 50€ for the evening."

"Yes, that's good, thank you."

Gaby drove down from the foot of the Sierra Blanca Mountains and came to the Pirelli monument which always reminded her of when she arrived in the rain.

She joined the carreterra and made her way home. She got in and was surprised to see the table was laid for dinner with candles and two place settings, was there something to celebrate?

"Jim?"

There was no one in the flat but he had a surprise or something to tell her as she checked the fridge. It was full of smoked salmon and various dishes that she loved. She was excited, what was he up to?

She packed up her files and went for a quick shower. She took a spare top and would change before coming home. She went to her pile of school lessons and flicked through the plans she wanted and nudged a pile that was Jims.' She went to tidy the papers and saw the name of the file on the top, it was Jedious Firelli. She stopped in her tracks, picked it up and quickly flicked through it. Why did Jim have a file on Jed? She wasn't sure whether to take it and read it. She decided against it and left the flat. She didn't want him to know that she'd stumbled on his surprise, let alone she'd seen or taken a file of her ex-lover.

This bothered her as she drove to Nuevo Andalucía. Rosalyn was working and she could work there and catch up with her at the same time. It was time to organise a night out with their partners. Rosalyn was on her break and waved for her to sit at the corner table, near the cafe` entrance.

"Hey, come and sit here. Perfect timing, what do you want to drink?"

"I'll have an Americano and con gas water, hun."

"Coming up, how you've been?"

"I'm not sure."

"Tell me; you seem to have more excitement than us, what's happening?"

"Why does an accountant who took time off from his own company, come here and become a plumber. Then suddenly he's in with the biggest lawyer in Marbella and has set up an

accountancy office in his building and is going to work there permanently."

"Nothing scary so far, go on."

"Then I tell him about my lover and my ex and suddenly he's a folder in our flat of Jed, which has nothing to do with him."

"Strange, have you tackled him?"

"No, just seen it as I was rummaging through papers of my own, I don't know what to think."

"Maybe he wants to track him down and tell him it's over or get you to finish it. After all, he's proposed and wants to marry you. They're not all crooks you know."

"No," she chuckled" but I seem to attract the naughty ones in more ways than one."

"Really, we're looking for a swinger's party, do you know of any?"

"Never, are you?"

"Yes, don't tell me you haven't been to a swinger party here, it's all the rage."

"Well, it might be, but no I haven't. I haven't exactly been a saint, but I've never done anything of the sort."

"I'll get Ben to check Jim out when we go out, it will be a laugh. Harmless fun but no pressure honey. Don't you think you're reading too much into this Jed thing?"

"Yes, you're right. Why don't we all go out to bar Tougana on Friday and then Banús and you can ask Jim about any swinger parties? I'm sure I can find out, where there is one. In fact, I do

know of a party which I can guarantee will be sexually motivated if you're desperate in the next few weeks."

"See, I knew you'd know someone."

She went to school and was glad that it was Friday the next day. This week seemed to have been a mixture of people wanting her company as well as for lessons. She was pleased that she'd been invited to Suzann's party, but she didn't want to get involved with her.

She was thankful she was with Jim. Rosalyn was right; she was reading too much into everything and needed to calm down. She looked forward to getting home and would "feign" surprise. She'd been disappointed that Rosalyn was into sex parties, she couldn't seem to get away from the whole subject.

She changed at school and checked the rota as Arrabella caught her as she was leaving.

"Gavee, can you work Monday morning, we're one short and I need to do our payroll and the Director's on holidays."

"Ok, Arrabella, I'll come for nine, yes?"

"Thank you."

She drove home and as she opened the apartment door a waft of paella came towards her. The classical music played softly in the corner as Jim came out of the kitchen with a bottle of red in his hand.

"Perfect timing my beauty," as he planted a big kiss on her lips.

"Oh, what's this surprise?"

"Sit and we shall have dinner."

"Yes, I'll just freshen up," she said as she went to fluff her hair and place perfume on her throat and wrists as Jim served the platter of smoked salmon.

"What's going on here?"

"It's time I showed you my romantic side, that's all," he said as he pulled the chair out for her.

The meal was perfect as they talked about their day. She couldn't bring herself to ask about that file, but she knew of a roundabout way of bringing her ex-lover into the conversation.

"Saw Rosalyn today, she wants us to go out with them on Friday. I said Bar Tougana, is that ok? Maybe we could go to Banús; we haven't done that for ages."

"No, we haven't, you're right. I'll taxi in, you can leave the car at the town hall and then the four of us can get a cab later."

"Sounds good, what's this?" as Jim handed her an envelope.

She opened the envelope, and it was two train tickets to Barcelona, where they would join a Cruise ship for a Mediterranean five-day break.

"We need to get away," he whispered.

"Jim, it's fabulous," as she got up to embrace him. He lifted her to the sofa. He was greedy for her as he unbuckled his belt and sprung to life. His urgency was apparent as he moved deliberately inside her. She felt that something had changed... *"Away from what,"* she thought as he moved his hand over....

⋯⋯◄◊►⋯⋯

26

Monday at School

Rosalyn and Ben met Gaby outside the school as she walked them the short distance to Bar Tougana which was crammed with local people.

"I didn't realise this existed," shouted Ben above the chatter. The waiter ushered them to where Jim was already seated.

"Sweetheart just in time. Hi, you must be Ben and Rosalyn. I've ordered Paella and are you ok on some G and T's?"

"Great, thanks," said Ben shaking Jim's hand as they all sat in the corner, the flamenco music started as the chatter around them continued.

"You'd never have thought it."

"I know, Gaby's students brought her, and we've been coming ever since."

"It's great as it's only locals who know about it."

"He's busy all the time, very clever to hide the door," said Rosalyn.

"The atmospheres like a fiesta," grinned Ben as they continued to chat. Rosalyn and Gaby were in discussion about

the cruise that Jim had booked and there was excitement all around.

The Paella arrived and she wondered how he was going to react when Ben asked him about a swinger's party. He'd been shocked when she mentioned it after their love making on the sofa. Something wasn't right and she knew it was him. She'd looked at that file and there was a dossier about Jed and his activities. There was nothing scary; it mentioned bars, casinos, and restaurants. There was a photo of her in Harry's bar with him, but no other mention of her. She'd been disappointed and still hadn't had the courage to ask him, why he had a file on her ex? Furthermore, how on earth had he got hold of this file and from whom?

"Gaby, what do you say?"

"Sorry, Jim."

"I was suggesting we all go to Banús. I can show Ben and Rosalyn the nightclub they're looking for."

"You know of one?" she asked wondering who this Jim was becoming?"

"Are you going to come along?" asked Rosalyn.

"I don't think it's my thing, quite frankly," said Gaby frowning at Rosalyn as she knew what she thought, and she was pushing it in front of Jim.

"It will be a laugh Gaby, why not?" said Jim.

Her world was falling apart; this man who had saved her from all the promiscuity and seedy goings on was now suggesting a swinger's night out. She didn't know what to say.

"Let's find out what the joining criteria are, first."

"I don't mean us; I'll show Roslyn and Ben where it is, and they can join if they want. We haven't talked about it guys; we'll decide in our own time."

Gaby felt relieved as surely, he wasn't expecting her to join such a club.

"Of course, it's ok," said Ben. *"Ros and I have an arrangement; we swing once a month or so as it keeps our sex life alive. We wouldn't want to jeopardise your friendship because of our fetish."*

"No, it's ok, believe me we all love sex but if I'm going to put it about, I'd rather get paid for it," said Gaby sounding rather prudish but felt it right at that moment. She was not going to get carried away with this notion. She needed to talk to Jim about it and furthermore she needed to talk to Jim about Jim. She decided she would talk to him over the weekend.

Banús yet again was brimming with Arabs and a different type of tourist being early May. The yachts all bobbing at the quay side were busy with affluent families enjoying the warmth without the abundance of tourists. Sinatra's was out on its island and the Gin and Tonics were flowing. Tall men in dark glasses and suited bodyguards milled around with various sheiks. Glamorous women in high heels walked a foot behind them. The women were heavily guarded as they went from designer boutique to the next.

"They couldn't run, even if they wanted to," remarked Rosalyn as the four of them walked to the club entrance.

"You mean because of their high heels or because of their bodyguards," laughed Gaby as they all acknowledged her humour.

"Pearls," was situated in-between three designer boutiques; the side door of the entrance was next to an apartment block security gate and looked more of a prison gate than a club.

"Here it is," said Jim.

"I'll see if I can get joining info now as we're here," said Ben as he pressed the buzzer and waited.

Within ten minutes a big black man appeared and looked him up and down.

"Si?" he enquired.

"How can we join?"

"Enveetacion solamente Senior," and closed the door.

"Well, that's that then," said Ben, his curly blond hair falling over his eyes as he brushed it away and grabbed Ros's hand. *"Come on, let's get back to Sinatra's, we'll find a way. Thanks Jim once we're members we'll invite you."*

"Great stuff," said Gaby somewhat relieved.

The evening was balmy and throughout the entire night, she felt uncomfortable and had no idea why. She didn't say a word to him, but she felt as if she was being watched. She must stop looking at everyone as crooks. They went their separate ways after three o' clock as Ben had come across someone who was going to the club.

"Tell me Monday, I'll pop into the café to see you," whispered Gaby as Rosalyn merry with drink gave her a warm embrace.

"Yes, honey, see you then. I'll be at work from eleven."

"Ok, have a safe time guys."

They taxied home in silence, and she didn't want to ask him while she was feeling a bit drunk.

"Would you go then?" asked Jim as they got in the lift.

"Go where? You mean go swinging," as she leant on him as they got out of the lift, and he opened the door to their apartment.

"No," she said.

"I'm surprised."

"Why, whatever do you think of me?"

"Well, you've had two men going on at the same time, what's the difference?"

She stopped in her tracks and paused for a deep breath.

"Ok, something's wrong; I think we need to make coffee and talk."

She went into the kitchen; something was bugging him and what better time than the moment. He'd brought it up.

"Ok, what is it? Things haven't been particularly good around here since you've come back from Granada and since I've seen that file. You've probably left it out on purpose. What's going on? To answer your question, I'm not the swinger type, even though I've had a few lovers. That's entirely different to what you're suggesting. Have you changed your mind about us?

*I've agreed to be your wife, you're now off on a tangent about my past. I've told you everything. Maybe **you** need to tell me exactly what you're playing at?"*

"I wanted information on Jed in order I could track him down for you to end it. The other one, Nick is harder to find."

"I should hope so. He's an undercover police officer and you'll not find him."

"I'm sorry. I just want you to end it with them as I don't feel that I can move on entirely with you. They seem to be in the back of my mind, and I can see by you that they're on your mind too. Rosalyn saw him, she told me."

"Yes, but she knew him already, you don't know what he looked like before he disappeared let alone what he looks like now. It was fluke that she saw him you know that."

"Look, if you want to join the swingers we can."

"Actually, how the fuck do you know about it anyway?"

"Antonio is a member, but don't tell Isabella."

"For Christ's sake Jim. You're a member aren't you; you've been with Antonio and the Mayor. That's why you didn't want to get involved earlier?"

"Yes," said Jim as he got up and walked into the bedroom knowing he'd lost her now.

Gaby sat shocked at the dining table and digested this information. If that's all he was mulling over, she'd done far worse.

He sat on the bed with his back to her. She embraced him from behind and whispered,

"Why didn't you just tell them at dinner and help them join as you're a member. I would have understood. I hate lies Jim. It would have saved Ben all night canvassing the bars," as she laughed finding that funny.

"Maybe you'll need to enrol me then, have you actually participated?"

"Never I swear."

"I believe you honey."

They kissed and that original kiss was back on his lips; it was amazing how one knew when a kiss was different.

"Anyway," he said pulling away for a moment," *It's a ten-grand joining fee, I can't afford it."*

She shrieked out loud,

"Oo for rich friends, can I go as your guest?"

"Yes, one female and one male guest only at a time, so we can go if you like. Find out on Monday how Rosalyn and Ben got on. I didn't think they'd have that sort of funds, but hey what do we know. You're sworn to secrecy; it's a select club full of rich men, women, and celebs. Come here."

"I'm sorry I doubted you; I'd seen the file and thought the worst. Is that why you want to get away?"

"Yes, I need to regroup. Well, that's how I'm feeling to be perfectly honest. I just need to be alone with you. You still want to go, right?"

They embraced and got into bed and held each other for a while and Gaby could feel their closeness returning. They slept into the early hours, and she woke up to her fiancé making breakfast and the pungent aromas of fresh coffee.

"I'm being spoilt."

"No more than you deserve, move over, and breakfast in bed for my baby."

Monday morning came quickly as they made a pact. They wanted to be with each other and that was the end of the swinging discussion. Gaby understood his need for her to get closure with Jed and after their cruise, she would make contact and end it.

She had to be at work to cover Arrabella. She drove into Marbella with a renewed feeling of contentment and reassurance that she'd made the right choice. She walked from her parking area and was surprised to see Arrabella standing outside.

"Lost your keys?"

"What's wrong, OMG, what's happened?"

Arrabella was pale with shock as Gaby stood outside the school with her mouth wide open. The school had gone. The whole building was boarded up and the windows had white paper covering the glass. There was a notice outside the door with a telephone number which Arrabella was trying to call.

"There's no answer."

"What happened over the weekend, we were here Friday night?"

"It looks like they've taken everything," she said as she peered through a crack in the paper.

"Who? I don't believe it and its pay day, which is why we're in. The students will start arriving soon Arrabella, what are we going to do?"

"I know, they've all paid up front the next term too, which means they'll have lost three thousand euros each."

"Oh, my goodness, that's awful," said Gaby shocked.

"Look it says there's a meeting tonight at the conference centre. Someone will explain then. I'll see if Antonio is at work and ask his help. We're all owed a month's wages at least."

"I'll stay here and explain the students that none of us knew until this morning, ok? I'll see you at six at this place, si?"

"Yes, see you later."

She walked to her car, stunned, and called Jim.

27

Pearls.

He'd nearly lost the plot in Sinatra's earlier as he'd tried to keep his back to her all evening. It had been difficult once he'd seen who she was with. They were with a couple who were trying to get into Pearls and in the end, he'd no choice but to get Daisy to take them.

He hoped she wasn't going to accompany the couple, and he was relieved that they'd disappeared the minute the blonde bloke had announced that they'd found someone to invite them in.

He was surprised, she was with Antonio's new accountant, but more than that, he knew she was going to have to choose. He couldn't approach her as it would blow his cover. Miguel and Aleksey had turned up with their hookers and he made his mind focus and return to the job in hand.

He insisted they all went to Pearls earlier than usual as he didn't want Rosalyn to pick up on him. He was grateful that she seemed drunk, as they were about to go themselves. They slipped in as the three hookers placed their palms to the imprint on the inside door, no trace to them. Aleksey,

Miguel, and Armando nodded at their fellow undercover bouncer and walked in. There was one job to complete, and they'd be able to action it right here.

"***Pearl necklace***" was an exclusive club for the exceedingly powerful and rich unless your mate was the bouncer. The select joining fee alone was 10,000€ and a waiver of discretion, signed.

Your fingerprints had to be verified before you could become a permanent member. For a guest, the member had to pay 1.600 € each, per night, for them to get a taste.

Every female member was given a link chain which had a silver key to unlock the padlock from her neck. Once she entered the club, she would be handed her necklace for the evening. She would lock it and in turn place the silver key in the silver bowl which was kept at the desk.

The men would choose a key from the bowl. There was no number or label on any key to depict who it belonged in the room. Whichever key you chose; was the woman you were going to have fun with that evening.

The process could take all evening as Miguel discovered the week previously. He'd bought several drinks for several ladies to discover the key he'd picked belonged to Daisy, which Armand had found hilarious.

Once a couple had unlocked a padlock, they could either go away to one of the secluded rooms as a couple or wait for the foursome room to become available. The ladies could book either room in advance, or the chosen suitor would follow suit.

Champagne and tapas flowed throughout the night. Opium scented candles and the aroma of light drugs was apparent and available if anyone asked a discreet waiter. The glass coffee tables had lines of coke on some and others had glass bowls of condoms, discreet amongst the abundance of scented fresh flowers.

The waiters wore tight black swim shorts, and their bronze bodies were glowing from body oil. They worked in pairs with a waitress who was topless and wore the thinnest, tiniest thong one could imagine. The girls were also covered in tanned oil. They were as beautiful as the guests. To book a waiter, or waitress you had to slip them a purple envelope from the side table in the green room. These waiters could easily earn 5,000€ on a given evening.

Armand and his men had three waiters undercover along with the bouncer at the door. Armand needed to locate the Arab. They had decided they'd take them all down the same time. It was going to be risky but the whole of the Guardia along with the British were on schedule to scoop. One piece of the puzzle was needed, and neither could he, Aleksey or Miguel afford not to invite the Arab to the Masquerade party, which was the venue for the exchange.

He turned his head and buried it in Dolly's thick mane as Rosalyn and her husband walked past with a partner each towards the foursome rooms. Miguel tossed him a nod as the Arab in question had walked in with three girls, one was the red head, he'd seen at that villa in Mijas.

"Perfect," he thought as he went over to the Arab beckoning him for champagne and they ushered the party into the pink

room, where the waiter was pouring glasses of *Tattinger* in expectation.

***

Both Jim and Antonio were in a meeting as was Valentino and she decided to see Rosalyn at the café. She was stunned. She waved at Rosalyn who was serving customers, and she eventually came over with some coffee for her.

"You're not going to believe this," she said as Rosalyn was brimming to tell her news also.

"Give me five minutes and then I'll take my break."

"Ok."

Whilst she waited, she left a message for Eugenio, Isabella, José, and Mercedes. She knew that they'd all paid their next semester fees which was in the region of 2-3,000€ and they'd be furious. As they only came to her class on a Friday, they needed to know what had happened.

She also left a message for Jasmine as she would go in earlier the following day to see if she could take that full-time job. She guessed it was too late as she'd already turned her down twice, but there was no harm in asking.

Thankfully, with Jim's new position, it wasn't a crisis, and her nest egg hadn't been touched. It wasn't the point; she wanted to manage on her own two feet.

How could a business disappear overnight?

"What's happened?" said Rosalyn bringing a tray of drinks to their table.

"The school has gone."

254

"*What do you mean?*"

"*The school has disappeared; it's boarded up, computers gone for what we can see from outside. There's a notice to say there's a meeting tonight. The teachers haven't been paid, and the students have all paid in advance for their next three months, it's terrible.*"

"*Oh, my God, how awful. How can anyone do that?*"

"*Well, they've just did. Apparently, Eugenio's daughter, who is twenty got fired by text last week, it's just the way people seem to be.*"

"*But this is business, Gaby. They just can't close, disappear without notice.*"

"*They've just done that Ros; anyway, I'll go to the meeting tonight and find out more. I've tried to tell Jim but he's not answering my calls. What happened at the club?*"

"*Nick was there undercover, I didn't acknowledge him, thought it best not to. I was a bit drunk though but had a fun time; Ben's joining us this week.*"

"*Oh, my God! Did he participate, he is undercover? I do hope he finds me soon.*"

"*Look Gaby, he knew I was there, I acted drunk when I walked past him. He was with three men and those hookers we saw in Sinatra's, the other evening. I noticed them as they were incredibly attractive but drunk and high. I don't know if he participated, maybe you ought to join as you might get his key, then you could catch up with him, with Jim being none the wiser. Unless Jim wants a foursome of course and then you're in trouble gal,*" she laughed.

"You're funny, that's probably why I felt that someone was watching me all night, why didn't you say?"

"He's undercover and you don't want Jim to know who he is quite frankly."

"You're right, have you got the money then?"

"Yes, Ben's paying. It's actually 10,000€ a couple and he's into the selectiveness of it, no riff raff and all that!"

"Good for you, did you have sex with a new guy, tell me"

"Once you sign in, even as a guest you're given a necklace, well it's a silver chain necklace but you get the Pearl bit. Anyway, I put my silver key in the bowl straight away, they prefer it if you lock the chain at reception. Ben chose a key immediately, it was well orchestrated, the key belonged to an exotic flamenco dancer, she was hot, and an Arab had my key, he was equally hot. It was funny Gaby; he had the most piercing turquoise eyes for an Arab."

"Don't tell me his name was Abdul."

"Oh fuck, how do you know him?"

"He sold a house to my friend in Banús."

"Have you been there, then?"

"Certainly not, but Maud gave him head on the rug carpet in the new house she'd just bought in the middle of a party," giggled Gaby finding the scene quite funny.

"It's a small world."

"It's certainly is," sighed Gaby not knowing if she liked it suddenly.

"Was he good?" she whispered not being able to contain herself, she needed to know.

"See, you're interested?"

"No forget I asked."

"He was more interested in Ben; I'll have you know."

"Never!"

"Yes, Ben was out of his depth but between Abdul down on him and me on his chest, he was explosive and has been like a rampant rabbit since. Have you used the body gels they have there?

"Rosalyn, I haven't been there, and no what gels do they have?" *"They really make you feel drowsy; we were together most of the night, the four of us."*

"What about the hot exotic dancer?"

"She passed out on the bed, she was so drunk, but managed to join in later," and she winked. *"I've got to go; shall we meet up at Bar Tougana Friday night? You can fill me in on the School fiasco. If there's anything you want, I'm here all week."*

"Yes, see you then," as her mobile started to ring, and it didn't stop for an hour as she talked to her friends about the school closure and the meeting to be held at six.

She drove back to Marbella to catch Jasmine as although she was teaching at her school the next day, she wanted to know if there were any further lessons free.

"I'm glad to see you, Gaby. I'm a teacher short for the last hour, could you?

"Of course I can, which class is it?

*"It's Ivan's class actually; they're on "**professions and work.**""*

"Ok, I can do that, the school has gone. "

"What do you mean, Gaby?"

"I'll tell you after class, " as Ivan cheered as she entered his class, he seemed to like her a lot.

The forty-five minutes flew past, and the class had several professions and work on the board as they continued to answer the clues Gaby gave them.

"Who is the person who looks after you, if you're sick and you're in hospital?"

"I know, I know," shouted Ivan.

"What is it; write on the board, Ivan. "

Ivan scrambled to the front of the class and wrote "NUHRSE" on the board.

"Well done, who else looks after people?"

"I know," said another as she came up and wrote DOCHTOHR" on the board."

"Very good. "

"Anyone with a new profession we haven't got on the list. "

"My Mums job isn't on the list. "

"What does she do?" asked his friend sitting next to him.

Gaby cringed as this was going to be tricky as Ivan looked at her and he said,

"She makes things in the kitchen. "

"Come on class, ask Ivan more questions."

"Is she making brownies?" asked Margarita.

"No, she's breaking white stuff in bowls."

"Ah, is she mixing flour and making a cake?" asked Gaby as the penny dropped.

"Yes, but it's not a cake."

"She is a "baker," who can spell baker and write it on the blackboard."

"Well done, Petre, ok class that's it, home for lunch."

Jasmine came in and Ivan again needed a lift home.

"I can take him. I only wanted to tell you that the school has closed and maybe we can talk tomorrow. I have to go to the meeting at six to find out what's going on."

"Oh, my God, that's awful."

"I know, I'll take Ivan home, I've got time."

In the car, Gaby had to ask,

"What exactly is your mum doing Ivan, you might as well tell me, sweetheart."

"She is making pouches of drugs to sell."

"What's with the baking stuff?"

"I help her weigh it out by ounce and she puts crushed pain killers with it, so the druggie doesn't come around with a headache."

"Why does she do that?"

"They think it's good and buy more. Don't tell mum I've told you."

"Of course, not, what else does she do?"

"She copied people's passports and driving licences for money. I go every summer on the beach, that's my job."

"Ivan, I don't want to get involved, we'll keep this conversation to just us."

She pulled up outside the villa,

"Are you coming to the party?

"No, I'm away with Jim on holiday, next time."

"Are you coming in?"

"No, I've got an appointment in Marbella at six. Say hi to your mum for me."

She drove down the hill at a rapid pace and told herself that she wouldn't take Ivan home again, she wasn't comfortable. She always had an uneasy feeling every time she was there. No wonder. As she drove back to the apartment, she realised that Jim hadn't been in touch, even though she'd texted him several times.

"That's unusual for him," she thought as she parked up and made her way to the apartment. What a morning. The school was closed, Ivan's mum was dealing, and her estranged fiancé Nick had been spotted undercover in a swinger's private club, charming.

28

Malaga

The apartment was in a chaotic state and Jim had obviously been home. There were filled ashtrays on the dining room table and six lager glasses, bottles and tapa stuff piled in the kitchen. He was obviously tied up with something. Why didn't they go to the bar opposite the office? *Hum* she thought, whatever they had to discuss was obviously sensitive.

She was collecting Eugenio from the sardine restaurant, and they were going to Bar Tougana to discuss the schools' closure. She showered and changed and went into his room and that business card was out on the side again. The Black Beret details that José and Eugenio had checked out. A slight unease went through her, but she scribbled him a note and told him where she would be later.

She'd cleared up, took a blank notebook to make notes, and decided to call Sergio, Señora Izzie's son. She imagined she would need a Lawyer to get the money she was owed. She took his card from her bowl of business cards and left. She didn't know why, but she picked up the Guardia card and placed it in her purse.

Eugenio was waiting and his command of English was now exceptional as was all her advanced class. She was horrified when he told her, that he'd paid 3,500€ for the next two terms. She felt awful as she explained that she hadn't been paid and no-one had prior knowledge of what had happened, not even Arrabella.

Bar Tougana was full of students and all-day teachers apart from the Director of English who was conveniently on holiday. Yet no one knew anything. The atmosphere in the bar was tense and Sergio arrived at cheers from José and Mercedes who knew him.

"Oh good, Sergio can act for us all," said Mercedes as he beamed at them.

"Ok, I'll represent you, but let's see what happens at the meeting and we'll organise a claim later.

"The landlady has given us this round of drinks. She just said, we spend enough money here."

"That's typical of the Spanish support, how lovely," said Gaby as José handed out the drinks.

They walked to the conference centre and Sergio had briefed them. Having found out how much money her students had spent in advance lessons along with her wages, he had over 40,000€ missing from Gaby's class alone.

"Isabella isn't here," frowned Gaby as she checked her phone and realised that Jim hadn't been in touch.

"Maybe she's gone ahead," said José.

"Yes of course, she may be there already."

The conference centre housed two thousand seats and when they arrived the place was nearly full of irate students. On the stage was a long table and three men in suits sat and one was on the phone. At dead on six, the one on the phone put his hand up for everyone to be quiet.

"Por favor."

The gentleman spoke in rapid Spanish, and she didn't understand a word and was grateful that Sergio was sitting next to her. There was no sign of Isabella, as she tried to concentrate on the meeting. As a heated debate ensued, she found her mind wandering to recent events and Jim. Even though the atmosphere in the conference centre was tense, it wasn't the students' anger, which was upsetting her. She knew that her intuition wasn't far wrong and tried to work out what was bothering her.

"Gavee."

"Sorry, Sergio, I was miles away."

"Come on, we need to get to the bar, and I'll explain."

"Ok."

They made their way back and Maria their host had a line of shots lined up again on the bar as they all grabbed one and sat together in the corner.

"You must all complete these forms. Gavee, you've got to complete this extra form. We need to go to Malaga on Monday to file in front of the employment tribunal Lawyer. I'm acting for you all, but you must come with me to sign the official documents at the Notario, as your English teacher and not a student."

"Ok."

Everyone read and completed the papers. She still hadn't heard from Jim, and it was beginning to bother her. Isabella hadn't responded to her texts. She shrugged and ignored the warning knot in her stomach. She'd pop over to Isabella's on the way home, which would make her feel better.

She couldn't drink but her fellow students decided it was time to drown their sorrows as they'd all lost over three thousand Euros. It was going to take time for the company solicitors to unravel where the Director of English and his business partners had disappeared, seemingly with the money. She wanted to drive to Isabella's and then home. By Sergio's calculation, not only was she owed a months' salary, but she was also owed unpaid holidays, and his estimation was around 2,000€. He was going to place a claim for this sum on her behalf, and she realised that she'd taken an eye off her personal affairs.

They parted much later than she'd anticipated as she checked the time as she got to her car. She jumped in the car quickly and locked herself in as she suddenly felt scared. It was only ten o' clock: she called Isabella from the car to check she could visit as she scanned her rear mirror as she waited for her to answer.

"Gavee, it's Antonio, he's...."

"Muy despacio, Isabella. Tranquilo...Shall come to your house?" "Si, si Gaveee gratis, yes, thank you..."

Isabella was obviously distressed as Gaby started her engine and made her way to her villa. She wondered what had happened to Antonio. She hoped something hadn't happened to Jim as well. She turned right towards the mountains of Marbella as their villa was at the top of a long winding road. The views were breath taking and the lights of Marbella below looked like a sprinkling of stars as she turned into Isabella's gated drive.

Her maid was distressed as she ushered Gaby into the living room which was littered with papers and her three boys were in their pyjamas all upset.

"Whatever's happened?"

"It's Antonio; Jim is with him, he said to tell you, he's gone to the hospital."

"What happened?"

"Antonio was stabbed outside the villa an hour ago, Gavee, Jim was there. He'd gone to open the gate as it's stuck, the box is broken and as Jim's back wasn't looking, yes, someone crept up to the car and stabbed him through the window...........He's alive, I'm not sure if he's, what you say out the woods?"

"Oh, my god?"

"Jim came running here and called the paramedics, it's terrible. Jim managed to help the bleeding with his jacket, the boys saw him, was all upset."

"What time did this happen?"

"Hour ago, not long. We've had no signals. Have had four messages from you. We've had problems with phones all day."

"Ok," she said relieved that Jim hadn't called for this reason. She was getting either psychic or paranoid.

"What are you meant to do next?"

"Wait for Jim to call. He said for you to go home if you called, and he'll get a taxi back."

"Isabella, I'll wait with you until he calls and then we'll know he's all right. If you want to go to the hospital, I'll stay with the children."

"No, no. Antonio wants me to stay here. Can we have some tea and then you can talk to Jim when he calls."

An hour later, Isabella's mobile rung and Jim was relaying the diagnosis to her. Isabella nodded at Gaby as she responded,

"Gavee is here Jim talk to her. Thank you for helping. Yes, I'll see him in the morning," as she passed her phone to Gaby.

"You, ok?" she said not knowing what to say.

"Antonio is fine, it's a superficial stabbing. We haven't had signal all day. What's this about the school? I've had five messages from you all at once."

"Tell you later, as long as you're all right. Do you want me to get you?"

"No, I'll jump in a cab. I've got to give Valentino some files from Antonio. He's on his way here; I'll be home within the hour."

"Ok, I'll go now, Isabella is fine."

She drove down the winding road of the mountain in deep thought and wondered why someone had attempted to kill Antonio. It was too close to home for her liking, and she wondered how Jim felt. Furthermore, Jim had been with him at the time. She was deep in thought as she came to a crossroads on the mountain side and as she turned right a black van pulled out in front blocking her way. Before she had a moment to swerve or brake another black car skidded to a halt to her left and she was totally penned in. As she looked each way to see what was going on, her car door opened, and a hand went over her mouth as everything went black......

***

"What time did she leave you?"

"About midnight, why what's the problem, Jim?"

"She's not home; she's had an accident or something. Don't worry, I'll find her."

Jim put the phone in his pocket. What a day, where the hell was she? He paced the apartment it was two o' clock in the morning and there was no answer on her mobile and she hadn't parked the car. He needed to make some calls and then go and look for her.

Things were getting out of hand. Antonio had been delivered a warning. He wondered if he was next. He wasn't exactly sure about anything and then he paled as he sat in the apartment waiting a call from his Guardia buddy. They hadn't got to Gaby as a warning to him, surely not. She'd been in the wrong place at the wrong time. The sooner they went on holiday, the better. He felt sick as he called his friend again, he couldn't wait no longer.

"I'll be there now."

He charged out of the apartment as the car was waiting for him. He jumped in and they drove him to the edge of the mountain road where Gaby's car had been discovered. The driver door open, her bag on the seat, the keys in the ignition, but no Gaby.

"Oh fuck, they've taken her, why for fucks' sake, she's innocent. Who's taken her, Rodriguez, Marcello?"

"We don't know."

"For fuck's sake find her."

"Drive the car to your place, we'll come to you."

"Gracias, Marcello."

He drove the car and parked it quickly as the Guardia followed him. The apartment was full of green jackets as the word had got out. He went through her bag and there was nothing inside to give them a clue.

"Any ideas?" he asked as Aleksey walked in keeping his composure, knowing his boss couldn't know what he'd done. The Guardia were in deep conversation and Jim made a few calls.

"O.K., we will start searching, the school is closed, and where else she goes?" asked Aleksey knowing Rodriguez and Marcello mustn't pick up on his demeanour.

"I'll write down the places for you."

"We wait, as you can't declare her missing until the morning."

"Right," said Jim feeling sick and knowing this was partially his fault. He grabbed the brandy bottle and Marcello and Rodriguez stayed as Aleksey and his three men disappeared.

◆

29

Decisions

She stirred and wondered what had happened to her and where was she as she tried to move her head. It was thumping, she could hardly open her eyes as she squinted and tried to get her bearings. She patted herself slowly and she was intact at least. Her clothes were dishevelled but she had everything on. She sighed as she tried to remember what he'd said. She'd been thrown in the back of a van, and they'd brought her here. Wherever here was.

She was bruised and drugged. She was on the floor inside an apartment and there was no sign of anyone. She laid there waiting for the nausea feeling to subside. What he said, she couldn't remember, but he'd warned her about something as she'd blacked out the second time. She tried to concentrate and listen for any noises outside but fell asleep again, the sleeping draft still effective.

***

Jim was beside himself. Whatever had happened, he felt responsible. The Guardia came to the apartment and after a few huddled conversations they left with Jim in one car to locate her. They drove to Nueva Andalucía; they knew where they were heading. Jim's heart was in his mouth as he remembered that Ryan Marshall had been held in Nueva Andalucía before he was murdered. He knew Aleksey's cover couldn't be compromised but no one knew the connection.

What on earth had Gaby done to get abducted? Why had they targeted her? He couldn't fathom this out as he was told

269

to stay in the car. The Red Berets disappeared on foot around several privately gated villas on the top of the urbanisation. His mobile went off and he answered in Spanish.

"Digame, Isabella, Como Antonio?"

"Muy mechor, aqui a la casa. El quiero et tu, Jim."

"Ok, pero problema con Gaby, possible rapto/possible abduction"

"No!!!!!"

"Si, I'll come over later Isabella, the Guardia think they know where she is."

"Ok, Jim call me."

It had to be her past he thought and tried to think why this was happening. He wondered if it was Jed or that Nick. Jed probably, especially as he'd got the file. Maybe it was his entire fault. Nick was the undercover guy, and he was on a legitimate mission. Jed was the Italian thug. All of this scrambled his mind. She had come to the coast to find her true love and then he'd come along; and he'd fallen in love with her.

He felt worse as he thought this as two men carried a body out of the gates, covered in a sheet. Gaby was shoved in the back with Jim, and they sped away to Antonio's villa.

He felt her pulse, it was weak. She looked frail and he felt a wave of love towards her as she lay there semi-conscious. He placed his arms around her. Her black locks were stuck to her face, and she smelled sweet and sticky. Something was unusual for them to be going to Antonio's villa and not the hospital. The paramedics were already on the premises as they took her into the ambulance to check her over.

"What's happening?"

"Antonio's inside, see him. We'll take care of her and bring her in when she comes around," said the paramedic.

Rodriguez and Marcello, the two Guardia's stayed within the perimeter and Jim went inside. He needed to know why his future wife had been a victim. It would be interesting to hear what Antonio had to say on the matter. He walked into the living room as Isabella greeted him. Antonio was laid on the double sofa, heavily bandaged but propped up and drinking tea.

"Antonio, how're you feeling?

"Uncomfortable, what's the word."

"Sore," said Jim nodding.

"Yes, I was lucky."

"Who was it?"

"Not sure, but I'm making enemies, no? Because of my friends with Gil. It's the project we're working on; I think someone else wants the deal. The bid is between two people, and I represent one of them."

"What has this tender to do with Gaby, for Christ's sake Antonio?"

"A warning about you and me maybe, I don't know. Has she said anything yet?"

"She's out of it in the ambulance. Why isn't she at the hospital? Are you telling me everything? Actually Antonio, I don't want to know. I suggest you get better; I'll take Gaby away for our cruise. We can discuss this on my return."

"Jim, I've done nothing wrong, I think if I am out of the frame then the other client will win the job. Gil Y Gil is in the middle of it and because he's my client, I'm in the middle of it."

"It sounds terribly confusing; I don't want to get involved. I'll take Gaby home and I'll talk to you next week."

He left annoyed by all of it and knew he needed to salvage a fragile situation. He was beginning to feel fraught with concern as he approached the ambulance as one of the paramedics came out of the back.

"Is she, all right?"

"She must have complete resting."

"No problem, I'll take her home."

"No, we drive to your apartment and take her on stretcher."

"Oh, my god, she's still not conscious?"

"Not really. I've orders to take her to your place."

"Yes, I'll come in the ambulance with her. Let's go."

Marcello nodded as Rodriguez opened the villa gate and followed them down the hill towards Estepona. Jim was mortified as he sat holding her limp hand. They'd even turned on the silent blue light. This meant they could get her home sooner. Jim guessed they needed to get off the grid. They were authentic paramedics but on Antonio's books as well as the hospital. He couldn't quite grasp how many things were not what they seemed. He held Gaby's hand as they sped along the carreterra as Jim made a few poignant decisions.

He wasn't expecting more Guardia around the apartment block and on mass. The paramedics brought Gaby to the apartment and placed her in bed. They acknowledged Rodríguez and Marcello on their way out and nodded at their boss who walked in.

"What's the update?" asked Aleksey wanting to make sure he hadn't roughed her up too much. He'd got too fond of his two undercover mates and keeping this woman away from danger was more important, as Armand had eventually told them, who she was. *"Find out what happened and tell me. We need to know what they said to her. They'll have given her a message, call me on this number and leave the code. She's involved whether she likes it or not."*

"Yes of course," said Jim very clearly.

Aleksey left and knew that Jim must never find out, he may have compromised the whole undercover operation. His allegiance to Armand and Miguel had to be kept under control. However, they needed her safe and out of the way. He disappeared as the heist was imminent.

Jim checked on her. Her hair matted but away from her face as she slept off the chloroform she'd been subjected. The paramedic had warned him that she might be drowsy for a few more hours. She'd be shocked and scared. Whatever threat she'd been given, he hoped she'd remember and tell him. Activities in Antonio's office were reaching boiling point, and he didn't want the love of his life subjected to illegal activity.

She was meant to be travelling to Malaga on Monday to register her tribunal case. Three days later they were going on their getaway cruise. He couldn't have timed it better.

He went to cook; he was a natural in the kitchen and he toyed his few dilemmas as he made her favourite soup. He'd lied to her; she'd been subjected to all sorts of bad behaviour. He knew she hadn't been exactly a saint, but then again, she was a free-spirited person and that's why he was attracted to her. He knew that deep down she was a person of good morals and she'd told him everything. If anyone had lied, it had been him. He pondered his dilemmas and didn't hear the patter of her feet on the marble floor as she stood in the doorway, leaning on the frame looking at him chopping coriander.

"*Hi,*" she said quietly.

"*Hey, what are you doing up?*" as he dropped the knife and went to embrace her.

She buried her head on his chest and the tears flowed as he stood holding her, his own eyes swelling as he tried to blink them back. They held each other as he let her cry, he didn't need to say any more.

Eventually she prised away from him, her eyes black with smudged old makeup and tears,

"*He said something to me…. and… I ca… a. nt remember.*"

"*Shh, it'll come back, don't worry. Do you want to sit with me, while we wait for the soup to finish?*"

She nodded and felt frightened.

"Come on, go, and sit and I'll be there in a minute. I'll make you a cup of tea and we can talk."

She went to sit, and he knew by how frail she looked, that she wouldn't be fit for Malaga. Without applying pressure, he needed to know, what had been said to her.

She knew he'd said something; but she couldn't make out what it was. All she remembered that he sounded Russian. She knew half the sentence, but it was the other half she couldn't quite recall. Something told her that she needed to remember everything before she told him. It was obvious, that Jim had friends in the Guardia, and this was before her abduction. She realised this was why she'd never met any of them, they were law enforcement. She sighed, she was confused and drowsy still. Once her memory came back, she would decide.

"I'll go with Sergio tomorrow love; I need to register my wages claim against Wall Street the same time as the others."

"Are you sure? I'll come with you if you want. I don't have to be anywhere in particular."

"No, I'll be fine, I've got today and tonight to rest, I'll be fine. Especially after some decent food by this great cook I know," she laughed feebly.

He smiled and kissed her cheek and went back to check on lunch. She was at least in high spirits, and he felt relieved.

"Let's sit and watch a film after lunch and then by tonight, you may remember what happened. You can tell me when you're ready."

"Of course, I know one of the guys was Russian."
"How's that?"

"Because he said to someone, don't shoot."

"Oh, My God, were they going to shoot you? How do you know Russian?"

"I don't know I had a sac over my head and was passing out, but I clearly heard it. We had a lesson during my tefl Teaching course, I know now why they gave us a lesson in Russian," she said weakly.

"Why?"

"Obviously, the whole country is owned by Russians...."

"Hmm," said Jim a bit concerned to hear her say this. He knew one thing, this was going to make or break them, especially as he'd still not come clean totally with her. A decision he needed to act upon on their five days away.

30

Cruise

"It's done, and they've picked her up already," said Aleksey as Miguel nodded at Armando.

"We told her, don't worry. What's up with this broad anyway, you've been fancying her all the time Armand? "She's my fucking fiancée, long story, don't even go there, both of you."

"Fucking hell, Armand, what you are playing at?" said Aleksey slightly alarmed with this fact. *"She's with that prick, he mustn't know it was me, mate. I was doing you a favour."*

"Yes, I know, leave it. You warned her, that's all I needed you to do, ok. She doesn't know who he is. It's just the way it's happened. Let's get on with the job, it's going to be a fucking nightmare to pull off, but we're in it now, up to our fucking necks. When's the shipment due, Miguel?"

***

She was still feeling fragile as Sergio collected her on Monday morning for the Malaga meeting. Jim thought that she ought to rest some more but she was insistent on going.

This money was owed, and she wanted to add weight to the industrial tribunal case with her colleagues.

Sergio was shocked, as Jim relayed to him what had happened.

"Gavee will be safe in me; we should return by evening."

"Thanks Sergio," said Jim.

"I'm fine honey, it'll be good for me to think about something else, might help me remember," she said as she kissed him tenderly on the mouth, to reassure him.

"Yes, ok. Let me know when you're on your way home."

"Ok."

In the car, Gaby wasn't sure where to start, she had so much to think about and wasn't sure if she should even tell Sergio. He was a lawyer and although he had taken this case, she believed he was a criminal lawyer. She needed someone to confide in. Sergio had also asked her to go through some English with him, whilst they were in the car. He wasn't charging her, for this reason. All the teachers and her students had personal arrangements with him.

"Shall we start some of the lesson you want Sergio. On the way, back from Malaga, I want to talk to you about something private, is that ok?"

"Of course, Gavee, no problem."

The road into Malaga wasn't busy considering it was summer, even though the children were on half days. June was always a warm month and the warmth from the sun was pleasant as Gaby had her window down. As they approached the city, they could see the citadels of the Alcazaba and the ruins of the Gibraltar in the distance and standing overlooking the city, remnants of the Moorish rule. They could also see the magnificent Renaissance Cathedral which was nicknamed *"La Manquita"* / *"One armed lady"* because its towers had surprisingly not been built.

They made their way to Calle Victoria to the offices of the tribunal lawyer. Purple bougainvillea were everywhere along with potted shrubs and gardens showing off colourful plants and flower displays. Ahead, they could see an ocean liner was docked as Malaga was a favourite stopping point for Americans. The deep blue sky helped Gaby relax and she was glad Sergio was with her as she would never have found the street, let alone the underground car park.

She sported flip flops and loose linen trousers as she couldn't face walking on cobbled streets in high heels feeling the way she did. Sergio was great company and his lesson of the "past perfect and continual sentences," had been a success. She admired the pots of geraniums around the streets as they made their way to *Cafe`Sidoli*, where they were meeting her colleagues.

"Ah good, you're all here," Sergio nodded as Arrabella hugged her.

Sergio started to speak in rapid Spanish as Gaby picked up on a few odd words. They walked to the building, which was opposite the Plaza D La Merced, where Pablo Ruiz Picasso was born. The building was now a foundation building for promoting his work and new painters in the area. The office was on the third floor and there were no lifts as Gaby chuckled. They all climbed the six flights of stairs as she struggled a little, she was quietly pleased that no one had picked up on her fragility.

They were ushered into the boardroom by a young receptionist and as they sat and Sergio sorted out his papers on the table, the door opened. A tall buxom woman appeared beaming at them, wearing orange hair. She caught Arrabella' expression and they quietly smiled.

This lawyer was around forty-five and she was as tall as she was broad, her heavy bosom stretching the floral print of the top she was wearing which was red and yellow. Gaby wondered if she was colour blind as she wanted to put her sunglasses on but thought better of it. Her booming voice was kind, but her black rimmed glasses made her look more masculine than official as she gathered the information from Sergio.

She was going to represent them all, and she made it clear that the whole business could take at least two years to sort. Sergio, since the conference had discovered the culprits who had embezzled the funds and wages. The Director of English had been one of the mentioned persons involved which suddenly shocked her. She realised that everyone seemed to be into something they shouldn't be. The students apparently would have to wait longer as each case would have to be heard separately when the time came.

She sighed with relief as later Sergio explained that she didn't have to attend a court hearing as he and the Orange lawyer could deal with all the claims in due course.

They would all get their money eventually and they went back to *Café Sidoli* to have a farewell drink as they were going their separate ways. Arrabella was returning to Madrid where she'd found work in a different school.

On their way home, Gaby texted Jim to inform him they were on their way.

"What do you want to discuss, Gavee?"

"I've got a problem Sergio; can I tell you?"

"Yes of course, what is it?" as he pulled on to the carreterra towards Estepona.

***

Jim had cooked dinner and hoped that she'd remembered what threat she'd been given from her abductors. He'd had several meetings with Antonio in her absence at his villa. Antonio was recovering, but even Jim could see how much effect the stabbing had had on him. He opened a Rioja, one of Gaby's favourites and looked at his watch and knew she wouldn't be too long.

He had felt responsible and couldn't wait for the two of them to get on this cruise. He'd propose again and ask her to set a date. He needed to keep her focussed. Yes, that would be an important thing to do. He'd like that. First, he would tell her...

The front door opened, and he went to greet her as she embraced him.

"I'm glad to be home, you've never seen anyone with orange hair until today, Jim. The tribunal lawyer's going to scare them

all into paying us," she laughed as she sat at the table as Jim poured her a glass of red.

"Go on, tell me."

She rambled on about her day and the lawyer with the orange hair, which she described in minute detail. He hoped that she had the same detail, about her abduction. She avoided talk of the incident, she didn't want to lie to him, but she didn't want to tell him either, not yet. Especially since she'd relayed it all to Sergio.

"Ohm, that was delicious, shall I wash up?"

"No, I've a better idea," as he went towards her and kissed her slowly on the mouth. She placed her arms round his neck and murmured in agreement as he carried her to the bedroom. They lay in each other's arms as she apologised for not responding, she knew why. Jim was resigned to a lot of reasons but made light of it.

"Hey, you need to pack a case, we leave after tomorrow for a five- day break and then, Gabriella Daly you'll be exhausted by the amount of time I'm going to ravish on you. Five whole days, and nights, you'd better rest up," he teased as she threw the pillow at him laughing.

***

They were on the train to Barcelona to meet the cruise ship and she decided she would tell him once on board. He knew that she'd remembered, as she was different, he wasn't stupid. It was also time to tell her and risk her annoyance at his deceit. He couldn't go on any longer as she'd been threatened. She'd got involved unbeknown to her and she was going to be livid. It was disturbing him more than he'd let on, that she hadn't yet told him.

Gaby had been advised by Sergio what to say and she would tell him soon, she wanted to enjoy the cruise, sunbathe, and have quality time with him. There were eight cruise terminals at Barcelona Port and Gaby's cruise took in the west of the Mediterranean and was a popular choice for newlyweds, hen and stag parties and couples who wanted to recharge their batteries. She'd got it in her mind that she hadn't packed enough clothes.

"I'm sure you've enough, your suitcase is heavier than mine," said Jim as he embraced and kissed her cheek.

"I can always go without for two days," she whispered pleased they were getting away.

The ship was full and once they'd found their cabin and unpacked their suitcases it was time for lunch, and she knew it was best to tell him there and then, get it over with.

"Come on; let's find one of these many restaurants."

"I'm never going to find my way back to this cabin on my own."

"You're not going to be on your own, so don't worry."

"Come on then, I'm ravenous," she laughed pulling him as they made their way round the many decks to find the cafeterias.

The seafood was exceptional as they devoured a platter, finding their appetite and Gaby suddenly wanted to drink.

"This is fabulous, thank you," she said raising her glass to him as he smiled back at her relaxed. *"I've remembered; shall I leave it until we get home?"*

"It's up to you, if you want to tell me, then it's done, and I can call the Guardia. We can forget about it and enjoy our holiday."

"Of course," she took a deep breath.

"There were three of them I think, but the first black van drove right across me, making me swerve and stop. Before I could sort myself out, the second black car appeared and blocked me in. Before I knew it, my door was opened, and a thick cloth was placed on my mouth covering much of my face. Next thing a sac was put over my head and I recall someone shouting, "don't shoot" in a Russian accent. I tried to wriggle free of the hand over my face, but I must have blacked out. I don't remember being dragged or carried to the van but in the van; they took the rag from my mouth. Someone said, **"Get away (from Jim/ him,) leave (him) now, you're in danger. leave (him). This is your first and last warning."** *I could hardly hear him as he told me this and he repeated it twice. I opened my eyes briefly, I was scared stiff, but they'd tied a sac or something on my head. I vaguely remember when they blocked me in that they were wearing black balaclava type hoods. The other guy didn't say anything, but someone hit me over the head with a long rifle or a pole and the one who drove the van had a PSM Pistol."*

"How do you know so much about Russian arms, honey? Can you describe them at all?"

"No, they were all in black, no skin showing that I remember, but they were insistent that I left right away. Our Russian lesson in Seville was all about Russian fire arms and security. I guess it was handy after all," she tried to smile as Jim's face was showing grave concern for her story.

"Are you sure that's what they said?"

"Yes, that's all I remember. You sound as if you know something I don't."

"No, of course not, I need to relay it to the Guardia, that's all. Do you think they meant me or Estepona, or both?"

"I've no idea Jim," said Gaby having omitted the precise detail as advised by Sergio.

"I'll tell them tomorrow, shall we go for a siesta then, young lady?" he said his eyes twinkling with apparent relief.

"That would be acceptable, young man," she laughed knowing he hadn't believed her.

Their lovemaking was full of pretence all week. She knew there was something in the warning, she'd been given. She pretended to be more passionate knowing his kiss had changed again. He was harbouring something from her, and it was time to eradicate the seed of doubt.

They sat on the balcony restaurant as the liner made its way back to Barcelona, their sun kissed bodies benefiting from five days in the sun. They ordered food and Jim got up as the restaurant was in full swing. The last evening seemed romantic as the three guitarists ambled round the room.

He knelt near her as she put her glass down not expecting this as she watched him take something out of his inner jacket pocket,

"Will you marry me again, Miss Daly?"

"Oh, Jim, what's this?" as she opened the box which adorned another beautiful ring.

Again, she hesitated,

"Why yes, I'll marry you again," as she held his hand and pulled him up as the restaurant staff started to applaud and the three guitarists strummed over, and everyone started to dance.

"It's beautiful; I'll wear it on the other finger."

"Shall we set a date?"

"Yes, but what's on your mind? I think you're holding something back and now is the time to tell me."

"Yes, you're right."

"Let me go to the bathroom and then you can tell me. Give me a second."

She was nervous, she knew there was something and Sergio was right to tell her, to be economical with the threat she'd been given. She had to play along, even though she had agreed again to marry him. What a mess she was making of it all. She nearly missed her footing on the step as she came down to the restaurant entrance from the bathroom as a suited man caught her from toppling over.

"Steady."

"Why thank you," she said as she grabbed the rail and looked up and gasped in horror.

She stared right into Jed's deep brown eyes and fled back to the restaurant in total disbelief and shock, knowing she couldn't tell Jim as this would cause a diversion from his confession......

31

Masquerade party

"Whatever's wrong?"

"I feel quite sick. It just came over me."

"Come on, let's get back to the cabin, you look as if you've seen a ghost!"

She nodded, she'd seen a ghost all right, more of a blast from the past and on their fucking cruise of all places! He held her arm firmly as she suddenly felt nauseous and light headed.

"Goodness, Gaby, let me carry you."

"No, I'll make it, I feel quite ill."

They got to their cabin, and she fell on the bed and curled up, feeling wretched. Of all the people! Jim was as white as she felt as he brought her a glass of water. The conversation he wanted to have, temporarily forgotten. She laid her head back on the pillow and he comforted her, holding her close. The silence was intimate and heart breaking at the same time. Somehow, she guessed that whatever he was going to say was bigger than her feeling faint. That dreadful ache had returned to her stomach and she'd no idea how to tackle the confused feelings she had.

"We can talk in the morning; we can cuddle up and sleep unless you want me to get the ship's doctor. I'm more than happy to fetch him, you did look quite ill earlier," he suggested as she nodded.

"No, I just need to rest, thanks. I've had a lovely time, Jim."

He helped her undress and put her to bed and got in beside her with his arms around her. She'd never felt so wretched in all her life. This man, the only man she had trusted for a long time had a secret. Her ex-lover had been on board the same cruise as she and there was no sign of her original fiancé re-surfacing. She'd been warned against this man, who cared for her, but by whom. She drifted off to sleep as she decided she would tell him in the morning.

The ship's crew were buzzing all over the ship as Gaby took an early morning walk round the deck, to clear her head. Jim was fast asleep, and she needed to think. Maybe the warning about him was indirectly something to do with what he wanted to tell her. It didn't matter, she would discuss this at breakfast and if it caused her grief at least they would be on their way home. She couldn't fathom what on earth was so bad or important, that he hadn't told her. It might have something to do with Antonio and his office as he was heavily involved, more than he'd admitted to her.

She half hoped that she'd see Jed on her morning walk as that would save her from tracking him down. If he'd seen her all week, he would know and somehow, she realised that was why he'd "bumped" into her. That was his way of telling her.

Convinced this was the case she walked back to the cabin with renewed energy. It was time to cast him aside.

Her mobile was ringing as she got back as Jim went to answer it as she opened the door. He acknowledged her as he spoke,

"Yes David, she's right here."

"David, the Estate Agent, for you."

"Great thanks. Hi David."

"Really, how fantastic, when can we view?"

"Ok, call me once you've a date. Thanks."

"David has two villas in my price range for us to look at, probably end of next week."

"That's fantastic, are you sure?"

"Yes of course, he's also got a townhouse in Casco Antigo, Marbella that I might like, we might like."

"If you are alright about this, how exciting."

"Good, our own home can't wait."

"When are we setting the date then?"

"Once you've told me what's on your mind, over breakfast."

"Come on then," he said light heartedly but was dreading it.

They walked arm in arm up the flight of steps to the restaurant where everyone was hustling and bustling about the place as they were about to dock. The cafeteria where breakfast was served was packed with people and the chatter was infectious.

"Seems as if everyone is excited about getting back to shore," said Jim as he guided her through the maze to an empty table, overlooking the sea towards land.

"Yes, it's been great Jim, a lovely idea. We did need a break; you were right."

"Are you feeling better now?"

"Yes, I …."

Before she could admit to the reason of feeling faint, a tall dark figure emerged in their sight and Jim looked at Gaby and he knew.

"Ah, I see, you must be Jed, what a coincidence," he said sarcastically looking at Gaby with a frown.

"Sorry, I've come to congratulate you on your engagement; the ship's captain told us all at dinner. I wish you all the best. I'll never bother you again."

Jed walked away and a tall dark-haired beauty joined him as they disappeared down the flight of stairs.

"That's why you fell faint then?"

"I bumped in to him on the stairs when I went to the toilet last night; I was totally shocked and didn't want to spoil the evening. It's done now; he's out of our life."

"Have you seen him this week at all?"

"No, last night was the first time. I wasn't even looking or thinking about him, why are you asking such a thing?"

"As you've been distant with me all week, even though you've agreed to marry me. I know you needed to remember what the abductor said, but what is it?"

"Whatever do you mean.? I don't like your tone. I thought you wanted to tell me something; it's you that's not being honest here. I've been honest from the start with you. Why don't you come clean and then we can discuss it? I've told you what I remember from that night, trouble is you don't believe me. Which begs me the question, why don't you believe me? What do you know?"

The ships' hooter sounded interrupting their near disagreement as she got up knowing Sergio had said she needed to adhere to the warning. Until Jim told her what was on his mind, she would be cautious. He grabbed her wrist before she left the table in despair,

"I only want to tell you something, to reassure you. It's no big deal; we can talk, once we get on the train, as we need to leave."

"Ok, that'll be great."

The ship docked and eventually they departed and made their way to the train station. The carriages were busy, and they managed to squeeze themselves in -between a party of German tourists who had an abundance of luggage amongst them. It was impossible to have a talk let alone a private one. Whatever it was, Jim was beginning to get fraught about it. He didn't believe her regarding Jed; the trust was slowly deteriorating. For a couple who had agreed to marry twice, this wasn't right. Whatever he was bothered about, it was serious. She also had time to think about the mess she was suddenly in, again. Someone had gone to a great deal of trouble to warn her. She would decide on the whole mess, once he'd told her what was bothering him.

As she digested this her mobile rung loud in the carriage as everyone turned. She mouthed an apology as Eugenio talked to her in rapid Spanish,

"Muy despacio Eugenio, tener problema?" as Jim picked up on her question.

"No! I don't think so, si Eugenio, este tardes, Bar Tougana."

"What's up?" whispered Jim in her ear.

"It's Antonio. Have you heard from him?"

Jim searched in his pocket for his mobile and there were no messages from anyone,

"No there's nothing, why what's happened?"

"Eugenio says there's Guardia crawling all over the town hall and all the staff have been ordered in to work tomorrow. He can't get hold of Antonio as Gil Y Gil, the Mayor is looking for him."

"Something's going down, what's it got to do with me?"

"I don't know. You're thick with him, that's why he's called probably, you can ask him yourself. Whatever is going down, I don't want to be near it."

"Now you're being paranoid, I'm sure Antonio's still resting up. Eugenio's forgotten; he was attacked just over a week ago."

"Yes, I know," she said as the train pulled in to Nerja station.

Jim drove faster than normal as Gaby sensed there was something else wrong and not this so-called thing, he needed to disclose. She was frustrated with the whole atmosphere and enough was enough. As they drove passed Marbella toward Estepona, she couldn't stand it any longer.

"Are you going to tell me, what's on your mind?" she asked as he looked ahead at the carreterra, concentrating with the tourist traffic, which was heavier than normal.

"It's no big deal, but I need to tell you......."

His mobile rung interrupting them and he handed it to Gaby to answer.

"Oh, Hi Isabella, yes, he's driving, are you ok?"

"Si, denada, no problema, possible trente, si gracias Isabella, no, no problema, ok."

"Antonio?"

"Yes, can you pop over to see him once we get home? I said thirty minutes, she sounds stressed."

"What's wrong then?"

"She didn't say."

"Ok, are you going to meet Eugenio, and I'll join you there?"
"Yes, drop me off at the Pirelli monument and then I'll walk to the bar. My car is at the town hall."

"You'll be a bit early?"

"No, I've just had a text from Ros, they're going there for an early one, and I need to catch up with them, so that'll work."

The apartment seemed strange when they got in and Gaby went to shower as Jim checked his messages as suddenly they were bouncing in. She disappeared not bothered anymore; she'd tell Ros about what happened and ask her advice. As she came out of the shower, she pulled her towel round as he knocked on the door as she opened it. She couldn't see him through the steam filled room as he held her by the towel and kissed her tenderly on the lips.

He untied the knot, and the towel fell to the floor as she gasped with surprise as this was sudden. They're lovemaking throughout the cruise, had not been intimate at all. He grabbed her neckline, fondled her nipples, and moved his fingers all over her touching all her sensitive spots. She kissed him back gently as she realised his buckle and zip were undone as she felt for him.

"I've missed you," he smothered into her neck and whispered loving comments in her ear as she felt the prickle of response sear through her. He knelt as she lowered herself and wrapped the towel round him. He held her tight as they moved in union. The quick, sharp, and intense reaction was sudden as he continued to kiss her with a tenderness she'd not experienced throughout the cruise. She cried out loud as he responded with her, and they fell to the floor holding on to each other.

"I think we both need a shower now," he smiled. She said nothing.

He dropped her at the Pirelli monument, and she waved him away. She walked to Bar Tougana in rapid steps and realised this was the first time, she been out alone since the abduction. She didn't feel very sure of herself and was glad when she got inside the bar and joined Rosalyn and Ben.

"How was the cruise?" asked Ros as Ben went to get her a Gin & Tonic.

"Great for recovering after an abduction."

"You what?"

Gaby relayed the past events to her as Rosalyn went quite pale.

"Wait for Ben to hear this, this is dreadful."

"What's dreadful?" as he gave Gaby an exceptionally large Gin & Tonic as if he'd read her mind as she'd come through the door.

"I'll start again; I was abducted and threatened last week. Jim then took me on the cruise; you'll never believe who was on it?"

"Who, but hey hold on, who abducted you and what was the threat?"

"Promise, this is between us."

"Yes of course."

"The guy with a thick Russian accent told me to stay away from Jim and to leave right away."

"Never, why?"

"You tell me."

"Did you check him out Gaby before you agreed to live with him?"

"*Yes, Ben. I've called his office for a fictitious quote for business accounts, and it all seems legitimate. The website looks genuine; I don't think there's anything to worry about.*"

"*There must be, someone has warned you off, for Christ's sake. We need to find out who and why and what even,*" said Ben quite aerated by this news.

"*Have you tackled him about it?*"

"*No Ros, I told him that all I remember is that I've got to leave, but he knows I haven't told him everything. Also, he wants to tell me something and you're not going to believe this. As he was about to tell me Jed turns up at our breakfast table. He congratulates us on our engagement as Jim proposed the night before in the restaurant, so they must have seen us.*"

"*Oh, my God, what the fuck was he doing on the cruise?*"

"*I don't know but at least he knows about us and won't bother me again. He was with wife; I was right to let him go.*"

"*One down, one to go then.*"

"*Gosh, that's what Jim said.*"

"*Maybe he's found Nick and doesn't know how to tell you.*"

"*Yes, I've thought that I've no idea what's going on and who told me to leave Jim right away. It's still a bit blurry. This coast is so corrupted it's unbelievable, corrupt with crime and everything else,*"

Ros chortled and said,

"*Talking of everything else, fancy coming to Pearls with us later as we're up for some loving?*"

"*There's a masquerade party happening up in Estepona, we could always go there instead,*" said Ben.

"*I might just do both with you,*" she laughed as she saw Eugenio come in with José. "*By the way, Dave has found some properties for me to look at next week, isn't that exciting.*"

"*You need to sort Jim out before you buy anything with him,*" said Ben. "*Let's try and do some digging this week.*"

"*For Christ's sake, don't let on you know what the abductor said, I couldn't remember right?*"

"*Hey, don't worry, tranquilo,*" said Ben.

"*I'll catch up with these two and then join you. Don't go without me, Jim's on his way in a bit, we can decide then.*"

"*Eugenio, José, Como estas?*"

"*Bien Gavee, tiener vacaciones muy Bonita, si?*"

"*Si Eugenio, what's wrong, you sounded worried over the phone. Tell me?*" as the three of them sat at a corner table.

32

Confusion

"When do you leave for Granada, José? Bet you can't wait to go. Is Margarita coming down before you leave?"

"Yes, there's only three more weeks and I'll be home, a married man, it's happening quick."

"Are you going to get us all together, as we don't want to lose touch, just because the school is closed," suggested Gaby as she was going to miss him.

"Yes, I'm organising a party next Friday night. Can you tell Isabella, I think Margarita will come, it will be her hen's night too, yes?"

"Normally, hens and stags have separate parties but as you're leaving, you're probably sensible to have one party. I'm glad we'll see her before you marry. Has your replacement arrived at the bank?"

"Monday, it's a lady. Placido's replacement is a lady too, it's all change for everyone."

"At least you've got a good transfer José, I'll come to visit Granada and come and see you."

"*Yes, that will be good.*"

"*Eugenio, what's wrong, is your wife all right?*"

"*Yes, she's recovered, yes?*"

"*Recovering.*"

"*Oh right, yes, she's recovering well, Gavee. You can start her lessons again next week if you want.*"

"*Yes, I'll call her. What's happening at the town hall?*"

"*Is Jim coming here?*"

"*Yes, he's gone to check on Antonio and then he'll be with us, what's wrong, or do you want to wait for him? Before you tell me, I was abducted and threatened over a week ago. They told me to leave Jim, any ideas why?*"

"*Gavee, that's terrible, is it something to do with Antonio's stabbing?*"

"*I'm not sure if it's linked. Jim is the only person that's linked to Antonio and me. I've no idea what to do!*"

"*Does he know?*"

"*No, I've said that the threat mentioned I must leave. What do you think?*"

"*I've no idea; we wanted to ask Jim if he knew why the Mayor has asked us in on Saturday and if there's something wrong?*"

"*Because he works for Antonio's office?*"

"*Yes, and as Antonio is a bit recovering as you say, we didn't want to bother Isabella.*"

"*He's with Antonio as we speak, Eugenio. He knows you're waiting for him. We'll give him another hour and then I'll call him.*"

"Thank you."

"Drinks everyone, come and sit with Ros and Ben, it's getting a bit crowded in this corner."

An hour of chatter and general conversation and suddenly Gaby's mobile sprung into life. She looked at it and mouthed to Eugenio,

"It's Jim. Hi sweetheart, everything ok?"

"Something's happening here with Antonio. I'm doing some work for him and the Mayor. I can't make it, I'm sorry honey. I'll see you at home tonight, but I've no idea when. Make sure you get a cab home, ok."

"Don't worry, I'll tell Eugenio."

"Ok, Ciao."

"What's happening with the Mayor, that they need Jim?" asked Ben.

"He's an accountant; maybe he's sorting paperwork for you Eugenio and the staff at the town hall for tomorrow. I've no idea."

"We've got a huge bid, how you say, tender happening right now, which will bring in eight million to Marbella but the capital the winning contractor has to find is two million and prove it. The deadline is Monday," said Eugenio. *"Maybe it's all about this bid."*

"Why is the Mayor bidding, is he allowed?"

"No, he can't bid but his company can if they have the funds in place on Monday. The tender panel sits in the afternoon.

We've got Guardia booked for the whole week, until the decision is made."

"Gosh, that's it then, they're in the middle of helping the Mayor finish his bid."

"Why do they want us in?"

"You'll have to ask them tomorrow, Eugenio, we're only guessing, but this seems to make sense."

"Gaby, we're going to Pearls, fancy joining us as a guest, you don't have to participate."

"Do you know, I think I will, I'm intrigued by it and Jim's a member did I tell you."

"No!" everyone round the table said together.

"Yes, I was shocked too, but he claims it's because of Antonio."

"Gavee be careful," said José as he got up to leave.

"Yes, call me, but José is right, be careful as Jim said something's' happening."

The two Spanish men left chattering about the latest revelation about Jim as Ben interrupted her thoughts.

"Come on, you're coming with us. Jim's working and you need some fun, we'll look after you."

"I'll tell him; I'm coming with you to Pearls."

"No, I wouldn't bother, we all need to think if he's kosher, something doesn't add up."

"What do you mean," said Gaby alarmed at Ben's sudden comment as they hailed a taxi outside the bar for Banús.

"Where's your car, by the way?"

"Marbella town hall car park, it's been there over a week," she said as the taxi pulled up.

"Good old Eugenio."

"Yes, I'll go and get it tomorrow."

"You can spy and see what's going on," said Ben laughing as they all clambered in to the cab.

***

Puerto Banús was as usual jammed packed with tourists and plentiful of Arabs, glamorous women and men in black suits wearing Ray bans, even though it was midnight. **"*Pearls*"** opened its doors at 1am, and the three of them went to Sinatra's to enjoy a few large Gin & Tonics. The relaxing sound of the acoustic guitar in the background along with a warm breeze, people laughing and looking bronzed from the days sunbathing helped anyone forget their troubles or in Gaby's mind, that re-occurring niggle.

The waiters topped them up and she was in the mood to drink. She suddenly felt out of sorts, and she was going to have a bit of fun. They spent the hour discussing Jim, which was troubling her. The Cocktails were slipping down her throat faster than usual as Ben summoned the waiter yet again for more top ups.

"I don't know what to say, he wants to tell me something, but he keeps getting interrupted with one thing and another. He feels I need to know. I've no idea what that could be, Ben."

"Maybe once he helps Antonio sort out that tender, he'll tell you."

"Maybe we mustn't cast judgement until he does," said Rosalyn.

"I agree, let's wait, I don't want to talk about it anymore, if you don't mind."

Ben and Rosalyn agreed, and they made their way to Pearls.

"Gaby hi. Glad I've seen you."

"Dave hi, you, ok?"

"Yes, we can view those properties Monday?"

"That's great Dave, I'll call you Monday morning or shall we meet at Nueva?"

"Yes, meet there, have a good evening."

"Who's he?" asked Ben as they walked towards Pearls.

"He's looking at properties for me; he's found three in my budget."

"That's great news, come on we can celebrate some more in here, at least the booze is free."

"I should bloody well think so, the cost of being fucking members," said Ben under his breath as the girls laughed and followed him up the stairs once his palm print had been accepted.

Rosalyn placed the necklace round her neck as Ben was paying Gaby's guest fee. Gaby felt quite merry and nodded at the receptionist who handed her a necklace as Ben raised his eyebrows.

"You are sure, you don't have to."

"Actually, I want to and don't ask me why."

"Ok, but you can't change your mind or leave with it on."

"Yes, Jim explained come on let's get a drink."

They went into the green room which was already standing room only. A collection of bronzed waiters moved around with trays of Cava and Sangria as Gaby grabbed a glass. The place was buzzing, and the aroma of oils and incense seemed to intensify with each sip of her drink.

"It's packed in here, let's go to the purple room and mingle in there" said Ros as Ben had his silver key already to find the owner. *"Ben's not wasting time tonight,"* she whispered to Gaby. Ben started chatting up a red head asking permission to try her lock. It didn't open as Ben smiled and came back to the girls.

"Anyone tried your locks yet?"

"No, we've only been here two minutes, give the guys a chance to admire us," laughed Rosalyn as they giggled.

"Hello Gaby, didn't know you were a member, how are you?" *"Hi Abdul, good to see you, I'm great thanks,"* as she accepted a glass of cava from him.

"Do you want to unlock me?" she asked staring sultry into his turquoise blue contacts as he smiled at her and tried her padlock.

It didn't open and Gaby sighed with relief beneath her smile, what the fuck was she playing at? She couldn't leave without someone opening her fucking necklace and she wished whoever he was, he needed to hurry up, she didn't want to be here after all.

"Gaby, have another drink, look Bens' pulled," said Rosalyn as she tugged her dress to make her look as Ben escorted a lady towards them. He wanted a foursome and wanted Ros's key holder to appear.

The drinks flowed as Ben was flirting with the Swedish girl, and Rosalyn didn't seem fazed by it. Gaby knew they were now acting this part, and she understood the kicks they got.

"I'm going to the bathroom; I'll be back in a minute."

"Ok, honey, don't be long, we need to find our suitors."

"Hum, yes, ok."

The corridor was long to the bathroom and both rooms were fronted by an escort dressed as scantily as the waiters, leaving nothing to the imagination.

"Do you need assistance ma'am?"

"No, I'll be fine thanks."

The escort let her inside and she fled to the loo wanting to be sick! Several minutes later, she emerged feeling sober. She re-applied her makeup and decided there must be a way to get rid of the necklace without participating. She gave the girl outside a few Euros as she made her way back to the purple room, passing the red room on her way. She froze as she stood outside the doorway as the aroma of drugs filled the air along with smoke from Cuban cigars, making her squint, but there he was.

Jim was on the sofa with three women and Antonio, the Mayor opposite all laughing and joking. He had a silver key in his hand as he spoke to one of the girls who held his drink. She stood there horrified as she watched him try all the padlocks of the girls and the third one opened. She suddenly felt queasy and confused.

She hurried back to the others, but Rosalyn had found her man and the four had gone to the bedroom for some fun. She stood shaking and decided to stand in the corridor, in his path with a glass of cava in her hand. As she waited a tall rough looking man grabbed her arm and smiled at her. He tried her padlock, which opened.

She gasped and before she could look at her new suitor, Jim and Antonio walked towards her with their women as she stood her ground. He did a double take and ushered his party into the bedroom. The guy who chose her moved her quickly to an adjoining room and locked the door behind them. He placed his fingers on her mouth as they stood the other side of the door. This man listened to see if Jim had come out to find her. Gaby moved away suddenly so frightened she doubled up and sat on a chair, fear making her wretch.

"I can't do it, I'm sorry," she whispered.

"Glad to hear it, you don't recognise me?"

She looked at him again and fainted.

33

Something Happened

The black van drove through the campo at a safe speed not to disturb the terrain and general dust created by a speeding vehicle.

"Miguel, hurry up" commanded Armand his gruff voice perfected as Aleksey checked the package.

He stepped on the gas as the black van accelerated round a clump of trees, deep inside the campo of Benahavis, the signal received, loud and clear.

"This has got out of hand," said Armand quietly in the back of the van. The two men nodded knowing at some point they'd have to account for these actions.

"Under orders mate, we can't blow our cover, its tonight."

"I know."

"We told that broad, to keep away. Who the fuck is she again, you've been bothered every time we've bumped into her."

"Alex, mate, didn't you get it the first fucking time, she's, my fiancée."

"Fuck."

"Precisely."

"What you're going to do about that accountant she's been hanging around with?" as Aleksey continued to act a bit thick. *"We still haven't got any idea on him."*

"No, that's what I'm worried about, Jesus Miguel take it easy," ordered Armand as the van hit a boulder as they turned into narrow wasteland as guided by the GPS.

"Take a left, you then should see him," instructed Harry as he crawled up front ready to do the *drop*.

Armand and Aleksey both sat each side of the bagged body as Miguel followed Harry's instructions.

"Be fucking quick, we've got the drop tonight," reminded Armando.

Harry jumped out as did Aleksey as Miguel drove the van as close as possible. John the Dig was clearing round the grave as Miguel manoeuvred the van sideways.

"Right John."

"Right Harry, got the goods?"

"Yeah, in the back, let's do it."

Harry and John dragged the body and threw it in the grave as John immediately with Harry's help started to cover it.

Aleksey and Armand looked outwards as the dust covered them, the odd tumbleweed rolling past as the sun beat down on them. The olive tree, Harry's signature was dragged over the burial spot and stones were laid. The tumble weed rolling past was left to hide the signs of footprints and once satisfied, they jumped in the van and sped away so fast the dust acted as camouflage.

***

She woke up fully clothed but with three scantily clad waiters fanning her and the older one, trying to give her some water. She looked puzzled and the girl said,

"He left you this."

She propped herself up and looked again at the older girl.

"You fainted and the guy gave us instructions to look after you until you could read his message."

"Where is he?"

"He left with three others an hour ago; you've been out all this time."

"We can make you better," said the plumpest of the three as Gaby frowned trying to open the sealed envelope.

She read the note in disbelief, but it hadn't been a dream, Nick had rescued her, but his note didn't make sense. She knew she had to follow his instructions even though there was no explanation. She was surprised as his note said that he'd paid for the three girls, and it would be a pity to waste their time.

"What's the time?"

"It's four o' clock,"

She couldn't leave the building until six and as this was from her undercover estranged fiancé, she wasn't going to upset whatever plans were afoot, his words.

"Do you want the massage arranged for you?"

"Yes, that would be great."

"Plis lay on your front," said the older one fetching oils from the dressing table as the other two knelt side by side of her. They peeled off her clothes leaving her underwear as they grabbed a bottle of oil and started massaging her. She felt drowsy and relayed his conversation in her head as she heard a knock at the door. She tensed and a reassuring hand fell on her buttock as the girl whispered,

"Mr. Big guy has paid for your protection; no one will come. We escort you at six."

Fucking hell, she thought as she slumbered into a sense of uncertainty and tried to fathom what to do at six. His instructions were specific. She couldn't go home. She had no idea what was going down and she was in the way. She felt a warm finger moving under her lacy knickers.

She moved her leg up slightly giving the finger room to move towards her sweet spot. She felt her bra being unclipped and she decided to enjoy the moment. She was gently rolled over as the youngest girl poured oil over her sumptuous breasts. The plump girl had deft and soft fingers as she massaged her toes at the same time. The older one had poured cava and brought a glass for Gaby to drink as she propped her elbow up to sip some.

The two girls continued to massage her body inside and all over. The older one took some more cava and brushed her lips to her mouth as Gaby opened them and took the cava from her. Their tongues entwined and she kissed her delicately as a hot searing pain arrived from nowhere as the three girls loved her until five in the morning. Spent with attention, Gaby laid there and wondered how much he'd paid for this.

"Come," said the older one as she was escorted to the bathroom, where the bath was poured, and frothy bubbles floated everywhere. She sank in and picked up a scented soap.

"Shall I?"

She nodded as the older one joined her as they sat on their knees in the water. Her body was bronze perfect and her heart tattoos around her inner thighs were suddenly a turn on. The girl took over and the aromatic soap was massaged over her wet body. Gaby shuddered as the girl expertly and gently moved the soap within her, all over her teasing her and holding her waist as she moved her body in rhythm. A sudden shock seared her body again as she let out a scream as the girls' fingers went to her mouth to silence her.

They moved to the bed to dry each other as the girl eventually disappeared.

A loud knock on the door at nearly six made Gaby jump. She'd dressed and the three girls arrived, dressed seemingly for a funeral. She couldn't help but laugh at this sight and nodded as they were to take her out the concealed entrance only privy to the staff.

Once outside, she was alone and had no idea where to go and what to do. She needed her car and decided first things first. He hadn't said when she could go home. Her phone was dead which was annoying, and she walked to the second line to Hotel Pyr to see if Mercedes was on shift. She'd get a taxi from there and some coffee if Mercedes were working.

"Gave, what are you doing, so early?"

Relief hit her like a thunderbolt of lightning as she tried to brush the tears away.

"Come with me, what's wrong?"

Mercedes took her into the housekeeping laundry room which was where her desk was situated near a pile of freshly scented white towels.

"Sit, Tell me. Luis, dos Americano rapido," as her colleague who was at reception went to the restaurant to get drinks.

Gaby relayed everything apart from the girlie session at Pearls and Mercedes sat there dumbfounded and kept shaking her head.

"Jim is a good man, no?"

"I don't know, that's the whole problem, Mercedes."

"And this Nick, he's doing his job, right?"

"Yes, he's warned me to stay away from Jim. That's the second warning."

"What do you mean?"

She told her about the abduction as Mercedes couldn't keep her mouth shut with horror. Luis came in with a tray of hot drinks and pastries which were a welcome sight. Gaby grabbed a croissant; she was suddenly ravenous.

"Ok, Luis will go with you and get your car, and you come here. Park it in the bay I gave you."

"Thank you, can you charge my phone, its dead?"

"Yes, give it to me. You go with Luis now."

They left by taxi, and she checked her bag, everything was there as she located her keys. The taxi turned into the road for the Town Hall and was immediately stopped by the Guardia on a road block.

" Que?"

She understood the Guardia telling the taxi driver that he couldn't go any further. That gut feeling of trouble ahead washed over her as Luis got out to explain.

"Ah Professora Ingles, Gavee si?"

"Si, Rodriguez, Como estas, tener problema?

Relief came over her as she taught Rodriguez in Antonio's office as she explained that Luis was with her, to collect her car.

"It's ok, Eugenio is inside, and he saw your car. You can wait in the car park; I tell him you're here. You must not go inside, comprende?"

"Yes of course," said Gaby knowing something was wrong as Eugenio had told them.

" We'll walk to the car and wait for Eugenio, thanks Rodriguez. "

"Toto Bien, Gavee?"

"No Luis, no bien"

Eugenio looked drawn and suddenly old, as he stood at her car as they walked through the barriers.

"Eugenio, Cómo estás, Que pasa?"

"Gavee, they've arrested six people in the town hall, and they've taken the Mayor for questioning. Antonio has been called as their solicitor; there's a huge administration problem. I'm in temporary charge on Monday. Granada Town Hall is coming down to sort out the problem."

"Oh, my goodness is that why you were all summoned in this morning?" "Yes, the Mayor and three of his office were arrested at their homes, including his assistant and three bodyguards."

"Why have they all been arrested?"

"I don't know, but I'm going to ring round. Shall we meet tonight at Bar Tougana?"

"Yes, that would be great," said Gaby. *I'll tell Mercedes and you call José. I'll also call Isabella to check she's ok. I have stuff to tell you."*

"Ok, you better not park here until we know more, Gavee sorry."

"Eugenio, it's no problem, I'll go now as Luis needs to get back to work."

"Si ," said Luis nodding.

"Problemas con Mayor?"

"Si, Luis."

She drove quickly back to Hotel Pyr and parked up to locate Mercedes. Luis went ahead as he needed to be on shift. Gaby's' phone rang as she walked into the hotel. Mercedes handed it to her quickly seeing the name on the screen.

"Hi, honey."

"What the fuck are you playing at Jim, what's going on. Where are you?"

Her fingers crossed behind her back to see if he'd mention last night and that she hadn't been home.

"Sorry I didn't get home I'll explain later. I'm with Antonio, the Mayor has been arrested, and they need his financials. I'll see you tonight, ok"

Mercedes waved her to the café for a coffee, and she realised Jim had been with those hookers all night. He was in bed with Antonio and the Mayor, but why? She couldn't fathom it out, but Nick's warning was enough for her to play it cool and no; she wasn't going to be at the flat. His instructions had been clear. She sat with Mercedes telling her everything and she knew that Jim wasn't being honest.

"I come with you, Gavee. We'll go to your flat and get you a few things quickly. There's one room free tonight but then it's change over tomorrow, we worry about that tomorrow."

"Thanks Mercedes, let's go now, you're right."

Quickly they got to Estepona, and her heart dropped a beat as three Guardia cars were intermittently parked and surrounded the apartment block. A sure sign, she was either wanted, or she was going to be warned away.

"Gavee, this is bad. I'll get your things. Quick, write down what you need, and I'll go. You go and park from here, they don't know me."

"You're right, top drawer in bedroom, these things," as she scribbled a few garments down.

"Wardrobe, these three things, any jeans and the pink bag in bathroom, jewellery box in spare room."

"Ok, drive away and I'll walk to the Sardine bar and text you."

She drove round the one-way system and finally made her way to the sardine bar and parked. She kept her sunglasses on and placed a magazine in front of her, covering her face as she waited for Mercedes.

Thirty minutes later, she arrived, and they got away quickly, Mercedes had three big bags and a bunch of papers.

"These were through the door, post, yes? I thought you might as well take them as you should be home, yes?"

"Well done, I wouldn't have thought of that, have you done this before?"

Mercedes laughed,

"When we get back, you can check into room. The family are a day late as their child has been sick. I'll get Luis to organise the girls to make it up. If you leave by eleven in the morning, no one will know."

She parked the car in the enclosed bay for staff and Mercedes gave her a new pass for it. She disappeared as Gaby took the card key from Luis and made her way up to the fifth floor to her room. Mercedes had been efficient with her quick pack and apart from her toothbrush, she had everything. The girls had done the room and there was a basket of toiletries in the bathroom. She emptied the lot into her pink bag and was glad to see a toothbrush amongst the selection of goodies.

⋯⟨⟩⋯

34

The drug deal

It was only midday, and Gaby didn't want to look at the papers which were addressed to Jim and had been hand delivered. That was a mistake to bring but it was too late. He hadn't been home in the first instance to collect; he certainly wasn't going to challenge her about them. He probably thought she was home being a good girl and not hidden up in Hotel Pyr.

It was too early to go out for the night; she decided to pop into Marbella to see Jasmine as she hadn't seen her of late and she would make a good diversion for a few hours.

Jasmine was always pleased to see her, and they shared a coffee in Orange Square, and she finally agreed to take on a full-time job. Jasmine was delighted and Gaby felt good. At least Jasmine was genuine; she was beginning to doubt everyone else. She wanted to call Ben and Ros but didn't want to involve them. This was her dilemma. Nick, was who he said he was, even though he'd not told her for the length of their relationship, but she now understood why. It had taken the goings on here for her to realise he'd been in a tricky position.

She wanted to see Jim; he had a lot of explaining to do. She left Jasmine, pleased she'd made the effort to see her and relieved she had a full-time job. She would stop teaching at Antonio's office, it didn't seem safe anymore, however she'd wait for Jim's explanation.

As she drove towards the Pirelli to take the autopista for Estepona a young lad caught her eye walking towards the monument. *That's Ivan,* she thought as she pulled up and let her window down as he came running up to her car.

"Gavee, it's you. I missed the bus; can you take me home. Mum is expecting me soon as I have to help her party."

"Of course, I can, jump in."

Ivan was in full chatter mode as usual and he carried a bag which he held close to his chest on his lap.

"What time does the party start, Ivan?" as she pulled up the hill towards his villa.

"Late about midnight, I think, but you are coming, yes?"

"Maybe for an hour."

The hill was covered both sides in black sedans, Cadillac's and SUV'S as she turned around at the top and drove down to drop him off.

"Are you coming in?"

"Your mum is busy with the party, seems as if it's already started, the number of cars here, I won't stop."

"No, come in for a few minutes," as he dropped the bag, and a pile of passports fell out.

"Ivan, you've been stealing, you do know this is wrong, don't you?"

"I'm sorry Gavee, plees don't say to Mum, sorry, you mustn't know, you take to police station, no?"

"Will mum be angry that you have none?"

"Yes," he said quietly.

"Ok, take half and I will drop the other half in Polica, ok. Better half the people lose passports than all of them."

"You won't say anything."

"It's not my business, come on I'll take you in and explain that I offered you a lift as I saw you in Marbella, right?"

"Thank you."

Ivan replaced the passports and dropped a few on the floor of the car as they went inside. She could feel her shackles go up. The place was roaming with tall guys in black suits wearing ray bans and the atmosphere was strained. She walked in and Suzann pretended to look pleased at her sudden appearance.

"Hi Suzann, sorry for the interruption but I gave Ivan a lift home as I saw him in Marbella. I won't stay."

She couldn't miss it even though she tried to look away from the dining room table ahead of her. There were three open silver suitcases stacked high with white packs resembling flour, one suitcase bursting full of fifty euro notes in neat bundles. One of the black suits came over to stand in front of it as Gaby looked at Suzann.

"Thank you Gavee, I'm too busy now to give you tea, have you a mask for tonight?"

"Yes, uh, no, I didn't realise I needed one."

"Yes, here. Take this bag, there's a few in there, for your friends, no?"

"Great, thanks."

"No problem, I'll see you later, if I recognise you," as Suzann laughed as Gaby cringed and couldn't wait to leave. The two burly men outside gave her the creeps and suddenly she saw a Mercedes car she recognised, no surely, he wasn't here?

She decided she didn't want to know as something was happening at this villa, and it was obviously happening tonight.

"She's gone," whispered Miguel through his mike sounding relieved, Armand would have a fit if he knew she'd just walked in at the venue. Aleksey and a few other undercover police officers milling round, sighed quietly. Nothing could go wrong; it was too big. He was due here with one of the Barons and the biggest fish of all, was collecting here too.

The monies were in place, the place was rife with SAS, Guardia and undercover. Even Miguel's girls were on their way to liven up the party. Maar, the red head, was lining up coke on the glass table, ready for the big boys to try the goods at midnight.

Suzann had ordered out of town heavyweights and Miguel's undercover team had provided her with protection all day, ready for tonight. Maar had done an excellent job.

***

She forgot about the passports and went back to the hotel to get ready and have a sleep. She was exhausted and a siesta was in order before meeting Eugenio. She guessed what was going on at Suzann's and decided it was best not to go near the place. She would call Ros and Ben and tell them she had masks for their party. She knew they'd want to go, and she had an invite for them. She fell asleep and was woken up by her mobile, it was six o'clock what did Suzann want?

"Gavee sorry to bother you, but Ivan and the kids need to go to Benalmadena, where Roy lives, my boyfriend. His car has broken; can you help me. They need to leave for his boat on the pier."

Knowing she'd seen the stash of cash and drugs; she had no choice but say yes. Taking the kids away from whatever was happening at the villa was a good thing.

"I'll be there in half an hour Suzann, no problem."

She drove to collect the kids and wouldn't go in; she made one of the suited men fetch them as she saw that car again. Was that Jim's or Jed's? She remembered the passports on the floor and threw them in the glove compartment as the three kids came running out with a bag each waving good bye to Maar who nodded at her.

"Come on then, tell me about this boat?" as she tried to amuse the kids to Benalmadena.

Knowing the kids were safe, she drove back to Bar Tougana and decided to park behind the old school. She was pleased to see Ben and Rosalyn already there. She had to tell them; they were going to be shocked.

"Hi, guys, are you going to the party?"

"I think everyone is," said Ben as he went to fetch those drinks.

"Gaby, are you all right, you look preoccupied?"

"No, I'm fine Hun."

"Where's Jim?

"With Antonio, the Mayor has been arrested and there's a load of stuff going on at the town hall. Eugenio is on his way out for a drink; he's running the town hall until Granada people arrive in the week."

"Never, what's going down."

"I've no idea, Ben. All I know is that they were all summoned in for a meeting to be told that arrests had been made."

"This place is dreadful, kidnapping, your abduction, murder whatever next?"

"What happened to you at Pearls? We came out after a good hour, and you were gone?" said Ben passing round large Gin & Tonics to their table.

"No, it was longer than that; it must have been three hours."

"Actually, I found a quiet Arab and had a snogging session with him and to be honest I left," as she hoped she sounded convincing. Suddenly she didn't want to tell anyone anything. Mercedes had suggested she kept her distance, and she decided to listen to her friend.

"Whatever is your bag sweetie, at least you've been."

"Yes, it's an amazing place."

"By the way, I've got masks for you, if you're going to Suzann's party, it's invite only I meant to ask you before?"

"Abdul has the hots for Ben and sent him two invites to the office at Nuevo."

"Never."

"Oh yes, he's crazy about me," said Ben trying to sound amused.

"I suppose Pearls is good for contacts, it was full of business men the other night."

"We're going as Abdul's guests."

"Be careful Ros, with what's been going on. I'm going home tonight; I need to catch up and hope Jim has finished with Antonio."

"Look there's Eugenio, grab him a seat and I'll go and get him a bottle of red; he looks as if he needs it."

"You Ok, Eugenio?"

"I can't get an answer from José; I've left him messages and been to his house. There's no sign of him."

"I thought Margarita was coming tomorrow as the party is next week, he can't be far, Eugenio. Have you been to the bank, I know it's closed but he sometimes goes in to catch up on stuff?"

"I've been to his bank, his house and left messages, nothing. Something has happened Gavee, I know it."

"Calm down Eugenio, Placido's murder is one thing, but José don't be paranoid!"

"Look, you're upset with this morning's arrests, and the town hall is in chaos. I'm sure José has gone to visit his family or he's sorting out stuff. Don't forget he's moving and he's about to get married, he has a lot going on."

"Yes, I suppose. Margarita is here tomorrow and if there's something wrong, she'll call me."

"That's better Eugenio, have a glass of red."

Bar Tougana was buzzing, and the music was on at a higher notch than usual. They had to speak louder to each other to get heard over the din. It was packed and Eugenio was drinking his worries away. Ben and Ros were also drinking heavily as she offered to drop them off at the party, but she wasn't going to stay. She had decided earlier that she needed to have her wits about her and had started drinking water.

The last thing she wanted was to be stopped and breathalysed by the Guardia and cause more grief. She wished Jim would call; he was obviously involved with something too big to tell her. She felt an arm on her shoulder as she looked up temporarily distracted by her thoughts.

"Good night, Eugenio, call me tomorrow, once you've heard from José."

"Si Gracias, Gavee, Buenos noches mi amigos."

"Come on, we're ready to go, it's past midnight already, I need to find Abdul Abdullah," said Ben very merry as Gaby drove them to the villa. The party was evidently in full swing as the music could be heard from the bottom of the hill.

"I'll go further up the hill to turn around, then I'll drop you off," said Gaby knowing she could put her foot down as soon as they'd gone.

"Fantastic," said Rosalyn as drunk as Ben.

***

"Fuck, we've got a late arrival, wait," whispered Miguel through his mike in the Black Sedan. He held his breath recognising the ford fiesta and hoped she wasn't going to stay. This was going to get tricky. *"All units wait for these guests to get inside then we go."*

"We can't, Abdul wants some blonde bloke and he's not here. We need him to stay, and the big fish isn't here yet."

"Blonde bloke walking in with blonde girl."

"Black limo on route to you, it's going to block the fiesta, coming down the hill, we can't stop it."

"Shit," thought Miguel as the limo pulled up, the influential person stepped out with an entourage of four. One of Miguel's men stood in the middle of the road and put his hand out to stop Gaby from trying to manoeuvre past. Two of the men carried a suitcase each as they disappeared inside.

"Esperar, un moment, Señorita/ wait a moment," he said through her window as if he knew her.

She froze, where had she heard that voice before? She locked herself in and waited. It was pitch black and the only street light was the one above the back door of the villa entrance. She could just see Ben and Rosalyn go inside as three or four suited men followed in from the limo that was blocking her path.

Suddenly there was gunfire, and the music stopped. She could hear screams as Gaby clutched her stomach, wanting to drive away but the burly suit stood facing her.

She cried out loud as she watched the handcuffed men taken from the villa. She recognised Abdul even though his mask was on. She gasped as Suzann was handcuffed and being dragged to the van to her right. She looked straight at her and glared which made her stomach churn. Why or why had she offered to bring Ben to the party? She was rigid with shock as several cuffed men were being taken to various vehicles and then she saw him. The dreadlocked man, led a cuffed Jed, with three men around him to the SUV, his face full of rage. He looked across and saw her, his face turned to stone as he bore his black eyes through her as she shuddered.

The knock on her windscreen made her jump as the burly man beckoned for her to drive away. The limo had disappeared. The red head Maar appeared with Ben and Rosalyn in handcuffs and then she realised she was an undercover policewoman! She put the car in gear and drove like a mad woman, scared out of her wits towards Hotel Pyr.

Nick had warned her.

35

Margarita

She parked and quickly made her way to her room; she was shocked at what she'd witnessed. Nick had arrested Jed who was obviously in the thick of something huge. It didn't take a genius to work it out. Nick had been undercover all this time, and she'd had an affair with the very person he was stalking. She felt nauseous, what a bloody mess. She hoped that he'd come for her, once they'd finished what had obviously been a big scoop. She realised she could easily have messed it up, as she was sick, heaving in the toilet as she tried to get to bed.

She couldn't get Suzann's **"*Intimidating look*"** out of her mind along with Jed's. She felt fearful of them, but they'd been arrested, she mustn't worry.

She had no idea where she was sleeping Sunday evening as having seen the arrests, she didn't want to go back to the apartment. And where the fuck was Jim?

Her mobile rung seemingly a few hours later as she woke from a deep sleep and realised it was nearly ten. She had to vacate the room in an hour, and she was glad someone was calling her.

"Hola."

"Gavee, it's Margarita, José's gone?" she was hysterical as Gaby tried to calm her as she sat up in bed panicking.

"Have you called Eugenio?"

"Yes, can we meet?"

"Hotel Pyr, Mercedes hotel in Banus. Say in an hour?"

"Yes, yes, I'll tell Eugenio, Gracias."

She threw the phone on the bed and couldn't grasp what was going on. She got up, had a hot shower, and sorted her bags. She emptied the second lot of toiletries into her bag and took three towels. She took everything to her car and made her way to the restaurant and asked Luis to tell Mercedes they needed her advice.

She sat in the restaurant drinking coffee and Luis seemed to have taken her under his wing. *Tostada con tomate* arrived and fruit as she ate wondering where on earth was Jim. What was going on with José? It was unnerving as a very distressed Margarita ran into the Hotel. She evidently had been crying all morning and as she poured her a coffee, Eugenio arrived looking as terse as Margarita.

"Whatever's going on Eugenio?"

"I don't know," he sat, and Gaby poured more coffee as Mercedes arrived, and she issued some instructions to a few waiters and came to join them.

"Margarita, Tranquilo, Digame," said Eugenio.

Margarita looked at them in turn and took a deep breath and explained in rapid Spanish as Mercedes translated.

She'd arrived at his apartment yesterday afternoon as she hadn't seen or heard from him since Friday night. He always called to say goodnight but sometimes, with poor signal, she never worried. Saturday, when he hadn't called by lunchtime she left earlier. His apartment is normal, but his keys are there, and his wallet is on the side of the kitchen diary, where he keeps his things for his pocket.

"Strange, he would never leave the house without house keys and a phone, not a bank manager," said Gaby.

"Are the bank keys in the apartment?" asked Eugenio suddenly realising what had happened as he turned quite pale.

Margarita nodded her head, *"the bank keys are on the side with his wallet."*

"Someone came for him at the house as all his belongings are inside."

"Or they dropped them back after taking him."

"Eugenio, what's wrong?"

"We need to get inside the bank, we've got the keys, and I need to check on something."

"Do you have the password, otherwise you're going to set the alarms off?" said Margarita in Spanish as Mercedes was impressing Gaby by translating.

"You can't get involved Eugenio. You've got enough to do by keeping the town hall in order after yesterday's arrests."

"I think this is linked," he said quietly as Margarita started sobbing.

"Do you know anyone she can be with?"

"No, all their family are in Granada."

"We need to get someone here otherwise she'll do something silly, she's about to marry him in a fortnight, she needs a family member around her, until we find José."

"Si, Gavee, you're right, Margarita tener Mobil?"

"I'll call Rodriguez and see if he can shed light on José, she hasn't reported it yet, maybe we need to do that now Eugenio."

"Yes, call him and get him to come here."

Mercedes nodded as she retrieved Margaritas' mobile and started calling family members. It was a good two hours' drive, but this was beginning to look like a crisis.

Gaby went to the front desk and told Luis she was calling the Guardia. He needed to be discreet as tourists were leaving and checking in all day, the worst day to have Police presence at a major hotel.

"La officina mechor, hablo Mercedes, Gavee."

"Si Luis," as she went to tell them all to move into Mercedes office as Rodriguez answered his phone.

"Professora Gavee, Cómo estás, do you want to change lessons?"

"Are you working today, I've a problem?"

"Si, en Marbella con amigo, problema?"

"*Si, Puede conducir a Hotel Pyr, Possible soy aqui*"/Can you drive to Hotel Pyr as I'm here."

"*Si, vente minutos, Gavee.*"

"*Gracias.*"

"*Ok, Eugenio, Guardia are coming.*"

Margarita was much calmer as her sister was on her way to be with her. Gaby wanted to pop over to see Isabella but decided to wait and report José missing with Eugenio. She felt bereft already, she'd been through so much with her friends and now José had disappeared.

Two Guardia arrived and went straight to the back of reception. Margarita started to cry on seeing the green berets as the local Polica arrived and suddenly there was police activity all over the second line of Banús.

"*He works at Cajasur bank in Banús no?*"

Rodriguez looked at his mate and they walked away for a discussion and the walkie talkie started to get busy.

That feeling returned to her stomach as she looked at Eugenio as he nodded. Margarita was lying down on the floor, on a bed made of the hotel's spare linen. The Hotel doctor had been summoned, and he'd given her a sedative. Gaby fancied a sedative herself and decided to text Jim with urgency. She was afraid, worried sick and didn't know if she ought to go home. She wished Nick had been more specific about Jim.

The Guardia and Policia left as Rodriguez came to explain what was occurring.

"We unable to catch the new manager, yes?" looking at Gaby for his English assurance.

"Yes, that's fine," said Gaby not wanting to correct his English in the middle of a crisis.

"We all meet tomorrow at nine, when the bank opens."

"You don't need me to come, surely?"

"You bring José's amiga, plis."

"Yes, ok."

"What do you think's happened, Eugenio?" whispered Mercedes as the three of them went in to the restaurant, leaving Margarita to sleep. Mercedes hadn't worked all day, and Gaby was grateful for her support.

"José was helping the Mayor get his funds together, that's all I know. It will be interesting to see if the new bank manager can tell us anything in the morning. We'll have to wait."

"I'm going home, do you want a lift Eugenio, I can take you?"

"Yes, that will be good, Gavee thank you."

"Are you parking here tonight, Gavee?"

"I'll say yes, Mercedes, I'm going to see Isabella and then I'll decide. Margaritas' sister will be here by then."

"Tranquilo, no pasa nada, mi Amiga," as they embraced and left.

Eugenio was quiet as was Gaby as she drove him home. She was equally worried and told him what happened at Suzann's villa the night before. He was astonished when she mentioned that Ben and Ros had been arrested along with her ex and Suzann.

"How do you know her?"

"She's the mother of my student at Jasmines school."

"Oh goodness, innocent, what you say, wrong time, right...."

"Wrong place, wrong time in my case Eugenio."

"What are you going to do, have you heard from Jim? He must be involved with the Mayor; you haven't heard from him since you saw him the night before in Pearls."

"You're right; I've no idea what to do."

"Don't go home, Gavee. If you want to stay with us, you can," as she drove up his drive and he got out.

"No, if I can't go home, I can't implicate any friend either. I'm just an innocent teacher in the middle of it all."

"Take care, right?"

"Yes, I will."

She manoeuvred the car out of his drive and drove down to the cliff edge and sat looking at the sea thinking about her next move.

She wanted to see Isabella but didn't want to cause an awkward situation if she turned up. Last night was vivid in her mind as she recalled the cops taking all the culprits away. Another surprise had been seeing the red head Maar who had appeared stoned most of the time but had also been undercover.

Her phone shrilled loudly interrupting her thoughts and it was Suzann. Her heart fell to her stomach and wondered what on earth did she want?

"Hi Suzann," she said light heartedly.

"I saw you, I'm outside your apartment, when are you home? I need to talk, you're no teacher."

"Sorry Suzann I'm in Granada for a week, I'll talk to you when I get back, got to go, I'm driving."

She threw the phone down panicking. She'd been in the wrong place at the wrong time. That was it, she couldn't go home, unless Jim was with her, where the fuck was he? No response on text, she despaired as she locked the car and went for a walk on the beach to clear her head. Nick needed to find her as soon as possible, to help her conclude this mess. None of it was her doing, how had all this happened?

She got back in the car and placed her bags in the boot. She needed a pillow from the hotel, and she'd sleep in her car tonight. Suzann frightened her. She opened her glove compartment and two passports fell out, she'd forgotten about them. She looked at them and one was a British female and the other a Dutch female. She couldn't exactly hand these in, whilst the Guardia and the Policia were investigating José. She would pop them through the letter box tomorrow after the bank.

She drove to Isabella's villa and the place was closed. There was no sign of the guard or the guard dog that lived outside the servants' quarters. There was no sign of life. She rang the gated bell and waited for a response. There was none and she decided to drive back to Hotel Pyr and mingle with the guests round the pool.

The Hotel was busy, and Luis was off - shift. Mercedes had left her a note to say that Margarita had gone home with her sister, and they would all meet at the bank first thing. She had left her the passkeys to all the linen cupboards and Alberto in the restaurant had been instructed to look after her.

Satisfied she could mingle, went to the bathrooms on the ground floor, changed into a swimsuit and robe. She grabbed a beach towel and found a lounger, near the pool; it wasn't busy but enough people around for her to blend in. She kept her sunglass on and tied her hair up under a floppy sun hat and tried to relax.

36

Cajasur Bank

The pool area was deserted by seven o' clock. She went to the communal bathrooms and changed into linen trousers and a loose top and went to eat. Alberto waved for her to sit in the corner as she nodded.

Dinner felt like the last supper for some reason but she'd no idea why. Jim had not bothered to phone her which was disappointing. She was confused and she would ask Rodriguez's advice on Jim and Antonio's situation, in the morning.

She grabbed two pillows from the linen room and went to her car. It was colder than she'd imagine but eventually she dozed off in the back seat. Locked inside her car the towels acted as weights on her feet and the duvet had been an afterthought from Alberto, but she was now grateful for it. Luis was on shift at six and Mercedes started at seven.

A rustling sound woke her, but she couldn't move her neck; it was stiff as she saw the orange ball slowly rise in the distance. She blinked back the tears as she remembered what had happened. The trepidation of what the Guardia might tell them this morning bothered her. José was a good friend. Yet, no news was good news as she tried to move her neck slowly from the crevice between the back window and the seat knowing she needed to go and use the communal showers.

Luis was at the car door with a tray of coffee and pastries as she opened the side window. She drank her coffee, ate the two pastries, and got her bag and walked to the hotel. It was quiet and she got herself looking respectable. The bank was walking distance from the hotel and the walk would do her good.

She was a little early and sat in the bar opposite whilst she waited for them to arrive. Just before eight thirty, the new Assistant Manager arrived with a bunch of keys as she proceeded to open the bank. A few minutes later the second lady arrived, José's full-time replacement that was on handover. Five minutes to nine and the Guardia pulled up in two cars and blocked the road, each way. She got up and went outside as Eugenio, Margarita and one other walked towards her.

"Buenos Dias, Gavee, tu eres ok?"

"Si, Eugenio, et tu?"

"No, he dormido toda la noche/ haven't slept all night."

"Gavee Este es mi hermana, Maria/Gaby this is my sister Maria."

"Elcantado, Maria/nice to meet you, Maria."

They stood outside the bank as the Policia and Guardia went in to see the Managers. Rodriguez inside summoned them, who made them sit in the waiting area. Eugenio disappeared to the office with the manager who looked shocked as did her counterpart.

A few people stood waiting for the door to open but the Policia outside turned them away. Inside, they sat waiting for everybody to come back from the office. Gaby's phone beeped and she looked at it and her heart missed a beat, it was Jim.

"Now of all time," she thought.

The text was simple, it said, *"Where are you?"*

"Cajasur bank, Banús."

"Give me an hour."

She placed it back in her bag as Eugenio with Marta, and the new manager came out of the offices. The two Guardia were flying off instructions in rapid Spanish on their individual transmitters. One of them went outside and Marta was ordered to close the bank for the week.

"What's happened Eugenio, tell me."

Margarita sat clutching her sister as he took Gaby aside and sat away from the two ladies.

"It looks like José has fleeced the bank and all accounts with over €250,000 have disappeared along with current accounts with over € 5000."

Gaby's head started to spin, as she suddenly felt light headed and before the walls spun any faster, she whispered," *What do you mean?"*

"Anyone with more than €250,000 in their account has lost it, monies have been transferred out. José has left scratches on the desk in his office, we think he was made to do it. The Guardia also believe that they already know where he can be found."

"You mean he's dead?"

"Oh, most definitely, I have to tell Margarita. Gavee, what's wrong?"

The walls spun round, and she managed to say,

"Eugenio, my accou......."

She collapsed to the ground.

***

The room had ornate chandeliers hanging and there was a buzz around her ears, she couldn't quite focus and there was a mask over her mouth as she felt a hand in hers. She moved her head and saw smudged figures in and out of her radar as she tried to focus and concentrate. She felt another hand on her wrist, and she could just about see an outline of a paramedic. She was on a stretcher and as the mist cleared from her eyes, she recognised she was in the opposite bar by the open door. Alongside her on another stretcher was Margarita and her sister was holding her hand. She looked to her side and nearly fainted again as she stared into Nicks' blue eyes, the tears welling up...

"Do you prefer brown or blue," he squeezed her hand as her tears fell, *"Hey, it's ok, you've had a shock, you'll be all right in a bit."*

"What are you doing here?"

"I've been working with this lot for over a year sweetheart; our mission is over. I'm sorry but we believe José's dead, I've managed to tell them where I think he's buried."

"I don't understand I've lost all my money Nick."

"What do you mean?

"My next egg, my savings and my current account was in this bank, it's all gone."

She produced her balance slip that Eugenio had given her from her fist in her other hand and it showed a transfer out giving a zero balance. She spoke as he looked at the paper,

"I thought your mission was drugs and not money laundering."

"It's all the same, your new bloke, where is he?"

"You mean Jim; he's on his way here, why?"

"Good he's got something to tell you, hasn't he?"

"How do you know?"

"I know everything sweetheart. Are you fit enough to get off this stretcher for the paras to get out of here. You can sit with me, and we'll talk."

"Yes, I'm fine, just numb from this news; there must be something I can do, to get my money back."

"Let the guys go, look Margarita is going home, say goodbye and Eugenio is going to the Town hall. We're going to wait for Jim."

She let him help her from the stretcher and with a heavy heart embraced a numb Margarita, as a taxi arrived for them.

A Woman Police officer appeared, and Gaby promised to call them later.

She sat down with Nick as he ordered a bottle of brandy and two glasses. She looked at him. He looked odd with dreadlocks, and he was indeed scruffy, his eyes the only give away that it was him.

Relief overcame her, her heart raced again, and her insides churned as she knew, he was the only man who made her react that way. And he'd found her.

"I'm sorry about the villa, Ben and Rosalyn just wanted a lift. Tell me."

"We've wanted the drug cartel for this coast for over a year. Last night we arrested two, you know them both, along with the mules. How the fuck did you know that hooker, she's trouble?"

"My students' mother, Oh for Christ's sake Nick. Everyone I've been around is through one of the schools. Wall street, which fucking closed one weekend and Jasmines' school, where I met Jim."

"Ah, Jim, do you know anything about him."

"What do you mean?"

"Well, that's not my engagement ring you're wearing, it's his right?"

"Yes, I've gone with the flow. You should have told me; I can deal with anything if it's the truth."

"I know, the good news is, I want you back and the bad news is, you've got to decide," as he poured a large glass of brandy and handed it to her, *"Drink this; you're going to need it."*

"I've lost over €250,000 this morning; you're right I do need it. I have nothing, nada. Oh, my god, what am I going to do?" as she started to panic.

"Before Jim comes, take this," as he handed her all his cash from his wallet. *"Here's my card, get away from here tonight, use this number, leave me a concise message, and throw away this phone. Trust me enough to find you, baby."*

"Why, where are you going?"

"Next assignment is a follow up on this scoop, it's not long, and I will find you."

"What about Jim."

"You need to make your mind up right now; I'm going to disappear; Jim will be here soon; he mustn't see me."

"Why, for Christ's sake tell me."

"He's going to arrest me," as he kissed her on her brandy-soaked lips and disappeared out of the bar; jumped into Rodriguez car before Gaby could digest what he'd said.

"What...?"

She gulped the brandy as it burned her throat, she looked at the wad of notes in her hand and she stuffed them in her bag. What did he mean that Jim was...?

"Honey, sorry I've been longer than I said. Are you all right, you look as if you've had a shock?"

"Yes, sit; get a glass I'm on brandy. Where the fuck have you been?" she said sarcastically.

"The Mayor has been arrested for fraudulent activity and corruption. Antonio as his lawyer had to be with him. José from the bank has wiped the entire savings of customers to raise the funds for his tender. It's all hearsay as there's not much evidence. That's where I've been."

"Why were you with those hookers in Pearls on Friday night, I saw you?"

"Honey look, I'm an undercover Agent working as a spy for the Russian mafia, I've been trying to tell you."

She sipped her brandy slowly as she digested this statement as if he were ordering pizza. She looked at him as he sat there, the Armani suit and shiny shoes suddenly made sense. The cover story of an accountant as he'd got close to the target, he'd known all along what he was doing. She'd lost her lover; she'd lost her fiancé to another assignment who'd warned her about him. She didn't know this man in front of her anymore and worst of all; she'd lost her life savings, all in one morning.

"Why didn't you tell me at the beginning, you knew I'd left Nick for not being honest with me? You've done exactly that."

"The task was too big to compromise; I'd been undercover as a plumber for so long you helped me get close to Antonio much quicker through your students. I owe you for helping us get the result."

"Who killed Placido, Ryan and now José? You've known stuff all along, how could you lie so much?"

"I can't answer that question, but we've got questions for the British undercover cops. We're working together but not, it's complicated."

"I'm sure it is," as she slurred her words slightly. She gulped more brandy as her tongue got looser, she felt totally betrayed.

Her phone rang breaking the silence between them as he saw the name.

"Don't answer that, Suzann's dangerous and has been let off, on bail. She saw you at the villa; she'll make your life hell, believe me. She's got more clout than we thought, avoid her."

"How do you know all of this, were you there?"

"No, but I've just discovered who Nick is; your ex-fiancé reports to my second in command, he's so fucking good he doesn't leave a trail."

The brandy was kicking in and she didn't quite grasp what he'd said right away.

"How do I get my money back? You must have a way to retrieve funds for the innocent victims in this corruption case."

"Granada's town hall people are setting up a victim file, you need to see Eugenio and register your missing funds. It will take some time, but that's all you can do for now."

"What about us?"

"There's no us Gaby. I just needed to use you until we got the result."

He got up and walked away as the sun streamed in from the front door and prevented her from seeing his silhouette disappear. She drained her glass in disbelief. She poured another and sat there numb. She texted Eugenio and he agreed to bring the paperwork as she sipped her way through the remaining bottle of brandy.

Eugenio was shocked to learn about Jim and his hands shook as he wrote down her instructions. Between losing their friends and now Gaby was leaving, it had been a tough few weeks. She had to stay in Spain to reclaim her money, and she would have to keep her account linked to someone. She gave Eugenio power of attorney and her email address knowing she would soon lose her mobile, once she called Nick. The monies due from the school were now crucial for her survival and she gave Eugenio every contact detail for Sergio.

She was numb and stone cold sober as she walked to her car, having registered her claim. She rummaged for a few things. It was four o'clock and she decided to mingle with the holiday makers, find a sun bed, and try and get her head round the whole nightmare.

She sat on the lounger still shaking with disbelief as she re-lived her time with Jim. Two engagement rings, three silver necklaces and loads of tops and promises. He had manipulated the whole thing, how she agreed to move in with him, everything. She was sure, even the cruise, to bump into Jed was a set up. How could she have been so stupid? She'd never believe it if someone were telling her this story right now. She couldn't go to the apartment for any belongings, not after this revelation. She had nowhere to go.

At eight o'clock Mercedes came looking for her.

"Margarita has gone back to Granada; they've found a body, Gavee."

"Oh, Mercedes that's terrible."

"Here's my cousins' address in Garrucha, don't stay here, leave after you've had dinner. She's expecting you first thing."

"Can you help me, Mercedes?

***

With short dyed blond hair matching one of the stolen passports and a long black wig in a bag; she manoeuvred her car on to the Autopista. It was three in the morning, and she was headed for Garrucha, Almeria. She was bereft and crushed.

She had lost everything just by being a school teacher and innocently having deposited her nest egg in a reputable bank account. She had been used and abused, some of it her fault maybe, but she was innocent in all this. A pawn that had been so naïve she had been an easy walkover on all accounts.

Jim's flippant remark regarding their relationship and phoney engagement brought hot tears of humiliation down her cheeks as she drove away from the lights of Banús. He wasn't even a British Spy; she thought those jobs had gone down with the arc.

She had allowed her weaknesses for good looking handsome strangers to use her. She had allowed her heart to have fun. She had become reckless and now she had become a victim of her very own innocence and vulnerability. This had to change.

She checked the card that Nick had given her. It was safe inside her bra. Nick, had been her Knight and Saviour all along as she blinked back the hot tears.

How gullable she had been, she had let her guard down in all ways and she had been so naïve, she needed to get street wise right away. This experience had to mean something; it had to. She needed to find a way to change her financial dire situation and fast.

She headed towards Garrucha, her only way currently of surviving the chaos of the Costa Del Sol.

With € 78 to her name, she knew her life would never be quite the same again.........

With a deep breath and trying to maintain a positive outlook even in the middle of the worst scenario ever, Gaby put her foot down and decided she would turn this around. She would ensure these past few months was not going to be wasted......She couldn't return to the U.K., she needed to be here for the school money to be paid to her and now with this major fraud ongoing, Eugenio had said she needed to be in the country for when they sorted out the victims of the money laundering. She sighed, brushed away another tear. She would survive, somehow....

***

Marcello shifted unhappily in his seat as Rodriguez took the call. They'd given her Guardia escort to the Autopista, unbeknown to her.

He knew they shouldn't have accepted that bribe months ago. Now it was payback time. He reluctantly nodded at his mate as he answered the question.

"*Garrucha,*" whispered Rodriguez as Marcello nodded.

"*Bien, mañana,*" as Jim flipped his phone shut. She knew far too much and what she didn't know, she would soon work out, she was a loose end. A dangerous one at that.

He nodded at Aleksey as he bundled a bound and gagged Mercedes into the boot of his black Merc to meet her fate.

***

Key Characters

Operation Wilde Boar

Russian Mafia	British Intelligence	Guardia Beret Brigade
Jim Fernard-Mironoff	Nick Armand	Miguel Guerrero-*Black*
Aleksey Alokov	Maar Haigh	*Various* - Red Berets
		Green Berets
		Rodriguez Mariners
		Marcello Gonzalez
	Drug Cartels/ Barons	
Marbella Town Hall	Abdul Abdullah	*Drug Mules for coast*
Jesús Gil y Gil-**Mayor**	Jedious Firelli-(Jed)	Suzann Barangho
Marisol Yaguue -**Assistant Mayor**		Benjamin David
Eugenio Amador-**Accountant**		Ginger Greenwood
Antonio Marquiez-**Abagado/Lawyer**		

Newspaper report.

Marbella awaits new elections after most local politicians are accused of corruption

By Daniel González Herrera, Spain Editor

16 November 2006: **The sleaze scandal, which hit the southern Spanish resort city Marbella in spring 2006, soon proved to be only the tip of a massive corruption iceberg. During the spring operation, codenamed <u>Operation Malaya</u>, the police arrested the city's mayor and deputy mayor amid allegations of money laundering, property development offences, including building on land protected from development, manipulation of public tenders, the acceptance of bribes as well as schemes to alter the price of municipal services.**

During a second investigation, 'Operation Malaya 2' new offences came to light, resulting in some 30 city councillors and business people being accused of massive corruption. These accusations were in addition to the arrests made earlier in the year. Then. 29 people were arrested, including Mayor Marisol Yagüe, her deputy, Isabel García Marcos, and José

Antonio Roca, who was town planning advisor. During the investigation, Judge Miguel Ángel Torres said of Mr Roca that he was the driving force in Marbella City Hall and that the Mayor performed a mere symbolic role. In September 2006, the former mayor and her deputy were released from custody on 60,000-euro bail.

Those arrested as part of 'Malaya 2' included the former chief of Marbella's police Rafael del Pozo and TomásReñones, the city's second deputy mayor. Mr Reñones became acting mayor after the arrest of the mayor and the first deputy mayor. However, his involvement in the scandals became clear during the following-up investigations and Judge Torres ordered his unconditional detention. TomásReñones was football player and captain of Atlético de Madrid, the football club owned by the late Jesús Gil, the first of the big corrupted mayors of Marbella and founder of GIL, the political party whose members included the disgraced mayor Marisol Yagüe.